# Ivan Turgenev

# Fathers and Sons

*Introduction and Notes*
*by Ann Pasternak Slater*

The Constance Garnett translation
has been substantially revised by
Elizabeth Cheresh Allen

THE MODERN LIBRARY

NEW YORK

2001 Modern Library Paperback Edition

LIBRARY OF CONGRESS CATALOGING-IN-PUBLICATION DATA

Turgenev, Ivan Sergeevich, 1818–1883.
[Ottsy i deti. English]
Fathers and sons / Ivan Turgenev ; introduction and notes by Ann Pasternak
Slater ; the Constance Garnett translation has been substantially revised by
Elizabeth Cheresh Allen.
p. cm.—(Modern Library paperback classics)
ISBN 0-375-75839-9
1. Fathers and sons—Fiction. 2. Nihilism (Philosophy)—Fiction. 3. Russia—
Social conditions—1801–1917—Fiction. 4. Russia—Social life and
customs—1533–1917—Fiction. I. Garnett, Constance Black, 1862–1946.
II. Allen, Elizabeth Cheresh, 1951– III. Title. IV. Series.
PG3421 .O8 2001
891.73'3—dc21 2001031709

Modern Library website address: www.modernlibrary.com

Printed in the United States of America

2 4 6 8 9 7 5 3 1

# IVAN TURGENEV

Born to a retired cavalry officer and a wealthy heiress on October 28, 1818, in Orel, two hundred miles south of Moscow, Ivan Sergeevich Turgenev enjoyed a privileged childhood. He received his introduction to literature from a valet who recited the Russian epic poem *Rossiíada* to the boy in secret. Private tutors instructed Turgenev at home, where he learned French, German, and English, and stints at private boarding schools in Moscow followed. The lessons Turgenev gleaned from life on a country estate proved equally enduring. His mother, a cruel and capricious woman unloved by her husband, often visited abominable indignities upon her serfs; her own mother once smothered a boy serf who had irritated her. The impassioned aversion to every form of degradation that Turgenev developed then would animate his thought and fiction for the rest of his life.

After attending university in Moscow and St. Petersburg, Turgenev spent three terms studying philosophy in Berlin, where he developed a profound reverence for Western culture and absorbed the Hegelian idealism then agitating young Russian intellectuals studying abroad. A spell in the civil service when he returned to Russia left Turgenev unsatisfied, his sole consolation the acclaim heaped on his narrative poem *Parasha,* which was published in 1843. Biding time at his mother's estate, Turgenev fathered an illegitimate daughter by a seamstress employed there. In 1845, Turgenev decided to devote himself exclusively to literature. His mother, dismayed by her son's choice of occupation and enraged by his infatuation with the French opera singer Pauline Viardot, withdrew her financial support, though Turgenev recovered a considerable portion of her fortune upon her death in 1850. Turgenev would shadow Viardot around the world until his death.

In 1852, Turgenev published *The Sportsman's Sketches,* a collection of vignettes of country life that caused an unprecedented stir on both the literary and social scenes. Turgenev's matter-of-fact style mingled the authenticity of realism and the lyrical emotion of romanticism so unobtrusively that it amounted to a new genre altogether, with Aleksandr Pushkin as its patron saint. Turgenev's depiction of serfs as more humane and genuine than their masters, meanwhile, convulsed society. The stories supposedly inspired Czar Aleksandr II, who would ascend the throne three years later, to emancipate the serfs in 1861. For the moment, the infuriated authorities dismissed the censor who had passed the book and sentenced Turgenev to eighteen months of house arrest, though ostensibly for writing an exceedingly exuberant obituary of Nikolay Gogol.

Turgenev benefited enormously from the liberal spirit that saturated the first years of Aleksandr II's reign. He published three novels—*Rudin* (1855), *A Nest of the Gentry* (1859), and *On the Eve* (1860)—to awe and adulation. The radicals cherished Turgenev's commitment to social justice, and the conservatives savored his literary gifts. Driven by a lifelong desire to please all sides, Turgenev relished his relevance and popularity in turn. With the publication of *Fathers and Sons* in the spring of 1862, however, Turgenev's fortunes changed. The Right regretted Turgenev's idealization of the militant materialist Bazarov, while the radicals virulently denounced the author for drawing Bazarov as a caricature of their kind. Fyodor Dostoevsky was among the few who perceived Turgenev's actual intention: a measurement of "the incompetent ... against the unscrupulous," the well-meaning but inert fathers (who both irritated and charmed Turgenev) against the resolute but barbaric revolutionaries (who both horrified and dazzled him). In the polarized climate of the 1860s, most readers mistook Turgenev's "extreme moderation," to borrow Isaiah Berlin's phrase, for a fanaticism they themselves projected. The author's protests, complaints, and apologies—"Did I want to tear Bazarov to pieces or extol him? *I don't know that myself,* for I don't know whether I love him or hate him," he wrote in exasperation to the Russian poet A. A. Fet in April 1862—fell on deaf ears.

Profoundly wounded and disillusioned by the criticism, and unnerved by the prospect of an obsolete and irrelevant existence in Russia, Turgenev fled to Europe, where he remained for most of his life. From there, he wrote *Smoke* (1867), an invective against intellectual Russia so detached from reality that Dostoevsky advised Turgenev to procure a telescope in order to see Russia better, and *Virgin Soil* (1877), a roundly condemned attempt to depict the revolutionaries of the 1870s that betrayed how out of touch with his homeland Turgenev had become. Nonetheless, by dint of persistence and charm, Turgenev managed to repair his relations with the Left, and his homecoming in 1880 turned out to be a success. Turgenev enjoyed greater popularity in Europe, where he cultivated distinguished friends and admirers, Flaubert and Henry James among them, and received an honorary degree from the University of Oxford in 1879. After a year of illness, he died on August 22, 1883, in the commune of Bougival, on the Seine below Paris. At his request, he was buried in St. Petersburg near the critic Vissarion Belinskii, the beloved mentor who had rendered moral principle indivisible from Russian literature—and Turgenev's own.

# CONTENTS

# Introduction

*Ann Pasternak Slater*

*Fathers and Sons,* Ivan Turgenev's masterpiece, is set in Russia in 1859. It was published in 1862, the year after Russia's serfs, a third of the total population, were finally liberated by the Edict of Emancipation. The novel is delicately and deliberately balanced at the cusp of this change. Many liberal landlords had already anticipated the edict, assigning land to their own peasants in exchange for hired labor. Among them are the two fathers of Turgenev's novel. Opposing them were the new radicals, repudiators of traditional values, believing the old had to be destroyed before the new could be built. Among them are the two sons of Turgenev's novel, Arkadii and Bazarov, the self-proclaimed nihilists. They are not, however, militant extremists. Turgenev was sympathetically inclined to the moderates of both persuasions, and his treatment of the old and the new is scrupulously evenhanded.

By birth Turgenev was a member of the landed gentry. His mother had a large estate of five thousand souls, as the Russian puts it—five thousand serfs whom she ruled with callous despotism. "As a child," Isaiah Berlin tells us, "Turgenev had witnessed abominable cruelties and humiliations (including the murder of a child because it was crying) which she inflicted on her serfs and dependents." Her brutality was an early impetus to Turgenev's abiding sympathy for the downtrodden, and the prime source for his liberal principles. They were confirmed by a university education in Moscow, St. Petersburg, and Berlin. His love of Western values, and of the French singer Pauline Viardot, drove him to spend increasing periods abroad. For the French, he was "that gentle giant, that loveable barbarian," as Edmond de Goncourt called him. For the barbarian Russians, Turgenev's writing derives recognizably from a Western tradition of formal perfection quite alien to the massive, indigenous roughness of Tolstoy and Dostoevsky. In his life, as in his convictions and literary achievement, Turgenev straddles opposing worlds.

The catholicity of Turgenev's sympathies is evident from his probable originals, dim shadows cast, as it were, by the sharply delineated central figures of *Fathers and Sons.* Pavel Kirsanov, Arkadii's exquisitely civilized, impeccably dressed, and mildly mocked Anglophile uncle, was based on the author himself— according to hearsay reported by Turgenev's friend Henry James. Pavel Kirsanov, though neither a father nor a son, is the novel's painfully absurd antithesis to its powerful central character, the young nihilist Bazarov. Behind Bazarov can be seen two contrasting figures who influenced Turgenev profoundly. The first is the critic Vissarion Belinskii, whom Turgenev loved and admired, the dead master to whom he dedicated *Fathers and Sons.* All Turgenev's writing is modeled on Belinskii's realist, humanitarian, morally driven aesthetic principles. Bazarov shares elements of Belinskii's personality: his integrity, his commitment to deeply held convictions, his social intolerance, his inability to temporize. Both model and character are the sons of poor army doctors; both die young. Bazarov's second, antithetical original is Dobroliubov, the hard-line editor of the radical left-wing journal in which Turgenev had published his previous novel, *On the Eve* (1860). Dobroliubov reviewed it favorably for expressing a far more absolutist, militant slant than Turgenev intended. At his demurs, Dobroliubov cut Turgenev dead. His gloomy intransigence and ruthless radicalism may well have contributed to Bazarov's harsher edge. Turgenev changed editors, and *Fathers and Sons* was published by the right-wing Mikhail Katkov, who encouraged Turgenev to darken his portrait of Bazarov. In his turn, Turgenev later broke off with Katkov as an extreme reactionary.

Turgenev's potential originals display a doubleness riddling the novel's critical history. As Henry James says, *Fathers and Sons* is about "the battle of the old and the new, the past and the future, the ideas that arrive with the ideas that linger." Inevitably, its reception was correspondingly equivocal. Turgenev contrived to please neither party. The gentle liberals of the older generation felt that they had been rendered absurd. The young radicals thought Bazarov was an antagonistic portrait of all they stood for. The Right criticized Turgenev for crawling to the young by conferring heroic, even tragic status on Bazarov. The Left vilified him—more viciously—as the pusillanimous champion of the ineffectual privileged classes. Subsequent novels did not diminish the controversy. Turgenev suffered. "They are all attacking me, Reds and Whites, from above and below, and from the sides, especially from the sides," he wrote later to the Russian revolutionary leader and author Aleksandr Herzen.

The debate has continued for over a hundred years. Hostile commentators point to Turgenev's many contradictory statements about Bazarov, tailored to the inclinations of the individual auditor. Prince D. S. Mirsky, the émigré critic, called him "a consummate trimmer." The Soviet critics squandered their impoverished literary skills on a tedious ideological debate devoted solely to the status of Bazarov, proto-Bolshevik activist, or dilettante nihilist. Only now, in the twenty-first century, are Russian high school students taught to read the novel in a more integrated way: Bazarov is roundly condemned because he plays no part in nature's harmony. The focus is still on Bazarov. It is still judgmental.

Turgenev's ambivalence is the point and not the problem. He

knew what he wanted to achieve. Many years later, still smarting, he wrote, "I am told that I am on the side of the fathers—I, who in the person of Pavel Kirsanov, actually sinned against artistic truth, went too far, exaggerated his defects to the point of travesty, and made him ridiculous." It is an ironic tribute to Turgenev's success that the novel continues to be debated in the search for partisan affiliations that it refuses to render up. It is the critics and the readers who are at fault, not the author. Bazarov's dualities, which have always dominated the novel's reception, are only one part of a larger whole. *Fathers and Sons* scrupulously registers that "spark kindled by the innermost friction of things," as James called it. This is its central concern. This is its artistic truth, free from the doctrinaire imperatives that have hexed Russian literature throughout its history.

———

The "innermost friction of things" is tellingly identified at an inconspicuous early moment in the novel, when Arkadii and Bazarov, fresh from university, are driving to Arkadii's father's estate. From the carriage window, Arkadii sees rickety barns, flaking plaster on the churches, dying willows stripped of their bark, their branches snapped. Shabby peasants on the sorriest of ponies. Emaciated cows tearing at the roadside grass. "How can one start to reform all this?" he thinks with a sinking heart. Within a single paragraph his perception swings full circle. "Everything around him was golden green, gently stirring in wide ripples under the soft breath of the warm breeze. Peewits hovered over the low-lying meadows; crows strutted among the half-grown spring corn." Arkadii's face lightens; he turns to his father and hugs him. The juxtaposition of these two paragraphs is striking in their extreme divergence. What is presented to us is not objective fact but fluctuating subjective impressions—the duality of Arkadii's feelings as he returns home, full of new ideas and old affections.

The moment is pointedly echoed later, when Arkadii and Bazarov are lying in the shade of a haystack on one of those drowsy, deadening summer afternoons. Arkadii has lost some of his wholehearted admiration for Bazarov. Bazarov is in a destructive mood. They try to go to sleep, and fail. Arkadii watches a dead maple leaf fall to the ground, and observes how like a butterfly it looks. "Isn't that strange? The saddest, most lifeless thing is so like the most cheerful and vital." Bazarov mocks him for his eloquence. He has no time for art and poetry and all that romantic rubbish. But the aesthetic and irrelevant is aesthetically relevant. The butterfly leaf twisting to the ground is an image of the novel's double vision, shared by Arkadii and Turgenev himself.

Turgenev fosters a comparable flexibility in his readers by the novel's construction. With the utmost economy, he rotates Arkadii and Bazarov through a small range of settings and secondary characters that create a sequence of parallels and contrasts, constantly casting changing lights and shadows on the central couple.

Arkadii and Bazarov are first played off against Arkadii's father, Nikolai Kirsanov, and his uncle Pavel. The older generation is wary and polite, flustered and distressed by the casual ruthlessness of the young men's opinions. Bazarov is careless, intellectually arrogant; Arkadii idolizes him. The complicit reader is mildly pained by Bazarov's indifference to his courteous hosts. The balance shifts when the young men leave for the neighboring town, where Turgenev sets Bazarov's intellectual superiority against two absurd progressives: the tawdry bluestocking Kukshina, a single woman of uncertain age and fame, and the sole habitué of her tatty salon, the craven Sitnikov, whose skipping ingratiation is reminiscent of Squealer in George Orwell's *Animal Farm*. Their laughable pretensions put Bazarov's genuine scientific rigor in a favorable light, which is intensified when Arkadii and Bazarov are invited to stay on the estate of the widowed Mrs. Odintsov. Her admiration for Bazarov heightens his charisma. Arkadii, falling into calf-love, is disregarded. An unfraught friendship develops between him and Katia, Mrs. Odintsov's younger sister. The network of parallels and contrasts grows more closely woven: double threads separate, new colors are worked in. Distinctions and differences emerge between Arkadii and Bazarov. Mrs. Odintsov, rich, beautiful, and intelligent, contrasts with the crass and sordid Kukshina. The growing discrimination of Arkadii's admiration for Bazarov contrasts with the strongly ironized adulation offered by Sitnikov. The innocent incipient tenderness between Arkadii and Katia contrasts with the wary intellectual attraction magnetizing the more mature Bazarov and Mrs. Odintsov.

Only two characters are missing: Bazarov's parents. He is their only child and they adore him. After half the novel, three years at university, and many weeks at Arkadii's and Mrs. Odintsov's, Bazarov finally, reluctantly, goes home, bringing Arkadii with him. Within three days, he is bored and the young men leave. Our sympathetic pain for the silenced, suffering parents is voiced by the gentle Arkadii, who is shocked at Bazarov's callous egotism.

Bazarov's parents complete the crisscross of contrasts. They are themselves contrasted: the father was born into poverty, is highly intelligent, shrewd, rational, and humane, a fitting father for a clever son. The mother is his antithesis: the wealthier of the two, an old-world soul, deeply superstitious, the embodiment of Old Russia with its feudalism, charity, warmheartedness, and ignorance. Bazarov's parents also inevitably contrast with Arkadii's father and uncle. The Kirsanovs have an estate of two hundred souls, the Bazarovs of a mere twenty-two. Materially much richer, the Kirsanovs are intellectually poorer. Arkadii's father is making a feeble job of his newly emancipated estate. Bazarov's father, a retired army doctor, is naturally omnicompetent. The multiple antitheses set up by the complex of contrasts prevent the simple division into two camps enticing most critics of *Fathers and Sons*. Bazarov and his father are the novel's most radical figures; his mother is the most feudal. Bazarov has an easy familiarity with the serf boys on Arkadii's estate; he has a natural sympathy with Fenechka, the peasant mistress of Arkadii's father, and her baby son is happy to be handled by him. But the peasants in Bazarov's village look on him with indulgent scorn as a toff who understands nothing of the realities of life, and he disdains their drunken, lazy ignorance.

Bazarov's love for Mrs. Odintsov ends in failure. For all their extreme ideological differences, he is no different from Pavel Kirsanov, who has nursed a comparable failed love for most of his adult life. Pavel Kirsanov and Bazarov both indulge in a brief tendresse for Fenechka, which leads to their duel, in which the clash of similarity is at its most obvious. Bazarov is even implicitly linked with Nikolai Kirsanov, Arkadii's father, in one of those ironic innuendos characteristic of Turgenev's delicate art. At the novel's very beginning, we are blandly told that in his adolescence the reluctant Nikolai was expected to follow his father into the army. "He broke his leg on the very day that word of his commission arrived." A lifetime's limp liberated him. At the novel's end, Bazarov nicks himself dissecting a typhus-ridden cadaver and fails to cauterize the wound until it is too late. Are both injuries deliberately self-inflicted? Bazarov's life has lost its meaning with Mrs. Odintsov's rejection of him. As a scientist Bazarov knows well enough the dangers of dissecting a typhoidal corpse. Pavel Kirsanov ends the novel in a kind of living death, an immaculate, highly glazed émigré in the spas of Europe. Bazarov dies for real, open-eyed, angry, and unwavering, tended and bitterly mourned by his parents to the end.

"He brings all his problems and characters to the test of love," Joseph Conrad said of Turgenev. Arkadii and his father pass a simple version of the test. Bazarov does not fail, although his love of Mrs. Odintsov is a failure. The fault is hers, not his; she rejects him from spiritual cowardice and emotional indolence. Bazarov's real test comes with the love of his parents. Their love is generous, absolute, and absolutely self-effacing. He fails them miserably when he leaves them, and his indifference darkens him in our eyes. When his other relationships—with Mrs. Odintsov and even Arkadii—grow barren, he returns home once again, to try to lose himself in science, infects himself, and dies. We watch his death through the eyes of his parents, and suffer with them. Their love is what first condemns and finally redeems him.

Bazarov's radicalism achieves nothing. But Nikolai Kirsanov, no political activist, marries Fenechka, his peasant mistress, and legitimizes their son. This is social change in quiet practice. The novel ends with the double wedding of Nikolai Kirsanov to Fenechka, Arkadii to Katia, the death of Bazarov, and Pavel's living death. In the novel's final pages we are shown the Kirsanovs' fertile Arcadian future, father and son, wives and children—and (*et in Arcadia ego*) Bazarov's parents mourning at his grave. The dead leaf and the living butterfly.

———

Turgenev's handling of narrative is workmanlike but rather rudimentary. The novel's events are not in themselves memorable. A ball, a duel, not one but *three* overheard conversations—all this seems a little conventional. Yet it was a conscious artistic choice on Turgenev's part. Narrative events are subordinated to structure. They hardly matter, except to serve as a vehicle for the play of character within an incomparably vivid setting. And Turgenev's eye for detail is extraordinary. Houses, accents, weather, mannerisms, the liveries of different servants, even the pets—everything contributes to a living whole. Old Bazarov's house, full of flies, with its six tiny rooms smelling of lamp oil and clover, and a broken electric generator in the corner of his study. The greyhound's nails tapping across the floor at Mrs. Odintsov's. Kukshina's forlorn snub nose and laugh that displays her upper gum. Bazarov's father, "constantly shifting his shoulders as though his jacket were cutting him under the armpits."

Turgenev is the archaeologist of social strata and the palimpsest of generations, the analyst of time's accretions and the minute distinctions of class. Henry James acutely noted his delineation of the "heredity of idiosyncracies." It is evident in the slightest of details: the way both Bazarovs, father and son, compress their lips when referring to an admired liberal model in their past, for instance, or their shared love of the latest scientific texts, now fifty years out of date in the father's case. Providing the notes for this edition of *Fathers and Sons* brought home vividly the accuracy with which Turgenev roots his characterization in a cultural history precisely attuned to each individual. Edmond de Goncourt says that when Turgenev was imprisoned for a month for the liberal views of his first work, *A Sportsman's Sketches* (1852), "his cell was the room housing the police archives of a whole district, whose secret dossiers he studied at leisure." It was the lesson of a lifetime. Henry James reports Turgenev's account of how he composed: "[H]e wrote out a sort of biography of each of his characters, and everything they had done and that had happened to them up to the opening of the story. He had their *dossier,* as the French say, and as the police has that of every conspicuous criminal." The technique can be seen in descriptive tours de force, like the portrait of Bazarov's mother, which James quotes in full in his essay on Turgenev, or the delectable account of Fenechka's room, smelling of fresh floor paint and chamomile, greenish jars of misspelled "Gouzeberry," Nikolai Kirsanov's favorite jam, lining the windows, a short-tailed finch in a cage scattering hemp seed on the floor with a light tapping sound. In the corner a portrait of General Ermolov, a luminary of Nikolai's father's military past, scowls at the distant Caucasian mountains from behind the little silk-shoe pincushion Fenechka has hung over his forehead.

Turgenev's dossiers depend on detail. Virginia Woolf had a fine eye, quoting (from another novel) the hero's "white chamois-leather gloves, recently washed, every finger of which had stretched at the tip and looked like a finger-biscuit." However, Woolf is nervous of the gift deteriorating into a mere novel of manners, and she is impatient with Turgenev's precise historical sense, which places Arkadii and Bazarov within the setting of not one but two sharply evoked preceding generations. "We are involved with great-grandfathers and great-grandmothers, much to our confusion," she complains, suffering, like most English readers, from the complexities of Russian nomenclature, and, more important, being fundamentally out of sympathy with Turgenev's sense of individual ancestry, the "heredity of idiosyncrasy" that James rightly relished.

Woolf's response to Turgenev is constrained by her own artistic imperative, to catch the evanescent moment. Turgenev is a little too old-fashioned for her wholehearted approval. Conrad is the only English author among Turgenev's near contemporaries who understands him as a fellow Slav rather than as a foreign exotic. He smarts at Turgenev's neglect from his Russian contemporaries, and his tribute, in a letter to Edward Garnett written in 1917, is at once sardonic and moving:

> In truth it is not the convulsed terror-haunted Dostoievski but the serene Turgenev who is under a curse. For only think! Every gift has been heaped on his cradle: absolute sanity and the deepest sensibility, the clearest vision and the quickest responsiveness, penetrating insight and unfailing generosity of judgement, an exquisite perception of the world and an unerring instinct for the significant, for the essential in the life of men and women, the clearest mind, the warmest heart, the largest sympathy—and all that in perfect measure. There's enough there to ruin the prospects of any writer.

However, the fullest and best criticism one writer can lavish on another comes from Henry James. With good reason he called Turgenev "the novelist's novelist." And for the incomparable warmth of a personal memoir, we come to James's portrait of his friend, written shortly after Turgenev's death in 1883:

> I always left him with a sense of "intimate" excitement, with a feeling that all sorts of valuable things had been suggested to me; the condition in which a man swings his cane as he walks, leaps lightly over gutters, and then stops, for no reason at all, to look, with an air of being struck, into a shop window where he sees nothing.
>
> He was the most generous, the most tender, the most delightful of men.

SELECT BIBLIOGRAPHY

Berlin, Isaiah. *Fathers and Children: The Romanes Lecture* (Oxford, 1972).

Conrad, Joseph. *Notes on Life and Letters* (London, 1921).

de Goncourt, Edmond and Jules. *Pages from the Goncourt Journal,* edited and translated by R. Baldick (London, 1962).

James, Henry. *Literary Criticism: French Writers, Other European Writers, Prefaces* (New York, 1984).

Turgenev, Ivan. *Fathers and Sons,* edited, with an introduction and notes by E. R. Sands (Cambridge, 1965).

Woodward, James. *Turgenev's "Fathers and Sons"* (Bristol, 1996).

Woolf, Virginia. *Collected Essays* I (London, 1966).

———

ANN PASTERNAK SLATER is a Fellow of St. Anne's College, Oxford. She is the author of *Shakespeare the Director;* the translator of the memoirs of Alexander Pasternak, *A Vanished Present;* and the editor of *The Complete English Works of George Herbert* and *The Complete Short Stories of Evelyn Waugh* for Everyman's Library.

*Dedicated to the memory of Vissarion Grigorevich Belinskii*

# FATHERS AND SONS

# I

"Well, Petr, no sight of him yet?" asked a gentleman about forty years old wearing a short, dusty coat and checkered trousers, standing hatless on the low steps of an inn on the *** road. It was the twentieth of May 1859. He was addressing his servant, a round-cheeked young man with whitish down on his chin and small, lackluster eyes.

The servant, whose turquoise earring, variegated hair plastered with grease, and refined movements all betokened a man belonging to the newest, most advanced generation, glanced down the road condescendingly, and replied: "No, sir, no sight of him at all."

"No sight of him?" repeated his master.

"No, sir," the servant responded a second time.

His master sighed and sat down on a little bench. Let's introduce him to the reader while he sits looking around thoughtfully, his feet tucked up underneath him.

His name is Nikolai Petrovich Kirsanov. He owns a fine estate located fifteen versts from the inn that has two hundred serfs or, as he puts it—ever since he arranged to share his land with the peasants—"a farm" of nearly five thousand acres. His father, an army general who served during 1812, was a coarse, half-educated, but not villainous Russian. He worked hard all his life, first commanding a brigade, then a division, and lived continually in the provinces where, by virtue of his rank, he played a fairly important role. Nikolai Petrovich was born in the south of Russia, as was his elder brother, Pavel, of whom more later. He was educated at home until he was fourteen, surrounded by underpaid tutors and casually obsequious adjutants, in addition to all the usual regimental and staff personnel. His mother, a member of the Koliazin family, was called Agathe as a girl but Agafokleia Kuzminishna Kirsanova as a general's wife. She was one of those "mother-commanders" who wore elaborate caps and rustling silk dresses. In church, she was the first to advance to kiss the cross; she talked a great deal in a loud voice; she let her children kiss her hand in the morning and gave them her blessing at night—in a word, she conducted her life just as she pleased.

As a general's son, Nikolai Petrovich was expected, like his brother Pavel, to enter the army, although he not only lacked courage but even deserved to be called a little coward. He broke his leg on the very day that word of his commission arrived, however, and had to lie in bed for two months, staying "gimpy" to the end of his days. His father gave up on him and let him pursue civilian life. He took Nikolai Petrovich to Petersburg as soon as his son was eighteen and enrolled him in the university. Pavel happened to have been made an officer in the Guards at about the same time. The young men started to live together in one apartment under the distant supervision of a cousin on their mother's side, Ilia Koliazin, a high-ranking official. Their father returned to his division and his wife, and every once in a while just sent his sons large gray sheets of paper with a military clerk's handwriting scrawled across them. At the bottom of these sheets, carefully encircled by a scroll design, were inscribed the words, "Petr Kirsanov, General-Major." In 1835, Nikolai Petrovich graduated from the university; General Kirsanov retired the same year after an unsuccessful review, and brought his wife to live in Petersburg. He was about to rent a house in the Tavricheskii garden and join the English Club when he suddenly died of a stroke. Agafokleia Kuzminishna died shortly thereafter—she couldn't ever accustom herself to the dull life of the capital; she was consumed by the emptiness of existence away from the regiment.

Meanwhile, before his parents' death and somewhat to their

chagrin, Nikolai Petrovich had managed to fall in love with the daughter of his former landlord, a minor official named Prepolovenskii. She was a pretty and, as they say, advanced young woman; she used to read serious articles in the "Science" column of journals. He married her as soon as the mourning period for his parents was over. Having left the civil service, in which his father had procured him a position through his connections, Nikolai Petrovich lived with his Masha in perfect bliss, first in a country villa near the Lesnii Institute, then in a pretty little apartment in town that had a clean staircase and a chilly drawing room, and after that in the countryside, where he finally settled down and where within a short time his son, Arkadii, was born. The young couple lived quite happily and tranquilly. They were hardly ever apart; they read books together, they sang and played duets together on the piano. She tended her flowers and looked after the poultry-yard; he occasionally went hunting and busied himself with the estate. Arkadii grew up just as happily and tranquilly.

Ten years passed like a dream. In 1847, Kirsanov's wife died. He almost succumbed to this blow—his hair turned gray in the space of just a few weeks. He got ready to go abroad in order to distract his mind a bit ... but then came the year 1848. He unwillingly returned to the countryside, and after a rather prolonged period of inactivity, he began to take an interest in improving the management of his estate. In 1855, he took his son to the university; he spent three winters with him in Petersburg, hardly going out anywhere and trying to make friends with Arkadii's youthful companions. He hadn't been able to go the previous winter—and thus we see him in May of 1859, already completely gray, somewhat stout, and slightly stooped. He was waiting for his son, who'd just graduated, as he'd once done himself.

The servant, motivated by a sense of propriety, and possibly not eager to remain under his master's eye anyway, had gone beyond the gate and was smoking a pipe. Nikolai Petrovich bowed his head and began to stare at the crumbling steps. A large, mottled hen walked toward him sedately, treading firmly on its long yellow legs; a muddy cat gave him an unfriendly look, coyly twisting itself around a railing. The sun was scorching; the odor of hot rye bread drifted out from the semidark passage of the inn. Nikolai Petrovich lapsed into daydreams. The words "my son ... a graduate ... Arkasha ..." continually revolved in his head. He tried to think about something else, but the same thoughts kept recurring. He recalled his deceased wife.... "She didn't live to see this!" he murmured sadly. A plump, dark-blue pigeon flew into the road and hastily took a drink from a puddle near the well. Nikolai Petrovich began to watch it, but his ear had already caught the sound of approaching wheels.

"It seems that they're coming, sir," the servant announced, returning from the gateway.

Nikolai Petrovich jumped up and directed his gaze along the road. An open carriage with three horses harnessed abreast appeared; he caught a glimpse of the blue band of a student's cap and the familiar outline of a beloved face inside the carriage.

"Arkasha! Arkasha!" Kirsanov cried and ran forward, waving his arms.... A few moments later, his lips were pressed against the beardless, dusty, sunburned cheek of the young graduate.

## II

"Let me dust myself off first, Papa," Arkadii said in a voice that was tired from the journey but boyish and clear as a bell, as he cheerily responded to his father's caresses. "I'll get you all dirty."

"It's nothing, it's nothing," Nikolai Petrovich assured him, smiling tenderly and slapping the collar of his son's coat as well as his own twice with his hand. "Let me take a look at you, let me take a look at you," he added, stepping back from him; then he immediately hurried toward the courtyard of the inn, calling out, "This way, this way, and bring the horses at once."

Nikolai Petrovich seemed to be much more agitated than his

son; it was as if he were a little lost, and a little shy. Arkadii stopped him.

"Papa," he said, "let me introduce you to my good friend, Bazarov, about whom I've written to you so often. He's been kind enough to promise to stay with us."

Nikolai Petrovich promptly turned around and, walking up to a tall man wearing a long, loose coat with tassels who'd just gotten out of the carriage, he warmly shook that man's bare, reddened hand, which hadn't been extended to him immediately.

"I'm extremely pleased," he began, "and grateful for your kind willingness to visit us.... May I ask your first name and patronymic?"

"Evgenii Vasilich," Bazarov answered in a lazy but powerful voice and, turning down the collar of his coat, revealed his entire face to Nikolai Petrovich. It was long and thin, with a broad forehead, a nose that was flat at the base and sharp at the tip, large greenish eyes, and drooping, sandy-colored sideburns. His face was illuminated by a calm smile, radiating self-assurance and intelligence.

"I hope you won't find it too boring at our home, dear Evgenii Vasilich," continued Nikolai Petrovich.

Bazarov's thin lips moved almost imperceptibly. He made no formal reply and merely took off his cap. His long, thick, dark-blond hair couldn't conceal some large protuberances on his capacious head.

"Well then, Arkadii," Nikolai Petrovich began again, turning to his son, "should the horses be harnessed right away, or would you like to rest?"

"We'll rest at home, Papa. Tell them to harness the horses."

"Right away, right away," his father assented. "Hey, Petr, do you hear? Get everything ready, my boy—hurry now."

Petr, as an up-to-date servant, hadn't kissed the young master's hand but had merely bowed to him from a distance. He vanished through the gateway again.

"I came here with our carriage, but there are three horses for your carriage, too," Nikolai Petrovich remarked fussily, while Arkadii drank some water from an iron dipper the innkeeper brought to him and Bazarov began to smoke a pipe as he walked up to the coachman who was unharnessing the horses.

"It's only a two-seated carriage, and I don't know how your friend...."

"He'll go in the open carriage," Arkadii interrupted in an undertone. "You mustn't stand on ceremony with him, please. He's a wonderful person, and utterly unpretentious—you'll see."

Nikolai Petrovich's driver brought out the fresh horses.

"Well, hurry up, bushy beard!" Bazarov urged, addressing the coachman.

"Do you hear what the gentleman called you, Mitiukha?" interjected another coachman who was standing nearby, his arms thrust behind him through a slit in his sheepskin coat. "It's a bushy beard you have, too."

Mitiukha merely tugged at his cap and pulled the reins off a sweaty shaft-horse.

"Faster, faster, boys, lend a hand," cried Nikolai Petrovich. "There'll be some vodka for you!"

The horses were harnessed within a few minutes; father and son were installed in the two-seated carriage; Petr climbed up onto its box; Bazarov jumped into the open carriage and nestled his head against a leather cushion—and both vehicles rolled away.

## III

"So here you are, a university graduate at last, and you've come home," Nikolai Petrovich said, repeatedly touching Arkadii, first on the shoulder and then on the knee. "At last!"

"And how's my uncle? Is he well?" asked Arkadii. In spite of the genuine, almost childlike delight filling his heart, he wanted to shift the conversation from an emotional to an everyday tone as soon as possible.

"Quite well. He was considering coming with me to meet you, but for some reason or other he gave up on the idea."

"How long have you been waiting for me?" Arkadii inquired.

"Oh, about five hours."

"Dear old Papa!"

Arkadii energetically turned toward his father and planted a noisy kiss on his cheek. Nikolai Petrovich chuckled softly.

"I've got such a marvelous horse for you!" he began. "You'll see. And your room's been freshly wallpapered."

"But is there a room for Bazarov?"

"We'll find one for him, too."

"Please, Papa, make a fuss over him. I can't tell you how much I prize his friendship."

"Have you gotten to know him recently?"

"Yes, quite recently."

"Ah, that's why I didn't see him last winter. What's he's studying?"

"His main subject is the natural sciences. But he knows everything. Next year he wants to get a physician's diploma."

"Ah! He's in the department of medicine," Nikolai Petrovich observed, and he fell silent for a moment. "Petr," he began again, stretching out his hand, "aren't those our peasants going past?"

Petr looked where his master was pointing. Some carts harnessed with unbridled horses were rapidly rolling along a narrow side road. There were one or two peasants wearing unbuttoned sheepskin coats in each cart.

"Yes indeed, sir," Petr replied.

"Where are they going—to town?"

"To town, I should think. To the tavern," he added contemptuously, turning toward the driver slightly, as though appealing to him for reinforcement. But the latter didn't move a muscle; he was an old-fashioned individual, and didn't share the newest attitudes.

"I've had a lot of trouble with the peasants this year," Nikolai Petrovich continued, addressing his son. "They won't pay their rent. What can one do?"

"But are you satisfied with your hired laborers?"

"Yes," Nikolai Petrovich said between clenched teeth. "They're being turned against me, that's the problem—and they don't really try very hard. They spoil the tools. But they've tilled the land fairly well. When things have settled down a bit, it'll be all right. Are you interested in farming now?"

"You don't have any shade. That's a pity," remarked Arkadii, without answering the last question.

"I've had a large awning put up on the north side, above the balcony," Nikolai Petrovich noted. "Now we can even have dinner outside."

"That'd be too much like a summer dacha somehow.... Still, this is all trivial. What wonderful air there is here, though! How delicious it smells! Really, it seems to me there's no place on earth as fragrant as the regions around here! And the sky here...."

Arkadii suddenly stopped short, cast a stealthy glance behind him, and fell silent.

"Of course," Nikolai Petrovich observed, "you were born here, and so everything's bound to strike you in a special...."

"Come on, Papa, it doesn't matter where a person was born."

"But...."

"No, it doesn't matter at all."

Nikolai Petrovich gave his son a sidelong glance. The carriage traveled half a verst farther before the conversation between them was renewed.

"I don't recall whether I wrote to you," Nikolai Petrovich began, "that Egorovna, your old nursemaid, died."

"Really? Poor old woman! Is Prokofich still alive?"

"Yes, and he hasn't changed a bit—grumbles as much as ever. In fact, you won't find many changes at Marino."

"Do you still have the same bailiff?"

"Well, in fact, I've made a change there. I decided not to keep any emancipated serfs with me who'd been house servants, or at least not to entrust them with responsibilities of any significance." (Arkadii glanced toward Petr.) *"Il est libre, en effet,"* Nikolai

Petrovich commented under his breath, "but, you see, he's only a valet. So now I have a bailiff from town who seems to be a sensible person. I pay him two hundred and fifty rubles a year. But," Nikolai Petrovich added, rubbing his forehead and eyebrows with his hand, which always indicated some inner turmoil, "I just told you that you wouldn't find changes at Marino.... That's not quite true. I consider it my duty to warn you, although...."

He hesitated for an instant, and then continued in French.

"A strict moralist would regard my candor as improper, but, in the first place, this can't be concealed and, in the second, you're aware that I've always had unique ideas regarding the relationship between parent and child. Yet, of course, you'd be justified in condemning me. At my age.... In short, that ... that young woman about whom you've probably already heard...."

"Fenechka?" Arkadii asked casually.

Nikolai Petrovich blushed. "Please don't mention her name out loud.... Well ... she's living with me now. I've installed her in the house ... in two little rooms there. But that can all be changed."

"For heaven's sake, Papa, why?"

"Your friend's going to stay with us.... It might be awkward...."

"Please don't worry on Bazarov's account. He's above all that."

"Well, there's you, too," Nikolai Petrovich added. "The little lodge is so awful—that's the problem."

"For heaven's sake, Papa," Arkadii interjected, "it's as though you were apologizing. You ought to be ashamed."

"Of course I ought to be ashamed," Nikolai Petrovich responded, becoming more and more flushed.

"That's enough, Papa, that's enough. Please don't!" Arkadii smiled affectionately. "What a thing to apologize for!" he thought to himself, and his soul was filled with a feeling of condescending tenderness toward his kind, gentle father that was mixed with some sort of veiled sense of superiority. "Please stop," he insisted once more, instinctively reveling in the consciousness of his own progressiveness and freedom from prejudice.

Nikolai Petrovich glanced at him from behind the hand with which he was still rubbing his forehead, and felt a pang in his heart.... But he instantly blamed that on himself.

"Here are our fields at last," he observed after a long silence.

"And that's our forest ahead of us, isn't it?" Arkadii asked.

"Yes. Only I've sold it. They're going to cut it down this year."

"Why did you sell it?"

"We needed the money. Besides, that land will go to the peasants."

"The ones who don't pay you their rent?"

"That's their business. Anyway, they'll pay it someday."

"I'm sorry about the forest," Arkadii remarked, and he began to look around.

The countryside through which they were driving couldn't be called picturesque. Field upon field stretched all the way to the very horizon, gently sloping upward in some spots, then slanting downward again in others; small forests were visible here and there; ravines covered with low, scanty bushes, reminiscent of their representations on ancient maps from the era of Catherine the Great, wound through the terrain. The travelers came across shallow streams with barren banks; tiny lakes with narrow dams; little villages with huts under dark, often decrepit roofs, rickety barns with woven brushwood walls and gaping doorways next to neglected threshing sheds; churches, some of which were brick, their plaster peeling off in patches, others of which were wood, their crosses hanging askew and their graveyards overgrown. Arkadii's heart slowly sank.

To complete the picture, the peasants they encountered were all shabbily dressed, riding the sorriest little ponies; the willows near the road, whose trunks had been stripped of bark and whose branches had been snapped, stood along the roadside like ragged beggars; emaciated, shaggy cows, pinched with hunger, were greedily tearing at the grass along the ditches—they looked as though they'd just been snatched from the murderous clutches of some hideous monster. The piteous aspect of the broken-down beasts in the midst of the lovely spring day evoked the white phantom of endless, dismal winter, with its storms, frosts, and snows.... "No," thought Arkadii, "this isn't a wealthy region, it doesn't impress one by its abundance of resources or its industry. It mustn't, it mustn't remain like this. Reforms are absolutely necessary ... but how can one carry them out—how can one start ... ?"

Such were Arkadii's reflections ... yet even as he reflected, the springtime began to take hold of him. Everything all around him was golden-green, everything—trees, bushes, and grass—was shimmering, gently stirring in wide ripples under the soft breath of the warm breeze; the endless trilling of larks poured forth from all sides; peewits either called out as they hovered over the low-lying meadows or silently ran across the mounds of grass; crows strutted among the half-grown spring corn, standing out darkly against its tender verdure, and disappeared in the rye that had already turned slightly white, occasionally sticking their heads out from amid its hazy waves. Arkadii gazed steadily, his reflections gradually becoming less focused and fading away.... He flung off his coat and turned toward Nikolai Petrovich with a face so bright and boyish that his father gave him another hug.

"We're not far away now," Nikolai Petrovich remarked. "We just have to go up this hill, and the house will be in sight. We'll get along beautifully together, Arkasha. You'll help me farm the estate, if that isn't too boring for you. We have to grow close to one another now, and get to know one another really well, don't we?"

"Of course," replied Arkadii. "But what a marvelous day it is today!"

"It's in honor of your arrival, my dear boy. Yes, it's spring in all its loveliness. Although I agree with Pushkin—do you remember, in *Eugene Onegin:*

> To me, how sad your advent is,
> Spring, spring, the time of love!
> What....

"Arkadii," Bazarov's voice called out from his carriage, "pass me a match. I don't have anything to light my pipe with."

Nikolai Petrovich fell silent, while Arkadii, who'd begun to listen to him not without surprise, albeit not without sympathy either, hastily pulled a silver matchbox out of his pocket and passed it to Petr to transmit.

"Do you want a cigar?" Bazarov shouted out again.

"All right," Arkadii answered.

Petr returned to the carriage and handed him a thick black cigar along with the matchbox. Arkadii promptly began to smoke, diffusing such a strong, pungent odor of cheap tobacco that Nikolai Petrovich, who'd never smoked, was forced to turn his head away as imperceptibly as he could, for fear of offending his son.

A quarter of an hour later, the two vehicles came to a stop before the steps of a new, gray, wooden house with a red iron roof. This was Marino, also known as New Village or, as the peasants had nicknamed it, Poverty Farm.

# IV

No crowd of house serfs ran out onto the steps to greet the gentlemen; no one but a little twelve-year-old girl appeared. Following behind her, a young man closely resembling Petr emerged from the house dressed in gray livery with white military buttons; he was Pavel Petrovich Kirsanov's personal servant. Without speaking, he opened the door of the two-seated carriage and unfastened the latch of the open carriage. Nikolai Petrovich accompanied his son and Bazarov down a dark, almost empty hall. They caught a glimpse of a young woman's face from behind a door before they entered a drawing room furnished in the most contemporary style.

"Here we are, at home," Nikolai Petrovich declared, taking off his cap and pushing his hair away from his forehead. "The most important thing now is to have some supper and to rest."

"Having something to eat wouldn't be a bad idea, in fact," Bazarov remarked, stretching his limbs and then sinking onto a sofa.

"Yes, yes, let's have supper, let's have supper as soon as possible." For no apparent reason, Nikolai Petrovich stamped his foot. "And here comes Prokofich just at the right moment."

A white-haired, thin, dark-complexioned man about sixty years old entered the room wearing a cinnamon-colored dress coat with brass buttons and a pink scarf around his neck. He beamed, went up to kiss Arkadii's hand, and then, bowing to the guest, retreated to the doorway and put his hands behind his back.

"Here he is, Prokofich," began Nikolai Petrovich. "He's come back to us at last. . . . Well, how does he look to you?"

"Never better, sir," responded the elderly man, beaming again, but he quickly knitted his bushy eyebrows. "Do you wish supper to be served?" he inquired impressively.

"Yes, yes, please. But wouldn't you like to go to your room first, Evgenii Vasilich?"

"No, thanks, I don't need to. Just have my little suitcase taken to it, along with this garment," he added, taking off his overcoat.

"Certainly. Prokofich, take the gentleman's coat." (Prokofich, as if bewildered, picked up Bazarov's "garment" in both hands and, holding it high above his head, retreated on tiptoe.) "And you, Arkadii, are you going to your room for a minute?"

"Yes, I want to wash up," Arkadii replied, and started to move toward the door, but at that instant a man of medium height, dressed in a dark English suit, a modishly short tie, and kid leather shoes, came into the drawing room. It was Pavel Petrovich Kirsanov. He appeared to be about forty-five; his short, gray hair shone with a dark luster, like new silver; his face was sallow but free of wrinkles, exceptionally even and fine-featured, as though carved by a light, delicate chisel, and contained traces of remarkable beauty; his clear, dark, almond-shaped eyes were especially attractive. In its aristocratic elegance, his entire body had preserved the gracefulness of youth and the impression of buoyancy, of the defiance of gravity, that's usually lost after one's twenties.

Pavel Petrovich extracted one of his exquisite hands with its long pink fingernails from his trouser pocket—a hand that seemed even more exquisite thanks to the snowy whiteness of the shirt cuff surrounding it, which was fastened by a single, large, opal cuff link—and offered it to his nephew. After a preliminary handshake in the European style, he kissed him three times in Russian fashion—that is to say, he touched Arkadii's cheek with his perfumed moustache three times—and said, "Welcome home."

Nikolai Petrovich introduced him to Bazarov. Pavel Petrovich greeted him with a slight inclination of his supple figure and a slight smile, but he didn't hold out his hand to Bazarov, and even put it back in his pocket.

"I'd begun to think you weren't coming today," he announced in a pleasing voice, nodding genially and shrugging his shoulders as he displayed his handsome white teeth. "Did anything happen on the road?"

"Nothing happened," Arkadii responded. "We just proceeded rather slowly. But we're as hungry as wolves now. Make Prokofich hurry, Papa, and I'll come back right away."

"Wait, I'm coming with you," Bazarov cried, suddenly pulling himself up from the sofa. Both young men went out.

"Who is he?" asked Pavel Petrovich.

"A friend of Arkasha—according to him, an intelligent young man."

"Is he going to stay with us?"

"Yes."

"That long-haired creature?"

"Why, yes."

Pavel Petrovich drummed his fingertips on the table. "I imagine Arkadii's *s'est dégourdi*," he observed. "I'm glad he's come back."

At supper, there was little conversation. Bazarov in particular said almost nothing, but he ate a great deal. Nikolai Petrovich recounted various incidents in what he termed his career as a farmer, talked about impending government measures, committees, deputations, the necessity of introducing machinery, and so forth. Pavel Petrovich slowly paced up and down the dining room (he never ate supper), periodically sipping a glass of red wine and occasionally uttering some remark, or rather exclamation, of the sort "Ah! Aha! Hmm!" Arkadii conveyed some news from Petersburg, but he felt a slight sense of discomfort, the discomfort that frequently overcomes a young man when he's just ceased to be a child and then returns to a place where people are accustomed to consider him a child. He made his sentences unnecessarily long, avoided the word "Papa," and sometimes even replaced it with the word "Father"—mumbled between his teeth, it's true. With exaggerated carelessness, he poured far more wine into his glass than he really wanted, and drank it all up. Prokofich, continually chewing on his lips, didn't take his eyes off Arkadii. After supper, everyone promptly separated.

"Your uncle's rather eccentric," Bazarov said to Arkadii, as he sat by Arkadii's bedside in his robe, smoking a small pipe. "Can you imagine such dandyism in the countryside! His fingernails, now, his fingernails—you ought to send them to an exhibition!"

"Well, of course, you don't know about him," Arkadii replied. "He was a social lion in his own day. I'll tell you about his past sometime. He was very handsome, you know, and used to attract lots of women."

"Oh, so that's it, is it? He keeps it up as a memorial to the past. It's a pity that there's no one for him to fascinate here, though. I kept staring at his amazing collars—they're like marble—and his chin was shaved to perfection. Come on, Arkadii Nikolaich, isn't that ridiculous?"

"Probably, and yet he's really a decent person."

"He's an archaic phenomenon! But your father's a fine man. He wastes his time reading poetry and he doesn't know much about farming, but he's a good soul."

"My father's worth his weight in gold."

"Did you notice that he seemed shy?"

Arkadii nodded his head as though he himself weren't shy.

"It's astonishing," Bazarov continued. "These old romantics—they continuously refine their nervous systems until those systems break down ... so that their equanimity is destroyed. And now, good night. There's an English washstand in my room, but the door won't lock. Still, that ought to be encouraged—an English washstand means progress!"

Bazarov left, and a joyous feeling swept over Arkadii. It's lovely to fall asleep in one's own home, in a familiar bed, under a blanket stitched together by loving hands—perhaps by a former nursemaid's hands—those affectionate, kindly, untiring hands. Arkadii recalled Egorovna, sighed, and wished her peace in heaven.... He didn't pray for himself.

Both he and Bazarov fell asleep soon, but other inhabitants of the house remained awake for a long while. His son's return had agitated Nikolai Petrovich. He got into bed but didn't put out the candles, and, propping his head on his hand, he lapsed into prolonged musing. His brother stayed in his study until well after midnight, sitting in a wide armchair before the fireplace, in which some embers were faintly smoldering. Pavel Petrovich hadn't undressed—he'd merely replaced the leather shoes on his feet with some red Chinese slippers. He held the most recent issue of *Galignani* in his hands, but he wasn't reading; he was steadily gazing at the fireplace, where a bluish flame flickered, dying down and then flaring up again.... God knows where his thoughts were wandering, but they weren't wandering solely in the past: the expression on his face was focused and grim, which isn't the case when someone is wholly absorbed in memories. And in a small back room, a young woman wearing a blue jacket and a white kerchief thrown over her dark hair was sitting on a large chest—this was Fenechka. She was half alert, half dozing, repeatedly looking toward an open door, through which a child's cradle was visible and the regular breathing of a slumbering infant could be heard.

# V

The next morning, Bazarov got up earlier than anyone else and went out of the house. "Ah," he thought, looking around him, "this little place isn't much to brag about!" When Nikolai Petrovich had divided his land with the peasants, he'd had to build a new residence on four acres of perfectly flat, barren fields. He'd constructed a house, offices, and a farmyard, laid out a garden, dug a pond, and sunk two wells. But the young trees hadn't thrived, very little water had collected in the pond, and the water in the wells tasted brackish. Only one arbor consisting of lilac and acacia bushes had done fairly well; the brothers occasionally had tea or ate dinner in it. Within a few minutes, Bazarov had traversed every one of the little garden paths, had visited the cattleyard and the stable, had sought out two farm boys, whom he promptly befriended, and had set off with them toward a small swamp about a verst from the house to find frogs.

"What do you want frogs for, master?" one of the boys asked him.

"I'll tell you what for," responded Bazarov, who possessed the special faculty of inspiring confidence in him among people of a lower social class, although he never tried to win them over, and treated them quite casually. "I'll cut a frog open and see what's going on inside, and then, because you and I are a lot like frogs, except that we walk on legs, I'll know what's going on inside us, too."

"And what do you want to know that for?"

"So as not to make a mistake if you get sick and I have to cure you."

"Are you a doctor, then?"

"Yes."

"Vaska, do you hear—the gentleman says you and I are the same as frogs. Weird!"

"I'm scared of frogs," remarked Vaska, a boy of about seven with hair as white as flax and bare feet, dressed in a long gray shirt with a stand-up collar.

"What's there to be scared about? Do they bite?"

"Come on, paddle into the water, philosophers," commanded Bazarov.

Meanwhile, Nikolai Petrovich had also woken up and gone to see Arkadii, whom he found already dressed. Father and son went out onto the terrace under the shelter of the awning; the samovar was already boiling on a table near the railing, amid large bouquets of lilacs. A little girl appeared, the same one who'd been the first to meet them at the steps upon their arrival the evening before. She announced in a shrill voice, "Fedosia Nikolaevna isn't feeling well—she can't come. She told me to ask you if you'd be so kind as to pour the tea yourself or if she should send Duniasha."

"I'll pour it myself, I'll do it," Nikolai Petrovich interjected hurriedly. "Arkadii, how do you drink your tea, with cream or with lemon?"

"With cream," Arkadii answered. After a brief silence, he tentatively said: "Papa?"

Nikolai Petrovich looked at his son disconcertedly.

"What?" he asked.

Arkadii lowered his eyes.

"Forgive me if my question seems inappropriate to you, Papa," he began, "but by your candor yesterday you yourself encourage me to be candid.... You won't get angry ...?"

"Go on."

"You give me the courage to ask you.... Isn't the reason Fen ... isn't the reason she won't come out here to pour the tea the fact that I'm here?"

Nikolai Petrovich turned away slightly.

"Perhaps," he eventually acknowledged. "She supposes.... She's ashamed...."

Arkadii cast a rapid glance at his father.

"She shouldn't be ashamed. In the first place, you're aware of my view of the matter" (it was highly pleasing to Arkadii to utter these words), "and in the second, would I want to constrain your life, your habits, the slightest bit? Besides, I'm sure you couldn't make a bad choice. If you've allowed her to live under the same roof with you, she must deserve it. In any case, a son can't judge his father—least of all me, and least of all a father like you, who's never constrained my freedom in any way."

Arkadii's voice was shaky at the beginning; he felt that he was being magnanimous, although at the same time he realized that he was delivering something in the nature of a lecture to his father. But the sound of his own voice has a powerful effect on any man, and Arkadii pronounced his concluding words resolutely, even emphatically.

"Thank you, Arkasha," Nikolai Petrovich replied hollowly, and his fingers strayed across his eyebrows and forehead once more. "Your suppositions are in fact correct. Of course, if this young woman hadn't deserved.... This isn't some frivolous caprice. It's awkward for me to talk to you about this, but you understand that it'd be difficult for her to come out here in your presence, especially the first day after you've returned home."

"In that case, I'll go and see her," Arkadii cried with a fresh burst of magnanimity, and he jumped up from his chair. "I'll explain to her that she doesn't need to be ashamed around me."

Nikolai Petrovich stood up as well.

"Arkadii," he began, "please ... how can ... there ... I haven't told you yet...."

But Arkadii didn't listen to him and ran off the terrace. Nikolai Petrovich watched him go, and then sank back into his chair, overwhelmed by embarrassment. His heart began to pound.... At that moment, was he envisioning the inevitable strangeness about to be introduced into the relationship between himself and his son? Was he acknowledging that Arkadii might have shown him greater respect by never touching on this subject at all? Was he reproaching himself for weakness? It's hard to say; all these feelings were occurring inside him, but only as sensations— vague sensations. Meanwhile, the flush on his face didn't subside, and his heart continued to pound.

The sound of hurrying footsteps became audible, and Arkadii came back out onto the terrace. "We've gotten acquainted, Father!" he exclaimed with some sort of affectionate, good-natured, triumphant expression on his face. "Fedosia Nikolaevna really isn't feeling well today, and she'll come out a little later. But why didn't you tell me I had a brother? I would have kissed him last night the way I just kissed him now."

Nikolai Petrovich tried to say something, tried to stand up and embrace his son.... Arkadii flung his arms around his father's neck.

"What's this? Embracing again?" the voice of Pavel Petrovich rang out from behind them.

Father and son were equally pleased by his appearance at that moment: there are genuinely touching situations from which one longs to escape as quickly as possible.

"Why should you be so surprised at that?" Nikolai Petrovich retorted cheerfully. "Think how many ages I've been waiting for Arkasha.... I haven't had a chance to get a good look at him since yesterday."

"I'm not the least bit surprised," remarked Pavel Petrovich. "I'm not opposed to embracing him myself."

Arkadii went up to his uncle and felt his cheeks caressed again by that perfumed moustache. Pavel Petrovich sat down at the table. He was wearing an elegant, English-style morning suit; a little fez adorned his head. This fez and his carelessly tied short tie betokened the informality of country life, but the stiff collar on his shirt—which wasn't white, of course, but striped, as is correct for morning attire—stood up as inexorably as ever under his well-shaved chin.

"Where's your new friend?" he asked Arkadii.

"He isn't inside the house. He usually gets up early and goes off somewhere. The important thing is not to pay any attention to him. He doesn't like formality."

"Yes, that's obvious." Pavel Petrovich began methodically spreading butter on his bread. "Is he going to stay with us for a long time?"

"Possibly. He came here on the way to his father's."

"And where does his father live?"

"In our district, about eighty versts from here. He has a small estate there. He used to be an army doctor."

"Hmm. So that's why I kept asking myself, 'Where have I heard that name, Bazarov?' Nikolai, do you remember, wasn't there a surgeon named Bazarov in our father's division?"

"I believe there was."

"Yes, yes, indeed. So that surgeon was his father. Hmm!" Pavel Petrovich stroked his moustache. "Well, and precisely what sort of person is Mr. Bazarov himself?" he asked in measured tones.

"What sort of person is Bazarov?" Arkadii smiled. "Would you like me to tell you precisely what sort of person he is, Uncle?"

"If you'd be so kind, Nephew."

"He's a nihilist."

"What?" responded Nikolai Petrovich, while Pavel Petrovich suspended his knife in the air, a small piece of butter on its tip, and held still.

"He's a nihilist," repeated Arkadii.

"A nihilist," echoed Nikolai Petrovich. "That's from the Latin, *nihil,* 'nothing,' as far as I can judge. The word must mean someone who ... who doesn't believe in anything?"

"Say, 'who doesn't respect anything,'" interjected Pavel Petrovich, and he began to spread his butter again.

"Who regards everything from a critical point of view," observed Arkadii.

"Isn't it all the same?" inquired Pavel Petrovich.

"No, it's not all the same. A nihilist is someone who doesn't bow down to any authority, who doesn't accept any principle on faith, no matter how revered that principle may be."

"Well, is this a good thing?" Pavel Petrovich interrupted.

"That depends, Uncle. For some people it's good, but for others it's very bad."

"Indeed. Well, I see that it's not our sort of thing—we're old-fashioned people. We imagine that without principles" (Pavel Petrovich uttered this word softly, the French way, whereas Arkadii pronounced it forcefully, with the accent on the first syllable), "without principles accepted on faith, as you put it, no one can take a single step, no one can breathe. *Vous avez changé tout cela.* May God grant you good health and a general's rank, while we'll merely sit back and marvel at your worthy ... what was the word?"

"Nihilists," Arkadii declared distinctly.

"Yes. There used to be Hegelians, and now there are nihilists. We'll see how you'll survive in isolation, in a vacuum. But now please call a servant, brother Nikolai Petrovich. It's time for my cocoa."

Nikolai Petrovich rang a bell and called out, "Duniasha!" But instead of Duniasha, Fenechka herself walked out onto the terrace. She was a young woman of about twenty-three, with white, soft skin, dark hair and eyes, red, childishly pouting lips, and gentle little hands. She wore a tidy print dress; a new blue scarf lay lightly across her plump shoulders. She was carrying a large cup of cocoa, and, setting it down in front of Pavel Petrovich, she was engulfed by shame: her pulsing blood sent a crimson wave across the delicate skin of her lovely face. She lowered her eyes and stood next to the table, leaning forward slightly on the very tips of her toes. It seemed that she felt guilty about having come there, and at the same time felt that she had a right to come there.

Pavel Petrovich furrowed his brow severely, and Nikolai Petrovich became embarrassed.

"Good morning, Fenechka," he muttered through his teeth.

"Good morning," she replied in a soft but resonant voice, and, casting a sidelong glance at Arkadii, who gave her a friendly smile, she left quietly. She had a slightly rolling gait, which suited her.

Silence reigned on the terrace for several moments. Pavel Petrovich sipped his cocoa. Suddenly he raised his head. "Here's Mr. Nihilist coming toward us," he observed under his breath.

Bazarov was indeed walking through the garden, stepping over the flower beds. His linen coat and trousers were smeared with mud; clinging marsh weeds were twined around the crown of his old, round-shaped hat; in his right hand, he was holding a small bag that had something alive moving in it. He rapidly approached the terrace and said with a nod: "Good morning, gentlemen. Sorry I was late for my tea. I'll be back in a minute. I just have to put these captives away."

"What do you have there—leeches?" queried Pavel Petrovich.

"No, frogs."

"Do you eat them—or take them apart?"

"For experiments," Bazarov stated matter-of-factly, and he went off into the house.

"So he's going to cut them up," remarked Pavel Petrovich. "He doesn't believe in principles, but he believes in frogs."

Arkadii looked at his uncle compassionately. Nikolai Petrovich stealthily shrugged his shoulders. Pavel Petrovich himself sensed that his witticism hadn't gone over well, and he began to talk about husbandry, then about the new bailiff who'd come to him the evening before to complain that a certain laborer, Foma, was "deboshed," and completely out of control. "He's such an Aesop," the bailiff had said, among other things. "He goes around everywhere declaring that he's a worthless human being—he gets away with anything as a result."

# VI

Bazarov returned, sat down at the table, and hastily began to drink tea. The two brothers gazed at him in silence, while Arkadii furtively looked first at his father and then at his uncle.

"Did you go far from here?" Nikolai Petrovich eventually inquired.

"Where you've got a little swamp, near the aspen grove. I startled five snipe or so. You could shoot them, Arkadii."

"Aren't you a hunter, then?"

"No."

"Is your particular field of study medical science?" Pavel Petrovich inquired in his turn.

"Medical science, yes, and the natural sciences in general."

"They say that the Teutons have recently made great advances in that area."

"Yes, the Germans are our instructors in this," Bazarov responded offhandedly.

Pavel Petrovich had used the word "Teutons" instead of the word "Germans" for ironic effect, which no one noticed, however.

"Do you have such a high opinion of the Germans?" Pavel Petrovich asked with exaggerated courtesy. He was secretly beginning to feel irritated. His aristocratic nature was revolted by Bazarov's thoroughgoing nonchalance. This surgeon's son not only wasn't intimidated, he replied to questions laconically, even dismissively, and there was something churlish, almost insolent, in his tone of voice.

"The scientists there are sensible people."

"Ah, I see. You probably don't have such high regard for Russian scientists?"

"I suppose that's so."

"That's most praiseworthy self-abnegation," Pavel Petrovich commented, straightening up and tossing his head back. "But why was Arkadii Nikolaich just telling us that you don't acknowledge any authorities? Don't you believe in *them*?"

"Why should I acknowledge any? And what should I believe in? They tell me the truth, and I agree—that's all."

"Do Germans always tell the truth?" rejoined Pavel Petrovich, and his face assumed an extremely austere, remote expression, as though he'd mentally withdrawn to some height above the clouds.

"Not all of them," Bazarov replied with a brief yawn. He obviously didn't want to continue this war of words.

Pavel Petrovich glanced at Arkadii, as if to say to him, "Your friend is certainly polite, isn't he?"

"For my part," he began again, not without some effort, "I'm so unregenerate as to dislike Germans. I'm not referring to Russian Germans now—we all know what sort of creatures they are. But even German Germans aren't much to my taste. There were a few in earlier times, here and there. Then they had— well, Schiller, I suppose, and Goethe.... My brother especially prefers them.... But now they've all turned into chemists and materialists...."

"A good chemist is twenty times as useful as any poet," Bazarov interjected.

"Oh, indeed," retorted Pavel Petrovich, and he faintly raised his eyebrows, as though he were falling asleep. "Then you don't believe in art, I gather?"

"The art of making money or of curing hemorrhoids!" Bazarov cried with a contemptuous laugh.

"Yes, yes. You enjoy making jokes, I see. You reject all that, no doubt? Granted. Then you believe solely in science?"

"I've already explained to you that I don't believe in anything. And what is science—science in the abstract? There are sciences, just as there are trades and crafts, but science in the abstract doesn't exist at all."

"That's very nice. Well, do you maintain the same negative attitude in regard to all the other traditions governing the conduct of human affairs?"

"What is this, an examination?" asked Bazarov.

Pavel Petrovich turned slightly pale.... Nikolai Petrovich decided that he was obligated to intervene in the conversation.

"We'll discuss this subject with you in more detail some other day, dear Evgenii Vasilich. We'll find out about your views and express our own. For my part, I'm heartily glad that you're studying the natural sciences. I've heard that Liebig has made some wonderful discoveries regarding the improvement of soils. You can help me in my agricultural labors—you can give me some useful advice."

"I'm at your service, Nikolai Petrovich, but Liebig is way over our heads! One has to learn the alphabet before beginning to read, and we haven't set our eyes on the letter 'a' yet."

"You certainly are a nihilist, I can see that," thought Nikolai Petrovich. "Nonetheless, permit me to turn to you occasionally," he added aloud. "And now, Brother, I believe it's time for us to have a little chat with the bailiff."

Pavel Petrovich got up from his chair.

"Yes," he said, without looking at anyone. "It's unfortunate to live in the countryside like this for five years or so, at such a distance from mighty intellects! You promptly turn into a fool. You may try not to forget what you've been taught, but then—just like that!—they'll prove it's all nonsense, tell you that sensible men don't concern themselves with such trifles any more and that you, if you please, are an antiquated old fogey. What can one do? Young people are evidently much smarter than we are!"

Pavel Petrovich slowly turned on his heel and slowly walked away; Nikolai Petrovich followed him.

"Is he always like that around you?" Bazarov asked Arkadii coolly as soon as the door had closed behind the two brothers.

"Listen, Evgenii, you dealt with him too sharply," Arkadii asserted. "You've hurt his feelings."

"Well, should I coddle them, these provincial aristocrats? Why, it's all pride, it's fashionable custom, it's foppishness. He should have continued to pursue his career in Petersburg, if that was his inclination. Anyway, the hell with him! I've found a rather rare species of water-beetle, *Dytiscus marginatus*. Do you know it? I'll show it to you."

"I promised to tell you about his past," Arkadii began.

"The beetle's past?"

"Come on, Evgenii, that's enough. My uncle's past. You'll see that he's not the sort of person you think he is. He deserves more pity than scorn."

"I don't deny it—but why are you so concerned about him?"

"One should be fair, Evgenii."

"How does that follow?"

"No, listen...."

And Arkadii told him about his uncle's past. The reader will find the gist of it in the next chapter.

# VII

Pavel Petrovich Kirsanov was educated first at home, like his younger brother, and subsequently in the Corps of Pages. From childhood on, he'd been distinguished by remarkable beauty; moreover, he was self-confident, slightly cynical, and had a rather cutting sense of humor—he couldn't fail to please. As soon as he'd received his officer's commission, he began to go everywhere. He was greatly admired in society, and indulged every whim, committed every folly, affecting a supercilious air— but even that was attractive in him. Women went out of their minds over him; men called him a dandy and secretly envied him. As has already been mentioned, he lived in the same apartment as his brother, whom he sincerely loved, although he didn't resemble him in the least. Nikolai Petrovich was slightly lame, had diminutive, pleasant, somewhat melancholy features, small, dark eyes, and thin, fine hair; he liked indolence, but he also liked to read, and he feared all social activities. Pavel Petrovich never spent a single evening at home, prided himself on his agility and daring (he was just introducing gymnastics to fashionable young men), and had read a total of five or six French books. At the age of twenty-eight, he was already a captain; a brilliant career awaited him. Suddenly everything changed.

At that time, a woman occasionally appeared in Petersburg society who hasn't been forgotten to this day, Princess R——. She had a well-bred, well-mannered, but rather stupid husband, and was childless. She used to go abroad suddenly, and just as suddenly return to Russia, generally leading a strange life. She had the reputation of being a frivolous coquette; she eagerly abandoned herself to every form of pleasure, danced to the point of exhaustion, and laughed and joked with the young people she entertained in her half-lit drawing room prior to dinner. But, at night, she wept and prayed, found no source of solace anywhere, and often paced around her room until morning, wringing her hands in anguish, or sat reading a psalter, pale and cold. Day would come, and she'd transform herself into a great lady once again; she'd go out once again, laughing, chattering, and seemingly flinging herself headlong into anything that could afford her the slightest distraction. She had a wonderful figure; her hair was the color of gold and hung down to her knees, as heavy as gold; but no one would have called her a beauty. Her only good facial features were her eyes, and not even her eyes themselves—they were small and gray—but their gaze, which was alert and deep, unconcerned to the point of audacity, and thoughtful to the point of melancholy—an enigmatic gaze. Some extraordinary light shone in that gaze, even while her tongue was lisping the most inane speeches. She dressed with elaborate care.

Pavel Petrovich met her at a ball, danced the mazurka with her—in the course of which she didn't utter a single significant word—and fell passionately in love with her. Accustomed to making romantic conquests, he quickly attained his object in this instance as well, but the ease of his success didn't dampen his ardor. On the contrary, he found himself in ever-increasing torment, in ever-increasing bondage to this woman who, even at the very moment when she wholly surrendered herself, always seemed to remain somehow mysterious and unfathomable, somehow unattainable. What lay hidden in that soul—God knows! It was as though she were in the grips of some sort of secret forces incomprehensible even to her—they played on her at will, and her intellect wasn't strong enough to tame their caprices. All her actions were characterized by inconsistency; she wrote the only letters that could have awakened her husband's legitimate suspicions to a man who was a virtual stranger to her. Her love always incorporated an element of sorrow: she ceased to laugh and joke with a man she'd chosen as a lover, listening to him and gazing at him with a bewildered look on her face. Sometimes, typically all of a sudden, this bewilderment would turn to icy horror: her face would assume a wild, deathlike expression; she'd lock herself up in her bedroom; her maid, putting one ear to the keyhole, could hear her smothered sobs. More than once, as he was going home after an intimate tryst, Kirsanov experienced the heartrending, bitter frustration that follows upon total failure.

"What more do I want?" he asked himself, as his heart ceaselessly ached. One day he gave her a ring with a sphinx engraved on the stone.

"What's this?" she asked. "A sphinx?"

"Yes," he answered, "and this sphinx is you."

"I?" she queried, slowly turning her enigmatic gaze toward him. "Do you know that this is very flattering?" she added with a meaningless smile, her eyes retaining the same strange look.

Pavel Petrovich suffered even while Princess R—— loved him, but when she cooled toward him—which happened fairly soon—he nearly lost his mind. He was in agony; he was jealous; he gave her no peace, following her everywhere. She got tired of his relentless pursuit and went abroad. He resigned his commission, despite the entreaties of his friends and the exhortations of his superiors, and set off after the princess; he spent some four years in foreign countries, at times seeking her out, at other times intentionally losing sight of her. He was ashamed of himself, he was disgusted at his own lack of spirit ... but nothing availed. Her image, that incomprehensible, almost senseless, but bewitching image, was deeply rooted in his soul. In Baden, he somehow regained his former status with her once more; it seemed as though she'd never loved him so passionately ... but it was all over in a month—the flame flared up for the final time and went out forever. Foreseeing an inevitable separation, he at least wanted to remain her friend, as though friendship with such a woman were possible.... She left Baden in secret, and from that time onward, she steadily avoided Kirsanov.

He returned to Russia and tried to resume his former life, but he couldn't get back into the old groove. He wandered from place to place like someone who'd been drugged. He still frequented society, maintaining the habits of a man of the world; he could boast of two or three fresh conquests; but he no longer expected anything much of himself or of anyone else, and he didn't undertake any new activity. He grew old and gray. Spending all his evenings at his club, where he became jaundiced and bored, he found dispassionately arguing in bachelor company ever more essential to him—a bad sign, as we all know. He didn't even consider marriage, understandably.

Ten years passed this way, colorlessly, fruitlessly, and quickly—terribly quickly. In no other country does time fly as fast as it does in Russia; in prison, they say, it flies even faster. One day during dinner at his club, Pavel Petrovich learned of Princess R——'s death. She'd died in Paris in a condition bordering on insanity. He got up from the table and walked around the rooms of the club for a long while, pausing to stand near the cardplayers as though carved in stone—but he didn't go home any earlier than usual. Days later, he received a packet addressed to him; it contained the ring he'd given the princess. She'd drawn lines above the sphinx in the shape of a cross and ordered the messenger to tell him that the solution to the enigma was—the cross.

This happened at the beginning of 1848, at the very time when Nikolai Petrovich came to Petersburg after losing his wife. Pavel Petrovich had hardly seen his brother since the latter had settled down in the countryside; Nikolai Petrovich's marriage had coincided with the very beginning of Pavel Petrovich's acquaintance with the princess. When Pavel Petrovich had returned from abroad, he'd gone to visit Nikolai Petrovich, intending to stay with him for a couple of months to admire his happiness, but he'd only managed to endure a week: the difference between the two brothers' situations had been too great. By 1848, this difference had diminished: Nikolai Petrovich had lost his wife and Pavel Petrovich had lost his memories—after the princess's death, he tried not to think about her. But Nikolai still possessed the sense of a well-spent life and a son growing up before his eyes; Pavel, by contrast, was a solitary bachelor entering upon that indefinite twilight period of regrets that are akin to hopes and hopes that are akin to regrets, when youth is over but old age still hasn't arrived. And this period was harder for Pavel

Petrovich than for other men: in losing his past, he'd lost everything.

"I won't invite you to Marino just now," Nikolai Petrovich told him one day (he'd named his estate that in honor of his wife). "You were bored there while my beloved wife was alive, and now I think you'd die of boredom."

"I was still foolish and fretful then," responded Pavel Petrovich. "Since that time, I've gotten calmer, if not wiser. On the contrary, if you'll let me, now I'm ready to settle down with you for good."

In place of an answer, Nikolai Petrovich just hugged him. But a year and a half passed after this conversation occurred before Pavel Petrovich decided to carry out his plan. Once he did settle down in the countryside, however, he didn't leave it, even during the three winters Nikolai Petrovich spent in Petersburg with his son. He began to read, chiefly in English; he arranged his entire life in English fashion, generally speaking; he rarely visited neighbors, and only attended local elections, where he typically remained silent, just occasionally making liberal sallies that annoyed and alarmed the old-fashioned landowners, while refusing to associate with representatives of the new generation. Both sides considered him arrogant, and both sides respected him. They respected him for his refined, aristocratic manners; for his reputation for amorous conquests; for the fact that he was dressed handsomely and always stayed in the best room of the best hotel; for the fact that he ordinarily dined well, and had once even dined with Wellington at Louis Philippe's residence; for the fact that he brought a real silver toiletry case and a portable bathtub with him everywhere; for the fact that he always wore some exceptionally "noble" fragrance; for the fact that he played whist in masterly fashion and always lost. Lastly, they respected him for his incorruptible honesty. Ladies found him enchantingly melancholic, but he didn't cultivate the acquaintance of ladies....

"So you see, Evgenii," Arkadii observed as he finished his narrative, "how unfairly you've judged my uncle! To say nothing of his having gotten my father out of trouble more than once, and having given my father all his money—the estate wasn't divided, as perhaps you don't know. He's happy to help anyone, and, among other things, he always sticks up for the peasants. It's true that he frowns and sniffs eau de cologne when he talks to them...."

"His nerves, no doubt," Bazarov interjected.

"Maybe, but he has the kindest of hearts. And he's far from stupid. He's given me such useful advice ... especially ... especially in regard to relationships with women."

"Aha! A scalded dog fears water, we know that!"

"In short," Arkadii concluded, "he's profoundly unhappy, believe me. It's a sin to despise him."

"Who despises him?" Bazarov retorted. "Still, I must say that a man who stakes his whole life on one card—a woman's love—and turns sour when that card loses, letting himself deteriorate until he's incapable of accomplishing anything, isn't a man, he's an animal. You say that he's unhappy—you know best—but he hasn't gotten rid of all his faults. I'm convinced that he seriously considers himself a useful individual because he reads *Galignani* and once a month saves a peasant from being flogged."

"But remember his upbringing, and the times in which he lived," Arkadii remarked.

"His upbringing?" Bazarov cried. "Every person has to bring himself up, like I've done, for instance.... And as for the times, why should I depend on them? Let them depend on me instead. No, my friend, that's all inanity and indiscipline! And what's all this about mysterious relationships between men and women? We physiologists know what these relationships are. You study the anatomy of the eye: where does that enigmatic gaze, as you put it, come from? The rest is all romanticism, nonsense, aesthetic garbage. We'd be much better off going and looking at the beetle."

And the two friends went to Bazarov's room, which was already permeated by some sort of medicinal-surgical odor mingled with the smell of cheap tobacco.

# VIII

Pavel Petrovich didn't stay for long at his brother's chat with the bailiff, a tall, thin man with a sickly sweet voice and devious eyes who responded, "Certainly, sir," to all Nikolai Petrovich's remarks and characterized all the peasants as thieves and drunkards. The estate had recently been put under a new system and was creaking like an ungreased wheel, warping and cracking like homemade furniture carved out of unseasoned wood. Nikolai Petrovich wasn't ready to give up, but he frequently sighed and became pensive; he felt that the enterprise couldn't go any further without more money, and his money was almost all gone. Arkadii had told the truth: Pavel Petrovich had helped his brother out more than once; more than once, seeing Nikolai Petrovich struggling and racking his brains, not knowing which way to turn, Pavel Petrovich had slowly moved to the window, his hands thrust into his pockets, had muttered between his teeth, *"Mais je puis vous donner de l'argent,"* and had given him some money. But he had none himself at the moment, and preferred to withdraw. The petty details of agricultural management bored him to tears; besides, it repeatedly occurred to him that Nikolai Petrovich, all his industry and zeal notwithstanding, wasn't handling things the right way, although he couldn't have indicated precisely where Nikolai Petrovich's mistakes lay. "My brother isn't sufficiently practical," Pavel Petrovich concluded to himself. "People deceive him." Nikolai Petrovich, by contrast, had the highest possible regard for Pavel Petrovich's practicality and always asked his advice. "I'm a mild, weak-willed sort of person. I've spent my entire life in a remote area," he'd say, "whereas you haven't lived in society so long for nothing. You see through people—you have an eagle eye." In response, Pavel Petrovich would merely turn away—but he never contradicted his brother.

Leaving Nikolai Petrovich in the study, he walked along the corridor that separated the front part of the house from the back. When he reached a low door, he paused in thought, and then, stroking his moustache, he knocked on it.

"Who's there? Come in," Fenechka's voice called out.

"It's I," Pavel Petrovich announced, and he opened the door.

Fenechka jumped up from the chair she was sitting in while holding her baby, and, thrusting him into the arms of a girl who promptly carried him out of the room, she hastily straightened her scarf.

"Pardon me if I'm disturbing you," Pavel Petrovich began, without looking at her. "I just wanted to ask you.... They're sending someone into town today, I think.... Please have that person buy me some green tea."

"Certainly," Fenechka replied. "How much do you want him to buy?"

"Oh, half a pound will be enough, I imagine. You've made some changes here, I see," he added, casting a quick glance around the room that glided across Fenechka's face as well. "These curtains," he explained, noticing that she didn't comprehend his remark.

"Oh, yes, the curtains. Nikolai Petrovich gave them to us as a present. But they've been up for a long while now."

"Yes, and it's been a long while since I've come to visit you. It's very nice in here now."

"Thanks to Nikolai Petrovich's kindness," Fenechka murmured.

"Are you more comfortable here than you were in the little lodge?" Pavel Petrovich inquired courteously, but without the slightest trace of a smile.

"Of course, this is better."

"Who's moved into that place now?"

"The laundry maids are there now."

"Ah!"

Pavel Petrovich fell silent. "Now he's going to leave," Fenechka thought. But he didn't leave, and she stood facing him as though rooted to the spot, feebly entwining her fingers.

"Why did you send your little one away?" Pavel Petrovich inquired at last. "I love children. Let me see him."

Fenechka blushed deeply with embarrassment and delight. She was afraid of Pavel Petrovich; he hardly ever spoke to her.

"Duniasha," she called out, "will you bring Mitia here, please?" (Fenechka addressed everyone in the house politely.) "But wait a minute. He should be wearing something nice," Fenechka declared as she moved toward the door.

"That doesn't matter," Pavel Petrovich remarked.

"I'll be right back," Fenechka responded, and she went out quickly.

Having been left alone, Pavel Petrovich looked around again, this time quite carefully. The small, low-ceilinged room in which he found himself was very clean and cozy. It smelled of the fresh paint on the floor and of chamomile. Chairs with lyre-shaped backs, purchased by the late general during his campaign in Poland, were lined up along the walls; a little bedstead under a muslin canopy stood in one corner beside an ironbound chest with a convex lid. A small lamp was burning in the opposite corner before a large, dark icon of Saint Nikolai the miracle-worker; a tiny porcelain egg hung down to the saint's breast on a red ribbon attached to a protruding gold halo. Carefully sealed, greenish glass jars filled with last year's jam were lined up by the windows; Fenechka herself had written "Gooseberry" in big letters on their paper labels—Nikolai Petrovich was especially fond of that flavor. A cage with a short-tailed finch in it hung on a long cord attached to the ceiling; the finch incessantly chirped and hopped around, as a result of which the cage constantly shook and swayed, and hemp seeds kept falling onto the floor with a light tapping sound. On the wall just above a small chest of drawers hung some rather poor photographs of Nikolai Petrovich in various poses that had been taken by an itinerant photographer. A photograph of Fenechka herself that was an absolute failure also hung there in a dingy frame: it displayed some eyeless face wearing a forced smile, and nothing more. And above Fenechka hung a portrait of General Ermolov wearing a Circassian cloak as he scowled menacingly toward the Caucasian mountains in the distance from beneath a little silk-shoe pincushion that fell right to his forehead.

Five minutes passed; bustling and whispering were audible from the next room. Pavel Petrovich picked up an old book off the chest of drawers, an odd volume of Masalskii's *Musketeers,* and turned a few pages.... The door opened and Fenechka came in, carrying Mitia. She'd dressed him in a little red smock with an embroidered collar, and had combed his hair and washed his face. He was breathing laboriously, his whole body was wriggling, and he was waving his little hands in the air, the way all healthy babies do, but his fancy smock had obviously impressed him—every part of his plump little body expressed delight. Fenechka had also combed her own hair and rearranged her scarf, but she might as well have stayed the way she was. For, in fact, is there anything on earth more appealing than a beautiful young mother with a healthy baby in her arms?

"What a chubby little boy!" Pavel Petrovich remarked graciously, and he tickled Mitia's small double chin with the tapered nail of his forefinger. The baby stared at the finch and giggled.

"That's your uncle," Fenechka told him, tilting her face toward Mitia and rocking him slightly, while Duniasha quietly set a smoldering perfumed candle in the window and placed a coin underneath it.

"How many months old is he?" Pavel Petrovich asked.

"Six months. It'll be seven soon, on the eleventh."

"Isn't it eight, Fedosia Nikolaevna?" Duniasha interjected, not without shyness.

"No, seven. How is that possible?" The baby giggled again, stared at the chest of drawers, and suddenly caught hold of his mother's nose and mouth with all five of the fingers on one of his hands. "Saucy little rascal," Fenechka commented, without drawing her face away.

"He looks like my brother," observed Pavel Petrovich.

"Who else would he look like?" Fenechka thought.

"Yes," Pavel Petrovich continued, as though speaking to himself, "there's an unmistakable likeness." He looked at Fenechka intently, almost sadly.

"That's your uncle," she repeated, this time in a whisper.

"Ah! Pavel! So you're in here!" Nikolai Petrovich's voice suddenly rang out.

Pavel Petrovich hurriedly turned around, frowning, but his brother gazed at him with such delight and such gratitude that Pavel Petrovich couldn't help responding to his brother's smile.

"You've got a handsome little cherub," he declared, and looked at his watch. "I came in here to inquire about some tea."

And assuming a nonchalant expression, Pavel Petrovich immediately left the room.

"Did he come by himself?" Nikolai Petrovich asked Fenechka.

"Yes, he knocked and came in."

"Has Arkasha been to see you again?"

"No. Shouldn't I move into the lodge, Nikolai Petrovich?"

"Why?"

"I wonder whether it wouldn't be better, if only at first."

"N-no," Nikolai Petrovich concluded hesitantly, rubbing his forehead. "We should have done it before.... How are you, pudgy?" he added, suddenly perking up, and going over to the baby, he kissed him on the cheek. Then he bent down slightly and pressed his lips to Fenechka's hand, which was lying on Mitia's little red smock, as white as milk.

"Nikolai Petrovich! What are you doing?" she whispered, lowering her eyes, then slowly raising them again. The expression in her eyes when she gazed at him a bit mistrustfully, while smiling tenderly and a little foolishly, was charming.

Nikolai Petrovich had met Fenechka in the following way. Once, three years earlier, he'd happened to stay overnight at an inn in a remote district town. He was pleasantly surprised by the cleanliness of the room allotted to him, as well as the freshness of its bed linen. "The lady of the house must be German," he concluded. But she turned out to be Russian, a woman of about fifty who dressed neatly and had an attractive, intelligent countenance, along with a discreet manner of speaking. He entered into conversation with her over tea; he liked her very much. Nikolai Petrovich had just moved into his new residence at that time, and, not wanting to keep serfs in the house, was searching for paid servants. The mistress of the inn, for her part, complained about the small number of visitors passing through town and the hard times. He invited her to come to his new residence in the capacity of housekeeper; she consented. Her husband had died long ago, leaving her an only daughter, Fenechka. Within a fortnight, Arina Savishna (that was the new housekeeper's name) arrived at Marino with her daughter and installed herself in the little lodge.

Nikolai Petrovich's choice proved to be a successful one— Arina imposed order on the entire household. As for Fenechka, who was seventeen at the time, no one ever mentioned her, and hardly anyone ever saw her; she led a quiet, sedate life; Nikolai Petrovich merely noticed the delicate profile of her pale face in church on Sundays, somewhere off to one side. More than a year passed this way.

One morning, Arina came into his study and, bowing deeply as usual, asked him if he could do anything to help her daughter, who'd gotten a cinder in her eye from the stove. Nikolai Petrovich, like all people who largely stay at home, had studied various remedies, and had even compiled a homeopathic guide. He immediately told Arina to bring the patient to see him. Fenechka became quite frightened when she heard that the master had sent for her, but she followed her mother to the study. Nikolai Petrovich led her up to the window and took her head in his hands. After thoroughly examining her red, swollen eye, he prescribed an eyewash, which he himself promptly concocted, and tearing his handkerchief into pieces, he showed her how it had to be applied. Fenechka listened to everything he said, and then wanted to leave.

"Kiss the master's hand, silly girl," Arina told her.

Nikolai Petrovich didn't offer her his hand; instead, in confusion, he himself kissed her bowed head on the part in her hair.

Fenechka's eye healed quickly, but the impression she'd made on Nikolai Petrovich didn't pass as quickly. He was constantly haunted by that pure, delicate, timidly raised face; he kept feeling that soft hair on the palms of his hands and kept seeing those innocent, slightly parted lips between which pearly teeth gleamed with moist brilliance in the sunshine. He began to watch her with greater attention in church, and tried to engage her in conversation. She stayed away from him at first, and one day, as evening was approaching, upon encountering him in a narrow footpath running through a field of rye, she fled into the tall, thick stalks, which were overgrown with cornflowers and wormwood, in order to avoid meeting him face-to-face. He caught sight of her small head through a golden network of ears of rye, from which she was peeping out like a little wild animal, and hailed her affectionately: "Hello, Fenechka! I don't bite."

"Hello," she whispered, refusing to come out of her hiding place.

She was gradually becoming more accustomed to him, but still behaving diffidently in his presence, when her mother, Arina, suddenly died of cholera. What was to become of Fenechka? She'd inherited her mother's love of order, sobriety, and respectability—but she was so young, so alone. Nikolai Petrovich himself was so kind, so unpretentious.... There's no need to describe the rest....

———

"So my brother came in to see you?" Nikolai Petrovich asked her. "He knocked and came in?"

"Yes."

"Well, that's nice. Let me give Mitia a swing."

And Nikolai Petrovich began tossing him nearly up to the ceiling, to the huge delight of the baby and the considerable concern of the mother, who stretched out her arms toward his bare little legs each time he flew upward.

Pavel Petrovich went back to his elegant study, whose walls were covered with handsome, bluish-gray wallpaper. Various weapons hung on a multicolored Persian rug nailed to one wall; the room contained walnut furniture upholstered in dark-green velveteen, a Renaissance bookcase made of old, dark oak, bronze statuettes arrayed on a magnificent desk, and a fireplace. He threw himself down on the sofa, clasped his hands behind his head, and lay still, gazing at the ceiling almost in despair. Whether he wanted to hide what was reflected in his face from the very walls—or for some other reason—he got up, closed the heavy window curtains against the light, and threw himself back down on the sofa.

# IX

Bazarov made Fenechka's acquaintance the same day. He was strolling in the garden with Arkadii, explaining to him why some of the trees, especially the oaks, weren't doing very well.

"They should have planted silver poplars here, as well as spruce firs and possibly lime trees, and given them some loam. That arbor over there has done well," he added, "because it's full of acacia and lilac bushes. They're easygoing types—they don't require much care. But there's someone there."

Fenechka was sitting in the arbor with Duniasha and Mitia. Bazarov paused, and Arkadii nodded to Fenechka like an old friend.

"Who's that?" Bazarov asked him as soon as they'd walked past the arbor. "What a pretty girl!"

"Whom are you referring to?"

"It's obvious—only one of them was pretty."

Not without embarrassment, Arkadii briefly explained to him who Fenechka was.

"Aha!" Bazarov responded. "Your father's got good taste, one can see that. I like your father, yes, I do! He's done well. We have to get acquainted, though," he added, and turned back toward the arbor.

"Evgenii!" Arkadii cried after him in dismay. "Be careful, for God's sake."

"Don't worry," Bazarov replied. "I know how to behave around most people—I'm no fool."

Approaching Fenechka, he took off his cap.

"Allow me to introduce myself," he began with a polite bow. "I'm a harmless person and a friend of Arkadii Nikolaevich."

Fenechka got up from the garden bench and gazed at him without speaking.

"What a handsome child!" Bazarov continued. "Don't be concerned—my compliments have never brought anyone bad luck yet. Why are his cheeks so flushed? Is he cutting his teeth?"

"Yes," Fenechka answered, "he's already cut four teeth, and now his gums are swollen again."

"Show me . . . and don't be afraid. I'm a doctor."

Bazarov picked the baby up in his arms and, to both Fenechka's and Duniasha's astonishment, the child offered no resistance—he wasn't frightened.

"I see, I see. . . . It's nothing, everything's in order. He'll have a good set of teeth. If anything goes wrong, let me know. And are you in good health yourself?"

"I'm quite well, thank God."

"Thank God, indeed—that's the most important thing of all. And you?" he added, turning to Duniasha.

Duniasha was a very prim girl inside the master's house, but a giddy one beyond its gates, and she merely giggled in reply.

"Well, that's fine. Here's your gallant warrior."

Fenechka took the baby back in her arms.

"How well behaved he was with you!" she commented in an undertone.

"Children are always well behaved around me," Bazarov responded. "I have a way with them."

"Children know who loves them," Duniasha remarked.

"Yes, they certainly do," Fenechka agreed. "Why, Mitia here won't let some people hold him for anything."

"Will he let me?" inquired Arkadii, who, after standing at a distance for some time, had approached the arbor.

He tried to entice Mitia into his arms, but Mitia threw his head back and screamed, to Fenechka's great embarrassment.

"Another day, when he's had time to get used to me," Arkadii said indulgently, and the two friends walked away.

"What's her name?" asked Bazarov.

"Fenechka ... Fedosia," answered Arkadii.

"And her patronymic? One should know that, too."

"Nikolaevna."

"*Bene.* What I like about her is that she isn't overly constrained. Some people would think badly of her for that, I suppose. What nonsense! Why should she be constrained? She's a mother—she has rights."

"She has rights," Arkadii observed, "but my father...."

"He has rights, too," Bazarov interrupted.

"Well, no, I don't think so."

"Evidently the existence of an extra heir doesn't thrill you?"

"You should be ashamed of yourself for attributing ideas like that to me!" Arkadii cried heatedly. "I don't consider my father wrong from that point of view—I think he ought to marry her."

"Aha!" Bazarov responded tranquilly. "What magnanimous people we are! You still attach significance to marriage—I didn't expect that of you."

The friends proceeded a few steps in silence.

"I've seen your father's entire establishment," Bazarov began again. "The cattle are inferior and the horses are worn out. The buildings aren't in good condition, either, and the workmen look like confirmed loafers, while the bailiff is an idiot or a thief—I haven't quite figured out which one yet."

"You're quite hard on everything today, Evgenii Vasilevich."

"And the kindhearted peasants are definitely swindling your father. You know the proverb, 'A Russian peasant will cheat God Himself.'"

"I'm beginning to agree with my uncle," Arkadii remarked. "You certainly do have a poor opinion of Russians."

"As though that mattered! The only good thing about a Russian is that he has the lowest possible opinion about himself.

What matters is that two times two makes four—all the rest is trivial."

"And is nature trivial?" Arkadii inquired, looking meditatively into the distance at the brightly colored fields beautifully and softly illuminated by the setting sun.

"Nature is also trivial in the sense that you mean it. Nature isn't a temple—it's a workshop, and a human being is the worker in it."

At that instant, the long, drawn-out notes of a cello floated across to them from the house. Someone was playing Schubert's "Expectation" with great feeling, albeit with an untrained hand, and the sweet melody flowed through the air like honey.

"What's that?" Bazarov asked in astonishment.

"It's my father."

"Your father plays the cello?"

"Yes."

"How old is your father?"

"Forty-four."

Bazarov suddenly burst into a roar of laughter.

"What are you laughing at?"

"For heaven's sake, a man of forty-four, a paterfamilias in the district of \*\*\*, playing the cello!"

Bazarov went on laughing, but, as much as he revered his teacher, this time Arkadii didn't even smile.


# X


About two weeks passed. Life at Marino continued to flow on its customary course. Arkadii relaxed and enjoyed himself while Bazarov worked. Everyone in the house had gotten used to Bazarov, to his casual manners and his curt, fragmentary way of speaking. Fenechka in particular had become so comfortable with him that one night she'd had a servant awaken him: Mitia had had convulsions. Bazarov had agreed to come, half joking and half yawning as usual, had stayed with her for two hours, and had assisted the child. By contrast, Pavel Petrovich had grown to detest Bazarov with all the strength of his soul: he considered Bazarov proud, insolent, cynical, and vulgar; he suspected that Bazarov didn't respect him, indeed, that he all but despised him—him, Pavel Kirsanov! Nikolai Petrovich was somewhat frightened of the young "nihilist" and doubted whether his influence over Arkadii was all to the good, yet he eagerly listened to Bazarov, eagerly attended his medical and chemical experiments—Bazarov had brought a microscope with him and occupied himself with it for hours on end. The servants also took to Bazarov, even though he made fun of them; they nonetheless felt that he was one of them, not one of the gentry. Duniasha loved to giggle at him, and cast meaningful glances at him whenever she ran past him "like a little quail." Petr, an extremely vain, unintelligent man who constantly furrowed his brow affectedly, whose entire worth consisted in the fact that he acted civilized, could spell out words, and diligently brushed his coat—even he grinned and livened up whenever Bazarov paid any attention to him. The boys on the farm simply ran after the "doctor" like puppies. Old Prokofich was the only one who didn't like him: he served Bazarov food at meals with a surly expression on his face, called him a "butcher" and an "upstart," and declared that Bazarov's sideburns made him look like a pig in a sty. In his own way, Prokofich was just as much of an aristocrat as Pavel Petrovich.

The best days of the year arrived—the first days of June. The weather was wonderful; some distance from there, it's true, another outbreak of cholera was threatening, but the inhabitants of that district had managed to become accustomed to its visits. Bazarov got up very early every day and walked for two or three versts, not on a stroll—he couldn't bear walking without an aim—but to collect plant and insect specimens. Sometimes he took Arkadii with him. On the way home, an argument usually sprang up and Arkadii was usually vanquished, although he talked more than his companion did.

One day they'd lingered rather late for some reason; Nikolai

Petrovich went out to the garden to look for them, and as he reached the arbor, he suddenly heard the rapid footsteps and the voices of the two young men. They were walking on the other side of the arbor and couldn't see him.

"You don't know my father well enough," Arkadii was saying. Nikolai Petrovich kept silent.

"Your father's a kind man," Bazarov declared, "but he's behind the times. His day is done."

Nikolai Petrovich listened intently.... Arkadii didn't respond.

The man who was "behind the times" stood still for about two minutes, and then slowly made his way home.

"The day before yesterday, I saw him reading Pushkin," Bazarov continued in the meantime. "Please explain to him that that's no use whatsoever. He's not a boy, you know—it's time to give up that rubbish. And the desire to be a romantic at the present moment! Give him something sensible to read."

"What should I give him?" asked Arkadii.

"Oh, Büchner's *Stoff und Kraft*, I suppose, to begin with."

"I think so too," Arkadii remarked approvingly. "*Stoff und Kraft* is written in popular language...."

"So, it seems," Nikolai Petrovich said to his brother that same day after dinner, as he sat in the latter's study, "you and I have fallen behind the times, and our day is done. Oh, well. Maybe Bazarov is right. But one thing is painful to me, I must confess— I did so hope to develop a close, friendly relationship with Arkadii now, and it turns out that I've fallen behind, whereas he's gone ahead, and we can't understand one another."

"In what sense has he gone ahead? And in what way is he so superior to us?" Pavel Petrovich cried impatiently. "It's that high-and-mighty gentleman, that nihilist, who's crammed all this into his head. I hate that medical man—in my opinion, he's nothing but a charlatan. I'm convinced that, for all his tadpoles, he hasn't gotten very far even in medicine."

"No, Brother, you can't say that—Bazarov's intelligent, and he knows his subject."

"And his conceit is absolutely revolting," Pavel Petrovich interrupted again.

"Yes," Nikolai Petrovich observed, "he is conceited. But one can't get anywhere without that, it seems—only that's what I didn't take into account. I thought I was doing everything to keep up with the times. I've provided for the peasants, and I've started a model farm, as a result of which they go so far as to call me a 'red radical' all over the district. I read, I study, I try to keep abreast of contemporary issues in general—and they say that my day is done. And I'm beginning to think that it is, Brother."

"Why so?"

"I'll tell you why. This morning I was sitting and reading Pushkin.... I remember, it happened to be *The Gypsies*.... All of a sudden, Arkadii came up to me and, without uttering a word, with the most affectionate compassion on his face, as gently as if I were a child, he took the book away from me, laid another one in front of me, a German book ... smiled, and went away, taking Pushkin with him."

"So that's it! What book did he give you?"

"This one."

And Nikolai Petrovich extracted the ninth edition of Büchner's famous treatise out of his back pocket.

Pavel Petrovich turned it over in his hands. "Hmm!" he growled. "Arkadii Nikolaevich is taking your education in hand. And so, did you try to read it?"

"Yes, I tried."

"Well, what did you think of it?"

"Either I'm stupid or it's all—nonsense. I must be stupid, I suppose."

"You haven't forgotten your German?" inquired Pavel Petrovich.

"Oh no, I understand the German."

Pavel Petrovich turned the book over in his hands again and glanced at his brother mistrustfully. Both fell silent.

"Oh, by the way," Nikolai Petrovich began again, obviously

seeking to change the subject, "I've gotten a letter from Koli-azin."

"Matvei Ilich?"

"Yes. He's come to \*\*\* on an inspection tour of the district. He's quite an important personage now and writes to me that he'd like to see us again, since we're relatives, so he's invited you and Arkadii and me to town."

"Will you go?" asked Pavel Petrovich.

"No. Will you?"

"No, I won't go either. What point would there be in dragging oneself across fifty versts on a wild-goose chase? *Mathieu* wants to display himself in all his glory, the devil take him! He'll have the entire district paying homage to him—he can get along without the likes of us. A great dignitary indeed, a privy councillor! If I'd stayed in military service, if I'd continued to slave away in that stupid harness, I'd have been a general-adjutant by now. Besides, you and I are behind the times, you know."

"Yes, brother, it seems that it's time to order a coffin and fold one's arms across one's breast," Nikolai Petrovich observed with a sigh.

"Well, I'm not going to surrender quite so fast," muttered his brother. "I've got a skirmish coming with that medical man, I predict."

The skirmish occurred that very evening, over tea. Pavel Petrovich came into the drawing room already prepared for the fray, irritable and determined. He was merely awaiting an excuse to attack the enemy, but an excuse didn't present itself for a long while. As a rule, Bazarov said little in the presence of the "old Kirsanovs" (that was how he referred to the brothers), and that evening he was in a bad mood, drinking cup after cup of tea without saying a word. Pavel Petrovich was aflame with impatience; his desires were eventually fulfilled.

The conversation turned to one of the neighboring land-owners. "Rotten aristocratic snob," Bazarov remarked matter-of-factly. He'd met the man in Petersburg.

"Permit me to inquire," began Pavel Petrovich, whose lips were trembling, "according to your views, do the words 'rotten' and 'aristocrat' mean the same thing?"

"I said 'aristocratic snob,'" Bazarov replied, lazily swallowing a sip of tea.

"Quite so, but I assume that you hold the same opinion of aristocrats as you do of aristocratic snobs. I consider it my duty to inform you that I don't share this opinion. I venture to say that everyone knows me to be a man of liberal ideas, one devoted to progress, but precisely because of that I respect aristocrats—real aristocrats. Be so good, my dear sir" (at these words, Bazarov raised his eyes and looked at Pavel Petrovich), "my dear sir," he repeated acrimoniously, "be so good as to recall the English aristocracy. They don't sacrifice one iota of their rights, and for that reason they respect the rights of others. They insist on the fulfillment of obligations to themselves, and for that reason they fulfill their own obligations to others. The aristocracy has given England her freedom, and maintains it for her."

"We've heard that song sung many times," Bazarov rejoined, "but what are you trying to prove by this?"

"What I'm trying to prove by *thifs*, my dear sir" (when Pavel Petrovich was angry, he intentionally said "thifs" and "thefse" instead of "this" and "these," although he knew very well that such forms aren't strictly correct. A vestige of the customs of the Alexandrine era was discernible in this fashionable mannerism. On the rare occasions when the nobility of that era spoke their own language, they employed either "thifs" or "thiks," as if to say, "Of course, we're native-born Russians, and, at the same time, we're worldly people who are free to disregard scholastic rules"), "what I'm trying to prove by *thifs* is that without a sense of personal dignity, without self-respect—and these two sentiments are highly developed in the aristocrat—there's no secure basis for the social ... *bien public* ... the social welfare. Individual character, my dear sir—that's the main thing. Individual character must be as solid as a rock, since everything is built upon it. I'm perfectly well aware, for instance, that you consider my habits, my clothes, and my various refinements ridiculous, but all of that proceeds from a sense of self-respect, from a sense of duty—yes indeed, of duty. I live in the countryside, in a remote area, but I won't demean myself. I respect the human being in myself."

"Let me ask you this, Pavel Petrovich," Bazarov commenced. "You respect yourself so much and sit with your hands folded. What sort of benefit does that provide the *bien public?* If you didn't respect yourself, you'd behave exactly the same way."

Pavel Petrovich turned pale. "That's a completely different question. It's absolutely unnecessary for me to explain to you now why I sit with my hands folded, as you put it. I merely want to say that aristocratism is a principle, and in our times no one but immoral or vapid people can live without principles. I said that to Arkadii the day after he came home, and I repeat it now. Isn't that so, Nikolai?"

Nikolai Petrovich nodded his head.

"Aristocratism, liberalism, progress, principles," Bazarov was saying in the meantime. "If you think about it, what a lot of foreign—and useless—words! To a Russian, they're utterly un-necessary."

"What *is* necessary to a Russian, in your opinion? If we listen to you, we'll find ourselves beyond all humanity, beyond its laws. For heaven's sake—the logic of history demands...."

"But what difference does that logic make to us? We can get along without that, too."

"What do you mean?"

"Why, just this. You don't need logic, I trust, to put a piece of bread in your mouth when you're hungry. Where do all these ab-stractions get us?"

Pavel Petrovich raised his hands in horror.

"I don't understand you when you say that. You insult the Russian people. I don't understand how it's possible not to ac-cept principles, rules! What gives you the strength to act, then?"

"I've already told you that we don't accept any authorities, Uncle," Arkadii interjected.

"We act on the strength of what we recognize to be useful," Bazarov declared. "At the present time, the most useful thing of all is negation—hence we negate."

"Everything?"

"Everything!"

"What? Not just art and poetry ... but even ... it's too horrible to say...."

"Everything," Bazarov repeated with inexpressible composure.

Pavel Petrovich stared at him—he hadn't expected this—while Arkadii fairly blushed with delight.

"Allow me to observe, though," began Nikolai Petrovich, "you negate everything, or, to put it more precisely, you destroy everything.... But one has to construct something, too, you know."

"That isn't our task right now.... The ground needs clearing first."

"The present condition of the people demands it," Arkadii added with dignity. "We're obligated to meet these demands. We have no right to indulge in the satisfaction of our personal egoism."

This last phrase evidently displeased Bazarov: it had a hint of philosophy—that is to say, romanticism, for Bazarov also called philosophy romanticism—about it. But he didn't deem it necessary to correct his young disciple.

"No, no!" Pavel Petrovich cried with sudden energy. "I'm not willing to believe that you gentlemen really know the Russian people, that you're the representatives of their demands or their aspirations! No! The Russian people aren't what you believe them to be. They hold tradition sacred. They're patriarchal people—they can't live without faith...."

"I won't dispute this," Bazarov interrupted. "I'm even prepared to agree that, in *this*, you're right."

"But if I'm right...."

"All the same, this proves nothing."

"This proves absolutely nothing," Arkadii repeated, with the confidence of an experienced chess player who's foreseen an apparently dangerous move on the part of an adversary and hence isn't the least bit disturbed by it.

"How can this prove nothing?" Pavel Petrovich muttered in amazement. "Are you opposed to your own people, then?"

"And what if we are?" shouted Bazarov. "The people imagine when it thunders that the prophet Ilia is riding across the sky in his chariot. What then? Should I agree with them? Besides, the people are Russian, and aren't I Russian as well?"

"No, you aren't Russian after everything you've just said! I can't acknowledge you to be Russian."

"My grandfather plowed the land," Bazarov responded with haughty pride. "Ask any of your peasants which one of us—you or me—he'd more readily acknowledge to be a compatriot. You don't even know how to talk to him."

"Whereas you talk to him and hold him in contempt at the same time."

"Well, suppose he deserves contempt! You criticize my attitude—but how do you know that I've developed it at random, that it isn't a product of the very national spirit in whose name you're arguing so vehemently?"

"Indeed! How worthwhile nihilists are!"

"Whether they're worthwhile or not isn't for us to decide. Why, even you don't consider yourself a useless person."

"Gentlemen, gentlemen, please, nothing personal!" Nikolai Petrovich exclaimed, standing up.

Pavel Petrovich smiled and, laying his hand on his brother's shoulder, forced him to sit down again.

"Don't worry," he said. "I won't forget myself, precisely by virtue of that sense of dignity our Mr.... Mr. Doctor mocks so mercilessly. Allow me to ask you this," he resumed, turning back to Bazarov. "Can you possibly suppose that your doctrine is new? You're sadly mistaken. The materialism you advocate has already been in vogue more than once, and has always proved to be insufficient...."

"Another foreign word!" interjected Bazarov. He was beginning to get angry, and his face assumed a sort of coarse, coppery hue. "In the first place, we advocate nothing—that's not among our customs...."

"What *do* you do, then?"

"I'll tell you what we do. Not long ago, we used to say that our officials took bribes, that we had no roads, no commerce, no real justice...."

"Oh, I see. You're reformers—that's what this is called, I believe. Even I would agree with many of your reforms, but...."

"Then we realized that talk—and nothing but talk—about our social ills isn't worth the effort, that it merely leads to banality and pedantry. We saw that our most intelligent individuals, the so-called leaders and reformers, are useless. We saw that we devote ourselves to absurdities, that we debate about art, unconscious creativity, parliamentarianism, trial by jury, and the devil knows what else, when the issue is getting enough bread to eat, when we're stifling under the grossest superstitions, when all our financial enterprises go bankrupt simply because there aren't enough honest people to run them, when the very emancipation our government has been fussing about will hardly do any good because our peasants are happy to rob even themselves in order to get drunk at the local tavern."

"Granted," Pavel Petrovich interrupted. "So—you became convinced of all this and decided not to undertake anything seriously yourselves."

"We decided not to undertake anything," Bazarov repeated grimly. He suddenly got annoyed with himself for having so extensively exposed his ideas before this gentleman.

"And to confine yourselves to criticism?"

"To confine ourselves to criticism."

"And that's called nihilism?"

"And that's called nihilism," Bazarov echoed, this time with particular insolence.

Pavel Petrovich squinted slightly. "So that's it!" he declared in a strangely composed voice. "Nihilism will cure all our woes, and you—you'll be our heroes and saviors. But why do you revile everyone else, even those reformers? Don't you do as much talking as everyone else?"

"Whatever our sins may be, that isn't one of them," Bazarov muttered between his teeth.

"What, then? Are you people of action? Are you preparing to act?"

Bazarov didn't answer. Pavel Petrovich seemed to tremble, but instantly regained control of himself.

"Hmm!... Action, destruction ...," he continued. "But how can you destroy without even knowing why?"

"We destroy because we're a force," Arkadii asserted.

Pavel Petrovich looked at his nephew and laughed.

"Yes, a force, which doesn't have to account for itself," Arkadii maintained, straightening up.

"Unhappy boy!" Pavel Petrovich lamented, utterly incapable of restraining himself any longer. "If only you realized what it is about Russia that you're affirming with your banal sententiousness. No—it's enough to try the patience of an angel! A force! There's a force in the savage Kalmuck, in the Mongolian—but what does that have to do with us? What's precious to us is civilization. Yes, yes, my dear sir, its fruits are the ones that are precious to us. And don't tell me that those fruits are worthless. The poorest dabbler in art, *un barbouilleur,* the man who plays dance music for five kopecks an evening, are all more useful than you are, because they're representatives of civilization and not of brute Mongolian force! You consider yourselves leaders, and all the while you're only fit for a Kalmuck's hovel! A force! And then remember, you forceful gentlemen, that you're a total of four and a half men, whereas there are millions of others who won't let you trample their most sacred beliefs underfoot, who'll crush you instead!"

"If we're crushed, it'll serve us right," Bazarov observed. "But that still remains to be seen. We aren't as few as you suppose."

"What? Do you seriously think that you can convert an entire people?"

"All Moscow was burned down by a cheap candle, you know," responded Bazarov.

"Yes, yes. First almost satanic pride, then mockery. This, this is what attracts the young, this is what wins over the inexperienced hearts of little boys! Here's one of them sitting beside you, ready to worship the ground you walk on. Look at him!" (Arkadii turned away and frowned.) "And this plague has already spread far and wide. I've been told that, when in Rome, our artists never set foot in the Vatican. They regard Raphael as virtually a fool because he's an authority, if you please, whereas they're all disgustingly sterile and inept beings whose imaginations don't rise above 'A Girl at a Fountain,' however hard they try! And even that girl is drawn incredibly poorly. In your view, they're courageous individuals, aren't they?"

"In my view," Bazarov retorted, "Raphael isn't worth a thing, and they're no better than he was."

"Bravo! Bravo! Listen, Arkadii … this is how youths of today have to express themselves! And if you think about it—how could they fail to follow you? In earlier times, young people had to study—they didn't want to be taken for ignoramuses, so they had to work hard whether they liked it or not. But now one just has to say, 'Everything on earth is absurd!' and the deed is done—young people are overjoyed. In fact, they were simply dolts before, whereas now they've suddenly become nihilists."

"Your praiseworthy sense of personal dignity has failed you," Bazarov remarked phlegmatically, even as Arkadii became thoroughly angry and his eyes began to flash. "Our argument has gone too far—it's better to break it off, I think. I'll be quite prepared to agree with you," he added as he stood up, "when you can name one single institution existing in our contemporary culture, either familial or societal, that doesn't merit complete, merciless destruction."

"I can name millions of such institutions," Pavel Petrovich averred, "millions! Take the commune, for instance."

An icy smile curved across Bazarov's lips. "Well, as regards the commune," he returned, "you'd better speak to your brother.

I suspect that he's seen by now what the commune actually is—what its reciprocal guarantees, its sobriety, and other features of that kind actually mean."

"The family, then—the family as it exists among our peasants!" cried Pavel Petrovich.

"I believe that you yourselves had better not explore this question in detail, either. Perhaps you've heard about the privileges the head of the family enjoys in choosing his daughters-in-law? Take my advice, Pavel Petrovich, and give yourself two days to mull it over—you probably won't find anything right away. Consider all our social classes, and think about each one carefully, while Arkadii and I will...."

"Continue to subject everything to ridicule," interjected Pavel Petrovich.

"No, continue to dissect frogs. Let's go, Arkadii. Goodbye, gentlemen!"

The two friends walked off. The brothers were left alone, and merely exchanged glances at first.

"So," Pavel Petrovich finally began, "that's what today's youths are like! They're our successors!"

"Our successors!" Nikolai Petrovich repeated with a dejected sigh. He'd been sitting as if he were on thorns throughout the argument, and had done nothing but stealthily glance at Arkadii with an aching heart. "Do you know what I was reminded of, brother? Once I had a disagreement with our poor mother. She was shouting and wouldn't listen to me. Ultimately, I said to her: 'Of course, you can't understand me. We belong to two different generations.' She was terribly offended, but I thought: 'What can one do? It's a bitter pill, but she has to swallow it.' Now our turn has come, you see, and our successors can say to us: 'You don't belong to our generation. Swallow your pill.' "

"You're much too generous and humble," replied Pavel Petrovich. "On the contrary, I'm convinced that you and I are far more in the right than these young gentlemen, even though perhaps we do express ourselves in somewhat old-fashioned language, *vieilli,* and don't have the same arrogant conceit.... Young people nowadays are so pretentious! You ask one of them, 'Do you want red wine or white?' 'I customarily prefer red!' he answers in a deep bass voice, with a face as solemn as if the whole universe were watching him at that instant...."

"Would you care for any more tea?" Fenechka inquired, sticking her head through the doorway. She hadn't dared to enter the drawing room while the sound of voices arguing in there was audible.

"No. You can tell them to take the samovar away," Nikolai Petrovich responded, and he rose to greet her. Pavel Petrovich abruptly said *"Bon soir"* to him and went off to his study.

## XI

Half an hour later, Nikolai Petrovich went out to his favorite arbor in the garden. A wave of unhappy thoughts washed over him. For the first time, he clearly perceived the gulf between himself and his son; he foresaw that it would grow wider and wider with every passing day. In vain, then, had he spent whole days reading the latest books during the winters in Petersburg; in vain had he listened to the conversations of young people; in vain had he rejoiced when he'd managed to interject his own ideas into their heated discussions. "My brother says we're right," he thought, "and, all vanity aside, I myself do believe that they're further from the truth than we are, although at the same time I do feel that there's something inside them we haven't got, some form of superiority over us.... Is it youth? No, it's not just youth. Doesn't their superiority consist in their having fewer traces of the landowner in them than we have in us?"

Nikolai Petrovich's head sank despondently, and he rubbed his hand across his face.

"But to renounce poetry?" he thought further. "To have no feeling for art, for nature...?" And he looked around him, as though trying to understand how it was possible to have no feeling for nature.

It was already evening; the sun was hidden behind a small aspen grove that lay half a verst from the garden; its shadow stretched across the motionless fields. A peasant on a little white horse was trotting along a dark, narrow path right next to the grove; his entire figure was clearly visible, right down to the patch on his shoulder, despite the fact that he was in the shade; his horse's hoofs flashed along in a smooth rhythm. The sun's rays fell across the grove from the far side, piercing its thickets to throw such a warm light over the aspens' trunks that they looked like pine trees, turning their leaves almost dark-blue, while a pale-blue sky faintly tinged by the glow of sunset spread above them. Swallows were flying high overhead; the wind had completely died away; some dilatory bees were humming lazily and drowsily among the lilac blossoms; a swarm of midges was hanging like a cloud over a lone branch delineated against the sky.

"My God, how beautiful!" Nikolai Petrovich marveled, and his favorite verses began to come to his lips—when he remembered Arkadii's *Stoff und Kraft* and fell silent. But he continued to sit there, he continued to give himself over to the sad and yet comforting play of solitary reflections. He liked to daydream, and his life in the countryside had enhanced this tendency in him. How recently had he been daydreaming like this, waiting for his son at the inn—and what a change had occurred since that day! Their relationship, then still undefined, was defined now—and defined in what way! His deceased wife came to his mind's eye, not as he'd known her for so many years, not as the thrifty, kind housewife, but as a young girl with a slim figure, innocently inquiring eyes, and a tight coil of hair fastened at her childlike neck. He recalled the first time he'd seen her—he was still a student then. He'd encountered her on the staircase of his lodgings, and jostling against her by accident, he'd wanted to apologize, but could only mutter, *"Pardon, monsieur,"* while she'd bowed, smiled, then had suddenly seemed frightened and had run away, although at a bend in the staircase she'd glanced at him quickly, donned a serious expression, and blushed. Afterward had come the first shy visits, the half-words and half-smiles, the embarrassment, the melancholy, the yearnings, and finally, that breathless rapture.... Where had it all gone? She'd become his wife, he'd been happy as few people on earth are happy....

"But," he wondered, "why couldn't one live an eternal, immortal life in those first, sweet moments?"

He didn't try to clarify his idea to himself, but he sensed that he longed to regain that blissful time through something stronger than memory; he longed to feel his Maria near him again, to feel her warmth, her breath—and after a little while, it seemed as if he could envision over his head....

"Nikolai Petrovich," Fenechka's voice rang out nearby. "Where are you?"

He was startled. He wasn't upset or ashamed.... He'd never even considered the possibility of comparing his wife and Fenechka—but he regretted the fact that she'd decided to come and look for him. Her voice instantly reminded him of his gray hair, his age, his present....

The enchanted world into which he'd just stepped, which had risen out of the dim mists of the past, shimmered—and vanished.

"I'm here," he answered, "I'm coming. Run along." "There they are, the traces of the landowner," the thought flashed through his mind. Fenechka silently glanced toward him in the arbor, then disappeared, and he noticed with astonishment that night had fallen while he'd been daydreaming. Everything around him was dark and hushed; Fenechka's face, ever so pale and small, had gleamed as she went past him. He stood up and started to go back to the house. But the emotions that had been stirred up in his heart couldn't be soothed all at once, and he began to walk slowly around the garden, at times staring at the ground beneath his feet, at other times raising his eyes skyward, where masses of stars were twinkling. He walked for a long while, until he was nearly exhausted, but the restlessness within him—some sort of searching, vague, mournful restlessness—still wasn't assuaged. Oh, how Bazarov would have laughed at him if he'd known what was going on inside Nikolai Petrovich at that moment! Even Arkadii would have condemned him. He, a forty-four-year-old man, an agriculturist and farmer, was shedding tears, groundless tears; this was a hundred times worse than the cello.

Nikolai Petrovich went on walking, unable to decide to go into the house, into the snug, peaceful nest that regarded him so hospitably from all its lighted windows; he didn't have the strength to tear himself away from the darkness, from the garden, from the sensation of fresh air on his face, or from that melancholy, that restless craving....

At a turn in the path, he ran into Pavel Petrovich. "What's the matter with you?" he asked Nikolai Petrovich. "You're as white as a ghost. You must not feel well. Why don't you go to bed?"

Nikolai Petrovich briefly described his spiritual condition to his brother and walked away. Pavel Petrovich went to the end of the garden, where he also grew pensive and also raised his eyes skyward. But nothing was reflected in his handsome dark eyes except the light of the stars. He hadn't been born a romantic, and his fastidiously dry, serious soul, with its inclination toward French misanthropy, wasn't capable of daydreaming....

———

"Do you know what?" Bazarov said to Arkadii the same night. "I've got a magnificent idea. Your father was saying today that he'd received an invitation to visit your illustrious relative. Your father's not going—so let's head for \*\*\* ourselves, since this gentleman invited you, too. You see what fine weather it is. We'll stroll around and take a look at the town. We'll enjoy ourselves for five or six days, and that's enough."

"Then you'll come back here again?"

"No, I have to go to my father's. You know that he lives about thirty versts from \*\*\*. I haven't seen him, or my mother either, in a long time. I should cheer the old folks up. They've been good to me, especially my father—he's priceless. I'm their only son, too."

"Will you stay with them for a long time?"

"I don't think so. It'll be boring, I suspect."

"And you'll drop in here on your way back?"

"I don't know.... I'll see. Well, what do you say? Do we go?"

"If you like," Arkadii replied languidly. In his heart, he was highly delighted at his friend's suggestion, but he considered it his duty to conceal his feelings. He wasn't a nihilist for nothing!

The next day he and Bazarov set off for ***. The younger members of the household at Marino were saddened by their departure—Duniasha even cried ... but the older inhabitants breathed more easily.

# XII

The town of ***, to which our friends headed, was under the jurisdiction of a young governor who was both a progressive and a despot, as is often the case in Russia. By the end of his first year of governance, he'd managed to quarrel not only with the marshal of the nobility, a retired officer of the Guards who entertained frequently and bred horses, but even with his own subordinates. The difficulties that ensued as a result eventually assumed such proportions that the ministry in Petersburg had deemed it necessary to send out some trusted representative, accompanied by a commission, to investigate the entire matter on the spot. By choice of the authorities, the job fell to Matvei Ilich Koliazin, son of the Koliazin under whose protection the Kirsanov brothers had found themselves at one time. He was also a "young man," that is to say, he'd recently turned forty, but he was already well on the way to becoming a statesman, and wore a star on each side of his chest—one of them was foreign, it's true, and not of the highest rank. Like the governor whom he'd come to pass judgment on, he was considered progressive. Even though he was already an important personage, he didn't resemble the majority of important personages. He had the highest possible opinion of himself—his vanity knew no bounds—but he behaved simply, gazed at people affably, listened indulgently, and laughed so good-naturedly that on first acquaintance he might even be taken for "a marvelous man." On important occasions, however, he knew how to make his authority felt, as they say.

"Energy is essential," he used to declare at those times, *"l'énergie est la première qualité d'un homme d'état."* Despite all that, he was readily deceived, and any moderately experienced official could twist him around his little finger. Matvei Ilich spoke of Guizot with great respect, and strove to impress upon everyone that he didn't belong to the category of *routiniers* and backward bureaucrats, that not one significant social event escaped his notice.... All such phrases were well known to him. He even followed developments in contemporary literature, albeit with dignified indifference, the same way that an adult who encounters a procession of small boys marching down the street will occasionally walk along behind it. In reality, Matvei Ilich hadn't progressed very far beyond those government officials of the Alexandrine era who used to prepare for an evening party at Mrs. Svechin's (she was living in Petersburg at that time) by reading a page of Condillac. But his methods were different, more modern. He was an adroit courtier, an expert conniver—and nothing more; he had no special aptitude for business, and no intellectual gifts. But he knew how to conduct his own affairs successfully—no one could get the better of him there—and that's the most important thing, after all.

Matvei Ilich welcomed Arkadii with the good cheer—we might even call it playfulness—characteristic of the enlightened high-ranking official. He was astonished, however, when he learned that the cousins he'd invited had stayed at home in the countryside. "Your papa always was an eccentric," he remarked, toying with the tassels on his magnificent velvet dressing gown. Then, suddenly turning to a young official wearing a discreetly buttoned-up uniform, he cried, "What?" with an air of concern. The young man, whose lips had become glued together from prolonged silence, stood up and looked perplexedly at his chief. But, having disconcerted his subordinate, Matvei Ilich paid no further attention to him. As a rule, our high-ranking officials are fond of disconcerting their subordinates, and the means to which they resort in order to attain this goal vary widely. The following means, among others, are widely employed, "are quite a favorite," as the English say: a high-ranking official suddenly ceases to understand even the simplest words, feigning total deafness.

He'll ask, for instance, "What day is today?"

He's respectfully informed, "Today's Friday, your Ex-x-x-x-lency."

"Eh? What? What's that? What are you saying?" the official repeats tensely.

"Today's Friday, your Ex-x-x-x-lency."

"Eh? What? What's Friday? Which Friday?"

"Friday, your Ex-x-x-x-lency, the day of the week."

"Well, well, so you dare to instruct me, eh?"

Matvei Ilich was precisely this sort of official, even though he was considered a liberal.

"I advise you to go and visit the governor, my dear boy," he said to Arkadii. "You realize that I don't advise you do so because I subscribe to the old-fashioned belief in the necessity of paying one's respects to the authorities, but simply because the governor is a very decent fellow. Besides, you probably want to meet the prominent members of society here.... You aren't antisocial, I trust? And he's giving a large ball the day after tomorrow."

"Will you be at the ball?" Arkadii inquired.

"He's giving it in my honor," Matvei Ilich responded almost pityingly. "Do you know how to dance?"

"Yes, I do, but not very well."

"That's a shame! There are some pretty girls here, and it's disgraceful for a young man not to be able to dance. Again, I don't say that because of any old-fashioned ideas—I don't believe for a moment that a man's wit lies in his feet. But Byronism is ridiculous—*il a fait son temps.*"

"But, Uncle, it's not at all because of Byronism that I...."

"I'll introduce you to the ladies here—I'll take you under my wing," Matvei Ilich interrupted, and he laughed complacently. "You'll find it warm enough there, eh?"

A servant entered and announced the arrival of the superintendent of public lands, a mild-looking elderly man with deep creases around his mouth who was extremely fond of nature, especially on a summer day when, in his words, "every busy little bee takes a little bribe from every little flower." Arkadii departed.

He found Bazarov at the inn in which they were staying; it took him a long time to persuade his friend to go to the governor's. "Well, there's no other choice," Bazarov finally said. "It's no good doing something halfway. We came to look at the townspeople—let's go and look at them!"

The governor welcomed the young men cordially enough, but he neither asked them to sit down nor sat down himself. He was constantly in a hurry; he donned a tight uniform and an extremely stiff tie each morning; he never ate or drank too much; he was always organizing things. They called him Bourdaloue around the district, hinting not at the famous French prophet but at the word *"burda,"* an indecisive person. He invited Kirsanov and Bazarov to his ball and, within a few minutes, invited them a second time, regarding them as brothers and calling them both Kirsanov.

They were on their way home from the governor's when a short man in a Slavophile overcoat suddenly leapt out of a passing carriage, crying, "Evgenii Vasilich!" and dashed up to Bazarov.

"Ah! It's you, Herr Sitnikov," Bazarov observed, continuing along the pavement. "What brought you here?"

"Can you imagine, I'm here completely by accident," he replied. Then, returning to the carriage, he waved his hand several times and shouted, "Follow us, follow us! My father had some business here," he continued, hopping across a ditch, "and so he invited me…. I heard about your arrival today, and I've already been to see you…." (On returning to their room, the friends did, in fact, find a card with turned-down corners that bore the name of Sitnikov, in French on one side, in Cyrillic characters on the other.) "You aren't coming from the governor's, I hope?"

"It's no use hoping—we've come straight from there."

"Ah! In that case, I'll visit him, too.... Evgenii Vasilich, introduce me to your ... to the...."

"Sitnikov, Kirsanov," Bazarov mumbled, without stopping.

"I'm most honored," Sitnikov began, walking sideways and smirking as he hurriedly pulled off his extremely elegant gloves. "I've heard so much.... I'm an old acquaintance of Evgenii Vasilich and, I may say—his disciple. I'm indebted to him for my regeneration...."

Arkadii looked at Bazarov's disciple. A combined expression of anxiety and stupidity was imprinted on the small but pleasant features of his sleek face; his little eyes, which seemed too close together, had a fixed, worried look, and his laugh—a sort of short, wooden laugh—was worried as well.

"Would you believe it," he continued, "when Evgenii Vasilich said for the first time in my presence that it wasn't right to accept any authorities, I experienced such ecstasy ... as though I'd been blind and had recovered my sight! Now, I thought, I've finally found an authentic human being! By the way, Evgenii Vasilich, you absolutely must get to know a lady here who's really capable of understanding you, and for whom a visit from you would be a real treat. You've heard of her, I presume?"

"Who is it?" Bazarov asked reluctantly.

"Kukshina, *Eudoxie,* Evdoksia Kukshina. She has a remarkable nature, *émancipée* in the true sense of the word—an advanced woman. Do you know what? Let's all go together to visit her right now. She lives a mere two steps from here. We'll have a meal there. Have you eaten yet?"

"No, not yet."

"Well, that's excellent. She's separated from her husband, you understand. She isn't dependent on anyone."

"Is she pretty?" Bazarov interrupted him.

"N-no, you couldn't say that."

"Then what the devil are you asking us to go and see her for?"

"Oh, you jokester, you.... She'll give us a bottle of champagne."

"So that's it. The practical person is now in evidence. By the way, is your father still in the gin business?"

"Yes," Sitnikov hurriedly replied, and he laughed shrilly. "Well? Will you come?"

"I really don't know."

"You wanted to look at people. Go ahead," Arkadii remarked under his breath.

"And what do *you* say, Mr. Kirsanov?" Sitnikov interjected. "You have to come, too. We can't go without you."

"But how can we all burst in on her at the same time?"

"That's no problem. Kukshina's a marvelous person!"

"There'll be a bottle of champagne?" Bazarov queried.

"Three!" Sitnikov exclaimed. "I'll swear to that."

"By what?"

"My own head."

"Your father's wallet would be better. However, let's go."

# XIII

The small, nobleman's house designed in the Moscow style inhabited by Avdotia Nikitishna—otherwise known as Evdoksia Kukshina—was located in one of the sections of *** that had recently burned down; it's well known that our provincial towns catch on fire every five years. By the door there was a bell-rope hanging above a visiting card nailed askew, and in the entryway the visitors were met by some woman, neither exactly a servant nor a companion, wearing a cap—these were unmistakable tokens of the progressive tendencies of the lady of the house. Sitnikov asked whether Avdotia Nikitishna was at home.

"Is that you, *Victor?*" piped a thin voice from the adjoining room. "Come in."

The woman in the cap promptly disappeared.

"I'm not alone," Sitnikov responded, casting a sharp glance at Arkadii and Bazarov as he briskly pulled off his overcoat, beneath which appeared something in the nature of a coachman's long velvet jacket.

"It doesn't matter," answered the voice. *"Entrez."*

The young men went in. The room into which they walked was more like an office than a drawing room. Sheets of papers, letters, and thick issues of Russian journals, their pages for the most part uncut, were strewn across dusty tables; white cigarette butts lay scattered in every direction. A fairly young lady was semi-reclining on a leather sofa. Her blond hair was somewhat disheveled; she was wearing a silk, not perfectly spotless dress, heavy bracelets on her short arms, and a lace scarf on her head. She rose from the sofa, casually drawing a velvet cape trimmed with yellowish ermine around her shoulders, languidly said, "Good morning, *Victor,*" and shook Sitnikov's hand.

"Bazarov, Kirsanov," he announced abruptly, in imitation of Bazarov.

"Pleased to meet you," Mrs. Kukshin responded, staring at Bazarov with a pair of round eyes, between which stood a small, forlorn, turned-up red nose. "I know you," she added, shaking his hand as well.

Bazarov scowled. There was nothing repulsive about the plain little figure of this emancipated woman, but her facial expression produced an unpleasant effect on the observer. One involuntarily felt compelled to ask her, "What's the matter? Are you hungry? Or bored? Or shy? Why are you so edgy?" Like Sitnikov, she was always perturbed in spirit. Her manner of speaking and moving was quite unconstrained and yet awkward at the same time. She obviously regarded herself as a good-natured, simple creature, and nonetheless, whatever she did, it always seemed that this was precisely what she didn't want to do; everything associated with her appeared to be done on purpose, as children say—that is, not simply, not naturally.

"Yes, yes, I know you, Bazarov," she repeated. (She had the habit peculiar to many provincial and Moscow ladies of calling men by their last names from the very first day of her acquaintance with them.) "Would you like a cigar?"

"A cigar's all well and good," interjected Sitnikov, who by now was lolling in an armchair, his legs dangling in the air, "but give us something to eat—we're awfully hungry. And tell them to bring us a little bottle of champagne."

"Sybarite," Evdoksia retorted, and she laughed. (Whenever she laughed, the gums above her upper teeth showed.) "Isn't it true that he's a sybarite, Bazarov?"

"I like comfort in life," Sitnikov affirmed self-importantly. "That doesn't prevent me from being a liberal."

"Yes, it does, it does prevent you!" Evdoksia cried. She gave instructions to her maid, however, regarding both the food and the champagne.

"What do you think about it?" she added, turning to Bazarov. "I'm confident that you share my opinion."

"Well, no," Bazarov demurred. "A piece of meat is better than a piece of bread, even from the chemical point of view."

"Are you studying chemistry? That's my passion. I've actually invented a new sort of compound myself."

"A compound? You?"

"Yes. And do you know what for? To make dolls' heads unbreakable. I'm practical as well, you see. But everything isn't quite ready yet—I still have to read Liebig. By the way, have you read Kisliakov's article on female labor in the *Moscow Gazette*? Read it, please. You're interested in the woman's question, I presume? And in the schools, too? What does your friend do? What's his name?"

Mrs. Kukshin let her questions fall one after another with affected nonchalance, without waiting for any reply. Spoiled children talk to their nursemaids that way.

"My name's Arkadii Nikolaich Kirsanov," Arkadii answered, "and I don't do anything."

Evdoksia giggled. "How charming! What, don't you smoke? You know, *Victor*, I'm very angry with you."

"What for?"

"They tell me you've begun to sing the praises of George Sand again. She's a retrograde woman, and nothing more! How can people compare her with Emerson? She doesn't have any ideas on education, or physiology, or anything. She's never heard of embryology, I'm sure, and these days—where can you get without that?" (Evdoksia even threw up her hands.) "Ah, what a wonderful article Elisevich has written on that subject! He's a gentleman of genius." (Evdoksia regularly employed the word "gentleman" instead of the word "person.") "Bazarov, come and sit by me on the sofa. Perhaps you don't know that I'm horribly afraid of you."

"Why so, if you'll permit me to inquire?"

"You're a dangerous gentleman—you're such a critic. Good God! Why, how ridiculous—I'm talking like some countrified landowner. I really am a landowner, though—I manage my estate myself. And can you imagine, my bailiff Erofei is a wonderful type—just like Cooper's Pathfinder. There's something so spontaneous about him! I've finally settled down here. It's an intolerable town, isn't it? But what can one do?"

"One town's like another," Bazarov remarked coolly.

"All its activities are such petty ones—that's what's so awful! I used to spend the winter in Moscow ... but now my lawful spouse, Mr. Kukshin, is residing there. And besides, Moscow nowadays ... I don't know ... it's not the same as it used to be. I'm considering going abroad. I was on the verge of setting off last year."

"To Paris, I presume?" Bazarov asked.

"To Paris and Heidelberg."

"Why Heidelberg?"

"For heaven's sake—Bunsen's there!"

Bazarov could find no reply to make to this.

"*Pierre* Sapozhnikov ... do you know him?"

"No, I don't."

"For heaven's sake, *Pierre* Sapozhnikov.... He's always at Lidia Khostatova's."

"I don't know her, either."

"Well, it was he who undertook to escort me. Thank God, I'm independent—I don't have any children.... What did I say? *Thank God!* It doesn't matter, though."

Evdoksia rolled a cigarette between her fingers, which were brown with tobacco stains, raised it to her tongue, licked it, and began to smoke. The maid came in carrying a tray.

"Ah, here's our meal! Would you like an appetizer first? *Victor,* open the bottle—that's your forte."

"Yes, that's my forte," Sitnikov grumbled, and then he laughed shrilly again.

"Are there any pretty women here?" Bazarov inquired as he drank a third glass of champagne.

"Yes, there are," Evdoksia replied, "but they're all such empty-headed creatures. *Mon amie* Mrs. Odintsov, for example, isn't bad-looking. It's a pity she has a certain reputation.... This wouldn't matter, however, except that she has no independence of thought, no breadth, nothing ... like that. The entire system of education needs changing. I've thought about this a great deal— our women are very badly educated."

"You can't get anywhere with them," Sitnikov averred. "One ought to despise them, and I do despise them, utterly and absolutely!" (The opportunity to feel and express contempt was most gratifying to Sitnikov. He attacked women in particular, never suspecting that he was fated to be cringing before his wife a few months later merely because she'd been born Princess Durdoleosova.) "Not one of them would be capable of understanding our conversation, not one of them deserves to be mentioned by serious men like us!"

"But there's no need whatsoever for them to understand our conversation," observed Bazarov.

"Whom do you mean?" Evdoksia inquired.

"Pretty women."

"What? Do you share Proudhon's views, then?"

Bazarov straightened up haughtily. "I don't share anyone's views—I have my own."

"Damn all authorities!" Sitnikov shouted, delighted to have a chance to express himself forcefully in front of the man he slavishly admired.

"But even Macaulay ... ," began Mrs. Kukshin.

"Damn Macaulay," thundered Sitnikov. "Are you going to stick up for mindless hussies?"

"For mindless hussies, no, but for the rights of women, which I've sworn to defend to the last drop of my blood."

"Damn ...," here Sitnikov stopped. "But I don't deny them," he asserted.

"No—I can see that you're a Slavophile."

"No, I'm not a Slavophile, although, of course...."

"No, no, no! You're a Slavophile. You're an advocate of the patriarchal despotism espoused by the *Domostroi*. You'd like to have a whip in your hand!"

"A whip's an excellent thing," Bazarov remarked, "but we've gotten to the last drop...."

"Of what?" Evdoksia interrupted.

"Of champagne, most honored Avdotia Nikitishna, of champagne—not of your blood."

"I can never listen calmly when women are attacked," Evdoksia continued. "It's awful, just awful. Instead of attacking them, you'd be better off reading Michelet's book *De l'amour*. It's marvelous! Gentlemen, let's talk about love," Evdoksia added, letting her arm languorously fall onto a rumpled sofa cushion.

A sudden silence ensued.

"No—why should we talk about love?" asked Bazarov. "But you just mentioned a Mrs. Odintsov ... that was what you called her, I believe. Who is this lady?"

"She's charming, charming!" Sitnikov piped up. "I'll introduce you. She's intelligent, wealthy, and a widow. Unfortunately, she isn't sufficiently advanced yet. She ought to get to know our Evdoksia better. I drink to your health, *Eudoxie*! Let's toast! *Et toc, et toc, et tin-tin-tin! Et toc, et toc, et tin-tin-tin!!!*"

"*Victor*, you're a naughty boy."

The meal continued for a long while. The first bottle of champagne was followed by another, then a third, and even a fourth....

Evdoksia chattered away without pausing; Sitnikov aided and abetted her. They had a long discussion about whether marriage is a prejudice or a crime, whether all human beings are born equal or not, and precisely what constitutes individuality. Things finally got to the point where Evdoksia, flushed from the wine she'd drunk, tapping her flat fingertips on the keys of a badly tuned piano, began to sing in a hoarse voice, first gypsy songs and then Seymour Schiff's ballad "Granada lies slumbering," while Sitnikov tied a scarf around his head and enacted the role of the dying lover at the words:

> And your lips with mine
> In a burning kiss entwine.

Finally, Arkadii couldn't stand it. "Ladies and gentlemen, it's getting to be like Bedlam in here," he stated out loud. Bazarov, who'd inserted an amused remark into the conversation at rare intervals—he'd paid more attention to the champagne—yawned loudly, stood up, and, without saying goodbye to their hostess, left with Arkadii. Sitnikov jumped up and followed them.

"Well, well, what do you think of her?" he inquired, obsequiously skipping from the right to the left of them. "Didn't I tell you she's a remarkable individual? If only we had more women like that! In her own way, she's a manifestation of the highest morality."

"And is the establishment that your father owns also a manifestation of morality?" Bazarov queried, pointing to a tavern they were passing at that moment.

Sitnikov gave another shrill laugh. He was deeply ashamed of his origins, and didn't know whether to feel flattered or offended by Bazarov's unexpected familiarity.

# XIV

A few days later, the ball at the governor's residence took place. Matvei Ilich was truly "the hero of the hour." The marshal of the nobility declared to one and all that he'd come purely out of respect for Matvei Ilich; meanwhile, even at the ball, even as he stood absolutely still, the governor kept on "organizing things." The geniality of Matvei Ilich's manner was equaled only by its stateliness. He was gracious to everyone—in some cases with a hint of disgust, in others with a hint of respect; he was all bows and smiles, *"en vrai chevalier français"* toward the ladies, and frequently burst into the hearty, sonorous laughter befitting a high-ranking official. He slapped Arkadii on the back and loudly called him "nephew"; he graced Bazarov, who was attired in a somewhat aged dress coat, with a sidelong glance in passing—a distracted but indulgent one—and with an indistinct but affable grunt, in which nothing could be distinguished but the words "I" and "very much"; he gave Sitnikov one finger to shake, accompanied by a smile, although his head was already averted; he even said *"Enchanté"* to Mrs. Kukshin, who appeared at the ball wearing dirty gloves, a dress with no crinoline, and a bird of paradise decoration in her hair.

There were scads of people, and no lack of men who could dance; the civilians for the most part crowded up against the walls, but the officers danced assiduously, especially one of them who'd spent six weeks in Paris, where he'd mastered various reckless interjections such as *"Zut," "Ah fichtrrre," "Pst, pst, mon bibi,"* and so forth. He pronounced them to perfection, with genuine Parisian *chic,* and yet said, *"si j'aurais"* for *"si j'avais," "absolument"* in the sense of "essentially"—in sum, employing that Russo-French dialect the French so ridicule when they needlessly assure us that we speak French like angels, *"comme des anges."*

Arkadii, as we already know, danced badly, and Bazarov didn't dance at all; they both took up positions in a little corner; Sitnikov attached himself to them. Exhibiting contemptuous scorn on his face, giving vent to spiteful comments, he kept looking around insolently, and sincerely seemed to be enjoying himself. Suddenly, his expression changed, and, turning toward Arkadii as if embarrassed, he announced, "Mrs. Odintsov's here!"

Arkadii glanced around and caught sight of a tall woman wearing a black dress who was standing in the doorway to the room. He was struck by the dignity of her bearing. Her uncovered arms gracefully rested beside her slender waist; some delicate sprays of fuchsia gracefully hung from her gleaming hair down to her sloping shoulders; her bright eyes looked out tranquilly and intelligently beneath a somewhat protruding white forehead—her look was definitely tranquil, not pensive—and her lips curved in a barely perceptible smile. Some sort of compassionate, gentle strength shone in her face.

"Are you acquainted with her?" Arkadii asked Sitnikov.

"Intimately. Would you like me to introduce you?"

"Please ... after this quadrille."

Bazarov likewise directed his attention toward Mrs. Odintsov.

"Who's that with the striking figure?" he inquired. "She doesn't look like the other females."

Having waited until the end of the quadrille, Sitnikov led Arkadii up to Mrs. Odintsov, but he hardly seemed to be intimately acquainted with her: he muddled his sentences, and she gazed at him with some surprise.

But her face assumed a pleased expression when she heard Arkadii's last name—she asked him whether he was the son of Nikolai Petrovich Kirsanov.

"Yes, indeed."

"I've met your father twice and have heard a great deal about him," she continued. "I'm very glad to meet you."

At that instant, some adjutant rushed up to her and begged her to dance a quadrille. She consented.

"Do you dance, then?" Arkadii asked respectfully.

"Yes, I do. Why would you suppose that I don't dance? Do you think I'm too old?"

"For heaven's sake, how could I possibly ...? But, in that case, let me ask you to join me for a mazurka."

Mrs. Odintsov smiled kindly. "Certainly," she said, and looked at Arkadii not exactly disdainfully, but the way married sisters look at very young brothers.

Mrs. Odintsov was a little older than Arkadii—she was almost twenty-nine—but he felt like a schoolboy, a young student, in her presence, as if their age difference were much greater. Matvei Ilich approached her with a majestic air and ingratiating remarks. Arkadii moved away, but he continued to watch her; he didn't take his eyes off her, even during the quadrille. She spoke with equal ease to her partner and to the official, quietly turning her head and eyes from one to the other, and quietly laughing twice. Her nose—like almost all Russian noses—was a bit thick, and her complexion wasn't perfectly clear; despite this, Arkadii concluded that he'd never met such an attractive woman before. He couldn't get the sound of her voice out of his ears; the very folds of her dress seemed to hang differently on her than on all the other women—more flatteringly and amply—and her movements were distinguished by both a special fluidity and naturalness.

Arkadii secretly felt somewhat shy when, at the first sounds of the mazurka, he began to sit out the dance beside his partner—he'd expected to embark upon a conversation with her, but he merely ran his hand through his hair without finding a single word to say. His shyness and discomfort didn't last long, however; Mrs. Odintsov's tranquillity communicated itself to him as well, and before a quarter of an hour had passed, he was talking to her freely about his father, his uncle, his life in Petersburg and in the countryside. Mrs. Odintsov listened to him with courteous attention, opening and closing her fan slightly; his chatter was interrupted when other partners sought her out—Sitnikov, among others, invited her to dance twice. She came back, sat down again, and picked up her fan, not even breathing more rapidly, as Arkadii began to chatter away again, filled by the happiness of being near her, of talking to her, of gazing at her eyes, her handsome forehead, her entire lovely, dignified, intelligent face. She herself said little, but her words reflected a knowledge of life; from some of her observations, Arkadii gathered that this young woman had already experienced and thought about a great deal....

"Whom were you standing with," she asked him, "when Mr. Sitnikov brought you over to meet me?"

"Did you notice him?" Arkadii asked in turn. "He has an impressive face, doesn't he? That's my friend Bazarov."

Arkadii started to discuss his "friend." He spoke of him in such detail, with such enthusiasm, that Mrs. Odintsov turned toward Bazarov and looked at him intently. Meanwhile, the mazurka was drawing to a close. Arkadii grew sorry to say good-bye to his partner—he'd spent nearly an hour with her so enjoyably! During the whole time, it's true, he'd continually felt as though she were condescending to him, as though he ought to be grateful to her ... but young hearts aren't weighed down by feelings like that. The music stopped.

*"Merci,"* Mrs. Odintsov remarked, standing up. "You've promised to come and visit me—bring your friend with you. I'd be very curious to meet someone who has the courage to believe in nothing."

The governor walked up to Mrs. Odintsov, announced that supper was ready, and offered her his arm with a careworn expression on his face. As she moved away, she turned to bestow a final smile and bow on Arkadii. He bowed low in return, watched her walk off (how graceful her figure seemed to him, draped in the grayish luster of black silk!), thinking, "She's forgotten my existence this very instant," and felt some sort of exquisite humility enter his soul....

"Well?" Bazarov questioned Arkadii as soon as he'd rejoined his friend in the corner. "Did you have a good time? A gentleman has just been telling me that this lady is 'oi-oi-oi,' but I gather that this gentleman is a fool. What do you think—is she really 'oi-oi-oi'?"

"I don't quite understand what that means," Arkadii replied.

"Oh my! What innocence!"

"In this case, I don't understand the gentleman you're referring to. Mrs. Odintsov is very nice—no doubt about it—but she behaves so coldly and strictly that...."

"Still waters ... as you know!" interjected Bazarov. "You say she's cold—that's just what adds a special flavor. Besides, you like ice cream, don't you?"

"Possibly," Arkadii muttered. "I can't decide about that. She wants to meet you, and asked me to bring you to visit her."

"I can imagine how you've described me! But you've done very well. Take me. Whatever she may be—whether she's simply a provincial social lioness or an 'emancipated woman' like Mrs. Kukshin—in any case, she's got a pair of shoulders of a sort I haven't seen in a long time."

Arkadii was offended by Bazarov's cynicism, but—as often happens—he didn't directly reproach his friend for what he didn't like about him. . . .

"Why are you unwilling to accept freedom of thought in women?" he inquired in a low voice.

"Because, my friend, as far as I can see, the only women who think freely are monsters."

Their conversation was cut short at this point. Both young men left immediately after supper, followed by Mrs. Kukshin's nervously hostile but not unconstrained laughter; her vanity had been deeply wounded by the fact that neither of them had paid any attention to her. She stayed at the ball later than anyone else, and at four o'clock in the morning, she was dancing a polka-mazurka in Parisian style with Sitnikov. This edifying spectacle constituted the final event of the governor's ball.

# XV

"Let's see what species of mammal this specimen belongs to," Bazarov said to Arkadii the following day as they mounted the staircase of the hotel in which Mrs. Odintsov was staying. "I smell something wrong here."

"I'm surprised at you!" Arkadii cried. "What? You, Bazarov, clinging to the narrow morality that. . . ."

"What an odd person you are!" Bazarov cut him off casually. "Don't you know that 'something wrong' means 'something right' in our dialect, to our sort? It's a virtue, of course. Didn't you yourself tell me this morning that she'd made a strange marriage—

although, in my opinion, marrying a wealthy old man is by no means a strange thing to do. On the contrary, it makes perfect sense. I don't believe the town gossip, but I'd like to think that it's justified, as our learned governor says."

Arkadii didn't respond and knocked on the door of the suite. A young servant dressed in livery conducted the two friends into a large room, which was badly furnished, like all rooms in Russian hotels, but was filled with flowers. Mrs. Odintsov herself appeared shortly, wearing a simple morning dress. She looked even younger in the spring sunlight. Arkadii introduced Bazarov, noticing with concealed amazement that he seemed ill at ease, whereas Mrs. Odintsov remained perfectly tranquil, just as she'd been the previous day. Bazarov himself was aware of being ill at ease, and became irritated. "Here we go—frightened of a female!" he thought and, lolling in an armchair no less informally than Sitnikov, began to speak with undue familiarity, while Mrs. Odintsov kept her clear eyes trained on him.

Anna Sergeevna Odintsova was the daughter of Sergei Nikolaevich Loktev, a man renowned for his handsome appearance, his schemes, and his gambling, who, after holding on and making a sensation in Petersburg and Moscow for fifteen years, had ended up completely ruining himself at cards and being forced to retire to the countryside, where he'd died shortly thereafter, leaving a small estate to his two daughters—Anna, a young woman of twenty, and Katerina, a child of twelve. Their mother—who was descended from an impoverished line of princes, the Kh——s—had died in Petersburg while her husband was still in his prime.

Anna's situation after her father's death had been very difficult. The brilliant education she'd received in Petersburg hadn't prepared her to cope with the cares of managing a household, or with a lonely existence in an out-of-the-way place. She'd known absolutely no one in the entire district, and she'd had no one to consult. Her father had tried to avoid all contact with the neighbors; he'd despised them in his way, and they'd despised him in theirs. She hadn't lost her self-possession, though, and had promptly sent for her mother's sister, Princess Avdotia Stepanovna Kh——, a spiteful, arrogant old lady who, upon installing herself in her niece's house, appropriated all the best rooms for her personal use, criticized and complained from morning to night, and wouldn't even take a walk in the garden without being accompanied by her one serf, a surly servant who wore a threadbare, pea-green suit of livery with light-blue trim and a three-cornered hat.

Anna had patiently put up with all her aunt's caprices, gradually proceeded with her sister's education, and seemed to have reconciled herself to the idea of wasting away in a remote area.... But destiny had decreed another fate for her. She happened to have been noticed by a certain Odintsov, a very wealthy man of about forty-six, who was an eccentric and a hypochondriac. Stout, morbid, and embittered, but not stupid and not evil, he'd fallen in love with her and had asked her to marry him. She'd consented to become his wife; he'd lived with her for six years and, upon his death, had left all his property to her. Anna Sergeevna had remained in the countryside for nearly a year after his death. After that, she'd gone abroad to travel with her sister, but had just spent time in Germany—she'd gotten bored, and had come back to live at her beloved Nikolskoe, which was located nearly forty versts from the town of ***. She owned a magnificent, wonderfully furnished house with a beautiful garden and conservatories there; her late husband had spared no expense to gratify his desires.

Anna Sergeevna very rarely went to town—generally only on business—and then she didn't stay long. She wasn't well liked in the district; there had been a fearful outcry at her marriage to Odintsov. All sorts of fictitious stories were told about her: it was alleged that she'd helped her father in his cardsharping activities, and even that she'd gone abroad for good reason, that it had been necessary to conceal the lamentable consequences.... "You understand why?" the indignant gossips would wind up. "She's gone through fire," they said of her, to which a noted local wit usually added, "and through the other elements as well." All this talk eventually reached her ears, but she ignored it; there was a good deal of independence and determination in her character.

Mrs. Odintsov leaned back in her armchair and listened to Bazarov with her hands folded. Contrary to his custom, he was talking a lot, and was obviously trying to engage her interest—which surprised Arkadii again. He couldn't decide whether Bazarov was achieving his goal, though. It was difficult to guess what impression was being made on Anna Sergeevna from her face: it constantly retained the same cordial, refined expression; her beautiful eyes glowed with attentiveness, but it was serene attentiveness. She was unpleasantly affected by Bazarov's artificial manner during the first minutes of the visit, as by a bad odor or a discordant sound, but she quickly gathered that he was ill at ease, and this actually flattered her. Nothing was repulsive to her but vulgarity, and no one could have accused Bazarov of vulgarity.

Arkadii was repeatedly forced to encounter surprises that day. He'd expected that Bazarov would talk to an intelligent woman like Mrs. Odintsov about his ideas and opinions—she herself had expressed a desire to listen to the man "who has the courage to believe in nothing"—but instead of that, Bazarov talked about medicine, about homeopathy, and about botany. It turned out that Mrs. Odintsov hadn't wasted her time in solitude: she'd read a number of excellent books and spoke perfectly correct Russian. She turned the conversation to music, but noticing that Bazarov didn't appreciate art, she subtly brought it back to botany, even though Arkadii was just launching into a discourse upon the significance of folk melodies. Mrs. Odintsov continued to treat him as though he were her younger brother; she seemed to appreciate his goodness and youthful simplicity—and that was all. Their lively, unhurried conversation went on for more than three hours, ranging freely over various subjects.

The friends finally stood up and began to say goodbye. Anna Sergeevna looked at them cordially, held out her beautiful, white hand to each one and, after a moment's thought, said with an uncertain but attractive smile, "If you aren't afraid of getting bored, gentlemen, come and see me at Nikolskoe."

"For heaven's sake, Anna Sergeevna," Arkadii cried, "I'd consider it a particular pleasure. . . ."

"And you, Monsieur Bazarov?"

Bazarov merely bowed—and a final surprise was in store for Arkadii: he noticed that his friend was blushing.

"Well?" Arkadii said to him on the street. "Do you still maintain your previous opinion of her—that she's 'oi-oi-oi' . . . ?"

"Who knows? You see how icy she is!" Bazarov retorted, and after a brief pause he added: "She's a grand duchess, a royal personage. She just needs a train trailing behind her and a crown on her head."

"Our grand duchesses don't speak Russian like that," Arkadii remarked.

"She's seen some ups and downs, my dear boy—she's eaten some of our bread!"

"Anyway, she's charming," Arkadii responded.

"What a magnificent body!" Bazarov continued. "If only I could see it on a dissection table now."

"Stop it, for God's sake, Evgenii! That's going too far."

"Well, don't get angry, you big baby. I just meant that it's of superior quality. We'll have to go and stay with her."

"When?"

"Well, why not the day after tomorrow? What's there for us to do here? Drink champagne with Mrs. Kukshin? Listen to your cousin, the liberal official? . . . Let's head out the day after tomorrow. By the way—my father's little place isn't far from there. Isn't this Nikolskoe on the S—— road?"

"Yes."

"*Optime*. Why hesitate? Leave that to fools—and intellectuals. I tell you, that's a magnificent body!"

Three days later, the two friends were driving along the road to Nikolskoe. The day was bright but not too hot, and the sleek horses trotted along merrily, lightly switching their bound, braided tails. Arkadii looked at the road, and without knowing why, he smiled.

"Congratulate me!" Bazarov suddenly exclaimed. "Today's the twenty-second of June, my guardian angel's day. Let's see whether he'll help me out somehow. They're expecting me home today," he added, lowering his voice.... "Well, they can go on expecting me a little longer. What difference does it make?"

## XVI

The estate inhabited by Anna Sergeevna stood on an exposed hill not far from a yellow stone church that had a green roof and white columns, with a fresco representing the resurrection of Christ painted in the "Italian" style over the main entrance. A swarthy warrior especially conspicuous for his rotund contours, wearing a helmet, was stretched out in the fresco's foreground. Beyond the church extended a village arranged in two long rows of houses whose chimneys peeped out here and there above the thatched roofs. The estate's manor house was built in the same style as the church, that known among us as the Alexandrine style: the house was also painted yellow and had a green roof and white columns, as well as a pediment with an escutcheon on it. The regional architect had designed both buildings with the approval of the late Odintsov, who couldn't stand—as he put it—any sort of pointless, arbitrary innovations. The house was sheltered on both sides by the dark trees of an old garden; an avenue of sculpted pines led up to the entrance.

Our friends were met in the hallway by two tall servants dressed in livery; one of them immediately ran to fetch the steward. That steward, a stout man in a black dress coat, promptly appeared and led the visitors up a staircase covered with rugs to a special room in which two beds had already been prepared for them, along with all the necessary toiletries. It was clear that order reigned supreme in the household: everything was clean, and the air was permeated with some sort of pleasant fragrance reminiscent of the reception rooms of government ministers.

"Anna Sergeevna requests that you join her in half an hour," the steward announced. "Do you have any orders to give in the meantime?"

"There won't be any orders, most respected sir," replied Bazarov. "Perhaps you'd be so kind as to bring me a glass of vodka."

"Yes, sir," the steward responded, not without perplexity, and he withdrew, his boots creaking as he walked.

"What *grande genre!*" Bazarov observed. "That's what it's called by your sort, isn't it? She's a duchess, and that's all there is to it."

"A nice duchess," Arkadii retorted. "At our very first encounter, she invited prominent aristocrats like you and me to visit her."

"Especially me, a future doctor, a doctor's son, and a village sexton's grandson.... I presume you know that I'm the grandson of a sexton? Like Speranskii," Bazarov added after a brief pause, compressing his lips. "At any rate, she indulges herself—oh, how she indulges herself, this lady! Shouldn't we put on evening clothes?"

Arkadii merely shrugged his shoulders ... but even he felt a little uncomfortable.

Half an hour later, Bazarov and Arkadii entered the drawing room. It was a large, lofty room furnished rather luxuriously, but not in particularly good taste. Heavy, expensive furniture stood in a conventionally stiff arrangement along the walls, which were covered by cinnamon-colored paper with gold flowers on it; Odintsov had ordered the furniture from Moscow through a friend and agent of his, a wine merchant. Above a sofa centered against one wall hung a portrait of a flabby, blond-haired man who seemed to be regarding the visitors in unfriendly fashion. "It must be the great man himself," Bazarov whispered to Arkadii, and wrinkling his nose he added, "Hadn't we better run for it ...?" But at that moment, the lady of the house came in. She wore a light, gauzy dress; her hair, which was smoothly combed back behind her ears, gave a girlish look to her clean, fresh face.

"Thank you for keeping your promise," she began. "You'll have to stay with me for a little while—it really isn't too bad here. I'll introduce you to my sister. She plays the piano well, which is a matter of indifference to you, Monsieur Bazarov, but you, Monsieur Kirsanov, like music, I believe. Besides my sister, an elderly aunt of mine lives with me, and one of our neighbors drops by occasionally to play cards. That comprises our entire social circle. And now let's sit down."

Mrs. Odintsov delivered this little speech with notable precision, as though she'd learned it by heart. Then she turned toward Arkadii: it appeared that her mother had known Arkadii's mother, and had even been the latter's confidante regarding her love for Nikolai Petrovich. Arkadii began to talk about his deceased mother with great warmth, while Bazarov started to leaf through picture albums. "What a tame beast I've become!" he thought to himself.

A beautiful greyhound wearing a blue collar ran into the drawing room, its nails tapping on the floor, followed by a dark-haired, dark-complexioned girl of about eighteen, who had a somewhat round but appealing face and small, dark eyes. She was holding a basket filled with flowers in her hands.

"This is my Katia," Mrs. Odintsov declared, gesturing toward her with a nod of the head. Katia made a slight curtsey, sat down beside her sister, and began picking through the flowers. The greyhound, whose name was Fifi, went up to each of the visitors in turn, wagging her tail and thrusting her cold nose into his hands.

"Did you pick all those yourself?" asked Mrs. Odintsov.

"Yes," answered Katia.

"Is our aunt coming to have tea?"

"Yes."

When Katia spoke, she smiled quite sweetly, shyly and naively, somehow looking up from under her eyebrows with comical severity. Everything about her was still young and immature: her voice, the rosy color that spread across her whole face, her pink hands with their whitish palms, and her slightly rounded shoulders.... She was constantly becoming flushed and out of breath.

Mrs. Odintsov turned to Bazarov. "You're looking at those pictures out of politeness, Evgenii Vasilich," she began. "That doesn't interest you. You'd better come over here by us and we'll argue a little about something."

Bazarov moved closer. "What subject do you have in mind?" he inquired.

"Any one you like. I warn you, I'm terribly argumentative."

"You?"

"Yes—that seems to surprise you. Why?"

"Because, as far as I can judge, you have a calm, cool temperament, and one has to get carried away to be argumentative."

"How could you have managed to comprehend me so quickly? In the first place, I'm impatient and obstinate—you should ask Katia—and, in the second, I get carried away very easily."

Bazarov looked at Anna Sergeevna. "Possibly. You'd know better than I. And so you're in the mood for an argument—by all means. I was looking at pictures of the Saxon mountains in your album, and you remarked that those couldn't interest me. You said so because you assume that I have no feeling for art—and in fact, I really don't have any. But those views might interest me from a geological standpoint—regarding the formation of the mountains, for instance."

"I beg your pardon. But as a geologist, you'd be more likely to resort to a book, to a specialized work on the subject, than to a drawing."

"The drawing shows me at glance what would be spread over ten pages in a book."

Anna Sergeevna fell silent for a moment.

"So you don't have the tiniest drop of artistic feeling?" she queried, putting her elbow on the table and by that very motion bringing her face closer to Bazarov's. "How can you get along without it?"

"And what do I need it for, may I ask?"

"Well, at least in order to study and comprehend people."
Bazarov smiled.

"In the first place, life experience takes care of that, and in the second, I assure you, studying separate individuals isn't worth the trouble. All human beings resemble one another, in soul as well as body. Each of us has an identically constructed brain, spleen, heart, and set of lungs. And the so-called moral qualities are also the same in everyone—the slight variations don't mean a thing. A single human specimen is sufficient to judge every other one by. People are like trees in a forest—no botanist would think of studying each individual birch tree."

Katia, who was arranging the flowers one at a time in leisurely fashion, raised her eyes to regard Bazarov quizzically, and upon encountering his quick, careless glance, she blushed all over. Anna Sergeevna shook her head.

"The trees in a forest," she repeated. "Then, in your view, there's no difference between a stupid person and an intelligent one, between a good one and an evil one?"

"No, there is a difference, just as there is between a sick one and a healthy one. The lungs of a tubercular patient aren't in the same condition as yours and mine, although they're constructed the same way. We more or less know where physical diseases come from. Moral diseases come from bad education, from all the inanities people's heads are stuffed with from childhood onward—from the defective state of society, in short. Reform society, and there won't be any diseases."

Bazarov uttered all this as though thinking to himself the entire time, "Believe me or not—it's all the same to me!" He slowly ran his long fingers through his sideburns while his eyes strayed around the room.

"And so," Anna Sergeevna said, "you conclude that when society has been reformed, there won't be either stupid or evil people?"

"At any rate, given the proper organization of society, it won't matter in the least whether someone is stupid or intelligent, evil or good."

"Yes, I understand. They'll all have the same spleen."

"Just so, madam."

Mrs. Odintsov turned to Arkadii. "And what's your opinion on his matter, Arkadii Nikolaevich?"

"I agree with Evgenii," he responded.

Katia looked at him mistrustfully.

"You surprise me, gentlemen," commented Mrs. Odintsov, "but we'll discuss this together further. Right now, I hear my aunt coming in to have tea. We should spare her ears."

Anna Sergeevna's aunt, Princess Kh——, a thin little woman with a pinched face and malevolent eyes staring out beneath a gray wig, came in and, barely bowing to the guests, lowered herself into a wide, velvet-covered armchair that no one was allowed to sit in except her. Katia put a footstool under her feet; the elderly lady didn't thank her, didn't even look at her, but merely shifted her hands under the yellow shawl that nearly covered her feeble body. The princess liked yellow: her cap had bright-yellow ribbons on it as well.

"How did you sleep, Aunt?" Mrs. Odintsov inquired, raising her voice.

"That dog is in here again," the elderly lady muttered in reply, and noticing that Fifi had taken two hesitant steps in her direction, she cried, "Shoo ... shoo!"

Katia summoned Fifi and opened the door for her.

Fifi rushed out in delight, hoping to be taken for a walk, but when she was left alone outside the door, she began scratching on it and whining. The princess scowled. Katia started to go out....

"I expect that the tea is ready," Mrs. Odintsov observed. "Let's go into the other room, gentlemen. Aunt, will you come and have some tea?"

The princess got up from her chair without speaking and led the way out of the drawing room. They all followed her into the dining room. An armchair covered with cushions, devoted to the princess's use, was drawn back from the table with a scraping noise by a young servant wearing livery; she sank into it. Katia, pouring the tea, handed her a cup emblazoned with a heraldic crest first of all. The elderly lady put some honey in the cup (she considered it both sinful and extravagant to drink tea with sugar in it, although she herself never spent any money on anything) and suddenly asked in a hoarse voice, "So what does Prince Ivan have to say?"

No one replied. Bazarov and Arkadii quickly realized that no one paid any attention to her, even though everyone addressed her respectfully.

"They keep her for the sake of status, because of her noble lineage . . . ," thought Bazarov.

After tea, Anna Sergeevna suggested that they go out for a walk, but it began to drizzle, and the entire group, with the exception of the princess, returned to the drawing room. The neighbor, a dedicated cardplayer, arrived; his name was Porfirii Platonych. He was a stoutish, grayish man with short, spindly legs who was highly polite and amusing. Anna Sergeevna, still conversing primarily with Bazarov, asked whether he'd like to play the card game of preference with them in the old-fashioned way. Bazarov assented, declaring that he ought to prepare himself in advance for the duties awaiting him as a country doctor.

"You'll have to be careful," Anna Sergeevna warned. "Porfirii Platonych and I will beat you. As for you, Katia," she added, "play something for Arkadii Nikolaevich. He likes music, and we can listen, too."

Katia reluctantly went over to the piano, and Arkadii, although he really did like music, reluctantly followed her—it seemed to him that Mrs. Odintsov was sending him away. Like every young man at his age, he was already experiencing some sort of vague, oppressive sensation that resembled a presentiment of love welling up in his heart. Katia raised the top of the piano and asked in a low voice, without looking at Arkadii, "What should I play for you?"

"Whatever you want," Arkadii responded indifferently.

"What sort of music do you like the best?" Katia inquired, without changing her position.

"Classical," Arkadii replied in the same tone of voice.

"Do you like Mozart?"

"Yes, I like Mozart."

Katia pulled out Mozart's Sonata-Fantasia in C minor. She played very well, albeit somewhat stiffy and unemotionally. She sat upright and immobile, her eyes fixed on the notes and her lips tightly compressed. Only at the conclusion of the sonata did her face begin to glow and her hair come loose, a little lock of it falling onto her dark forehead.

Arkadii was particularly affected by the last part of the sonata, the part in which, amid the bewitching gaiety of the carefree melody, sonorities of mournful, almost tragic, suffering suddenly intrude.... But the thoughts Mozart's music prompted in him had no connection to Katia. Looking at her, he simply thought, "Well, this young lady doesn't play badly—and she isn't bad-looking, either."

When she'd finished the sonata, without taking her hands off the keys, Katia asked, "Is that enough?" Arkadii declared that he wouldn't dare to trouble her further and began to chat about Mozart with her; he asked her whether she'd chosen that sonata herself or someone had recommended it to her. But Katia answered him in monosyllables; she withdrew into herself; she *hid*. Whenever this happened to her, she didn't come out of herself again very quickly; her face assumed an obstinate, almost obtuse expression at such times. She wasn't exactly shy, but she was mistrustful, and rather overawed by her sister, who'd brought her up and had no suspicion of that fact, naturally. Arkadii was finally forced to summon the reappearing Fifi and pat her on the head with an affable smile in order to make himself seem to be at ease. Katia began to arrange her flowers again.

Bazarov, meanwhile, kept losing—Anna Sergeevna played cards in masterly fashion, and Porfirii Platonych could hold his own at this game as well. Bazarov lost a sum that, although trifling in itself, wasn't altogether comfortable for him to lose. At supper, Anna Sergeevna once again turned the conversation to botany.

"Let's go for a walk tomorrow morning," she said to him. "I want you to teach me the Latin names and species of the wild-flowers."

"What good are the Latin names to you?" Bazarov inquired.

"Order is essential in everything," she replied.

"What an exquisite woman Anna Sergeevna is!" Arkadii exclaimed when he was alone with his friend in the room allotted to them.

"Yes," Bazarov responded, "a female with brains. And she's seen something of life, too."

"In what sense do you mean that, Evgenii Vasilich?"

"In a good sense, a good sense, my dear friend, Arkadii Nikolaich! I'm sure that she manages her estate superbly, too. But she isn't what's wonderful—it's her sister."

"What, that dark little thing?"

"Yes, that dark little thing. She's the one who's fresh and un-touched, and shy, and reticent, and everything you could want. She's someone worth devoting yourself to. You could make whatever you like out of her. But the other one—she's a stale loaf."

Arkadii didn't reply to Bazarov, and each of them got into bed with unaccustomed thoughts in his head.

Anna Sergeevna thought about her guests in turn that evening. She liked Bazarov for his lack of flirtatiousness, and even for his sharply defined views. She saw something new in him, something she'd never happened to encounter before, and it aroused her curiosity.

Anna Sergeevna was a rather strange creature. Having no prejudices of any kind, or even strong convictions, she never re-treated for any reason or went out of her way for anything. She'd seen many things quite clearly, and was interested in many things, but nothing had totally satisfied her; then again, she hardly desired total satisfaction. Her intellect was at once prob-ing and impartial; her doubts were never assuaged to the point of oblivion, and they never became strong enough to alarm her. If she hadn't been wealthy and independent, perhaps she would have thrown herself into some battle, would have discovered some passion.... But life was easy for her, although she got bored at times, and she continued to spend day after day without haste, only rarely becoming agitated. Dreams did occasionally burst into rainbow colors before her eyes, but she breathed more freely when they faded away, and she didn't regret their passing. Her imagination periodically overstepped the bounds of that which is deemed permissible by conventional morality, but even then her blood flowed as quietly as ever through her intriguingly graceful, tranquil body. Once in a while, emerging from a fragrant bath, thoroughly warm and enervated, she'd begin to muse on the insignificance of life, on its sorrows, its toil, its evil.... Her soul would become filled with sudden courage and would swell with noble ardor, but a draft would blow through a half-opened window, Anna Sergeevna would shrink back, feeling plaintive and almost angry, and only one thing would matter to her at that moment—to escape from that horrid draft.

Like all women who haven't truly been in love, she wanted something without knowing herself precisely what it was. Strictly speaking, she didn't want anything—but it seemed to her that she wanted everything. She'd barely been able to endure the late Odintsov (she'd married him out of calculation, although she probably wouldn't have agreed to become his wife if she hadn't believed he was a kind man), and had conceived a secret repugnance for all men, whom she could envision as nothing other than slovenly, ponderous, drowsy, and feebly importunate creatures. Once, somewhere abroad, she'd met a handsome young Swede with a chivalrous expression on his face and honest blue eyes under a broad forehead. He'd made a strong impression on her—but it hadn't prevented her from returning to Russia.

"What a strange person this doctor is!" she thought as she lay on the lace pillows of her magnificent bed under a light silk coverlet.... Anna Sergeevna had inherited a little of her father's inclination toward luxury. She'd loved her sinful but good-natured father dearly, and he'd adored her, had joked with her in friendly terms, as though she were an equal, and had confided in her fully, often asking her advice. She barely remembered her mother.

"What a strange person this doctor is!" she repeated to herself. She stretched, smiled, clasped her hands behind her head, then ran her eyes over two pages of a frivolous French novel, dropped the book—and fell asleep, perfectly clean and cool amid her clean, fragrant linen.

The following morning, Anna Sergeevna went off botanizing with Bazarov immediately after breakfast and returned just before midday. Arkadii didn't go anywhere and spent about an hour with Katia. He wasn't bored in her company—she herself offered to repeat the sonata of the day before—but when Mrs. Odintsov finally came back, when he caught sight of her, his heart momentarily contracted. She walked through the garden with somewhat tired steps; her cheeks were glowing and her eyes were shining more brightly than usual beneath her round straw hat. She was twirling the thin stalk of a wildflower in her fingers, a light mantilla had slipped down to her elbows, and the wide gray ribbons of her hat were clinging to her bosom. Bazarov walked behind her, as self-confident and casual as always, but the expression on his face, however cheerful and even friendly it was, didn't please Arkadii. Muttering "Good morning!" between his teeth, Bazarov went off to his room, while Mrs. Odintsov shook Arkadii's hand abstractedly and also walked past him.

"Good morning!" thought Arkadii.... "As though we hadn't already seen one another today!"

## XVII

Time, as is well known, sometimes flies like a bird and sometimes crawls like a worm, but human beings are generally particularly happy when they don't notice whether it's passing quickly or slowly. That was the condition in which Arkadii and Bazarov spent two weeks at Mrs. Odintsov's. The regimen she'd instituted in her household and her daily life partially made this possible. She strictly adhered to this regimen herself, and forced others to submit to it as well. Everything during the day was done at a fixed time: in the morning, precisely at eight o'clock, the whole group assembled to have tea; from that morning tea until noontime, everyone did whatever they pleased—the hostess herself was closeted with her bailiff (the estate was run on the rent system), her steward, and her head housekeeper; before dinner, the group reassembled to converse or read; the evening was devoted to strolls, cards, and music; at half past ten, Anna Sergeevna retired to her room, gave her orders for the following day, and went to bed.

Bazarov didn't like this measured, somewhat ceremonious punctuality in daily life—"like riding on rails," he averred; the livery-clad servants and the decorous stewards offended his democratic sensibilities. He declared that if one went this far, one might as well dine in the English style, wearing white tie and tails. He expressed his views on the subject to Anna Sergeevna one day. Her manner was such that no one ever hesitated to speak freely in front of her. She heard him out and then commented, "From your point of view, you're right—perhaps, in that respect, I truly am a noblewoman. But one can't live in the country without order—one would be consumed by boredom." And she continued to do things her way. Bazarov grumbled, but life was as easy as it was at Mrs. Odintsov's for him and Arkadii precisely because everything in the house "rode on rails."

Nonetheless, a change had taken place in both young men since the first days of their stay at Nikolskoe. Bazarov, whom Anna Sergeevna obviously favored, although she seldom agreed with him, had begun to show signs of unprecedented perturbation: he was easily irritated, reluctant to talk, he gazed around angrily, and couldn't sit still in one place, as though he were being swept away by some irresistible force; Arkadii, who'd definitely decided that he was in love with Mrs. Odintsov, had begun to yield to a gentle melancholy. This melancholy didn't hinder him from becoming better acquainted with Katia, however—

it even impelled him to pursue a friendly, warm relationship with her. "*She* doesn't appreciate me! So be it! ... But here's a gentle creature who won't turn away from me," he thought, and his heart tasted the sweetness of magnanimous sensations once more. Katia vaguely realized that he was seeking some sort of consolation in her company and didn't deny either him or herself the innocent pleasure of a half-shy, half-confiding friendship. They didn't converse with one another in Anna Sergeevna's presence; Katia always withdrew into herself under her sister's sharp gaze, and Arkadii, as befits a man in love, couldn't pay attention to anything else when he was near the object of his desire—but he was happy when he was alone with Katia. He sensed that he didn't possess the power to interest Mrs. Odintsov; he was intimidated and confused when he was alone with her. She didn't know what to say to him, either—he was too young for her. With Katia, by contrast, Arkadii felt at home; he treated her indulgently, encouraged her to express the impressions made on her by music, fiction, poetry, and other such trifles, without noticing or admitting that those trifles interested him as well. Katia, for her part, didn't try to dispel his melancholy.

Arkadii was comfortable with Katia, as Mrs. Odintsov was with Bazarov, and thus it usually worked out that the two couples, after being together for a little while, went their separate ways, especially during strolls. Katia adored nature, and Arkadii loved it too, although he didn't dare to admit it; Mrs. Odintsov was relatively indifferent to the beauties of nature, like Bazarov. The nearly continual separation of the two friends wasn't without its consequences: their relationship began to change. Bazarov ceased to talk to Arkadii about Mrs. Odintsov, even ceasing to criticize her "aristocratic ways." It's true that he praised Katia as much as before, merely recommending that her sentimental tendencies be restrained, but his praises were hasty, his advice was dry, and he generally spoke to Arkadii less than before. ... He seemed to be avoiding Arkadii, as if he were ashamed of his friend. ...

Arkadii observed all this, but he kept his observations to himself.

The real cause of this "change" was the feeling Mrs. Odintsov inspired in Bazarov, a feeling that tortured and maddened him, one that he would have instantly denied with scornful laughter and cynical derision if anyone had even remotely hinted at the possibility that it existed inside him. Bazarov was a great admirer of women and of female beauty, but love in the ideal or, as he put it, romantic sense he termed lunacy, unpardonable imbecility. He regarded chivalrous sentiments as something on the order of a deformity or disease, and had more than once expressed his surprise that Toggenburg hadn't been put into an insane asylum, along with all minnesingers and troubadours. "If you like a woman," he'd say, "try to achieve your goal. But if you can't, well, then turn your back on her—there are lots of fish in the sea."

He liked Mrs. Odintsov; the widespread rumors about her, the freedom and independence of her ideas, as well as her unmistakable inclination toward him—everything seemed to be in his favor. Still, he quickly saw that he wouldn't "achieve his goal" with her, and yet, to his own bewilderment, he found that it was beyond his strength to turn his back on her. His blood took fire as soon as he thought about her. He could have easily mastered his blood, but something else was taking hold of him, something he'd never accepted in any way, at which he'd always jeered, at which every bit of his pride revolted. In his conversations with Anna Sergeevna, he expressed his calm contempt for everything romantic more firmly than ever; when he was alone, though, he indignantly perceived the romantic in himself. Then he'd set off for the forest and tramp through it with long strides, smashing the twigs that got in his way and cursing both her and himself under his breath. Otherwise, he'd climb into the hayloft in the barn, and obstinately closing his eyes, he'd try to force himself to sleep—although he didn't always succeed, of course. He'd suddenly imagine those chaste arms entwining around his neck someday, and those proud lips responding to his kisses, and those intelligent eyes resting with tenderness—yes, tenderness—on his. Then his head would begin to spin and he'd lose consciousness for an instant, until indignation would boil up inside him again. He caught himself having all sorts of "shameful" thoughts, as though some devil were mocking him. Sometimes it seemed to him that a change was taking place in Mrs. Odintsov as well, that something special had appeared in the expression on her face, that maybe ... but at this point, he'd stamp his foot or grit his teeth, and clench his fists.

In fact, Bazarov wasn't altogether mistaken. He'd stirred Mrs. Odintsov's imagination, he'd intrigued her—she thought about him a great deal. She wasn't bored in his absence, she didn't wait for him, but she always became more animated upon his arrival; she liked to be left alone with him and she liked to talk to him, even when he made her angry or offended her tastes, her refined habits. She was seemingly eager both to test him and to examine herself.

One day, walking in the garden with her, he suddenly announced in a sullen voice that he intended to leave shortly for the village his father lived in.... She turned pale, as though something had stabbed her in the heart, stabbed her so hard that she was taken aback, and she wondered for a long while afterward what the significance of this feeling could be. Bazarov had informed her of his departure with no thought of testing her, of seeing what would come of it; he never "fabricated" anything. That morning he'd had a visit from his father's bailiff, Timofeich, who'd taken care of him when he was a child. This Timofeich, an experienced, astute little old man with faded blond hair, a weather-beaten, ruddy face, and tiny teardrops in his shrunken eyes, had unexpectedly presented himself to Bazarov wearing a short overcoat made of thick grayish-blue cloth belted with a strip of leather, and tar-covered boots.

"Hello, old man, how are you?" Bazarov cried.

"Hello, Evgenii Vasilich," began the little old man, and he smiled delightedly, as a result of which his whole face was suddenly covered with wrinkles.

"Why have you come? They've sent for me, is that it?"

"For heaven's sake, sir, how could they do that?" Timofeich mumbled. (He remembered the strict instructions he'd received from his master as he was leaving.) "I was sent to town on the master's business, and I heard that your honor was here, so I turned off along the way—to have a look at your honor, so to speak.... As if I'd ever want to disturb you!"

"Come on, don't tell lies!" Bazarov interrupted him. "Is this the road you take to town?"

Timofeich hesitated, and didn't answer.

"Is my father well?"

"Yes, thank God."

"And my mother?"

"Arina Vlasevna is well, too, praise be to God."

"They're expecting me, I suppose?"

The little old man leaned his small head to one side.

"Ah, Evgenii Vasilich, how could they not expect you? It makes my heart ache to look at your parents, I swear to God."

"All right, all right! Don't elaborate! Tell them I'll be there soon."

"Yes, sir," Timofeich replied with a sigh.

As he walked out of the house, he pulled his cap down on his head with both hands, clambered into a wretched-looking light-weight carriage he'd left by the gate, and set off at a trot—but not in the direction of town.

The evening of that same day, Mrs. Odintsov was ensconced in her study with Bazarov, while Arkadii paced around the main hall listening to Katia play the piano. The princess had gone upstairs to her room; she couldn't bear guests as a rule, especially this "new riffraff," as she dubbed them. She merely sulked in public; but she made up for it in private by bursting into such coarse language in front of her maid that the cap and wig on her head fairly danced. Mrs. Odintsov was well aware of all this.

"Why is it that you're preparing to leave?" she began. "What about your promise?"

Bazarov shivered. "Which one?"

"Have you forgotten? You were going to give me some chemistry lessons."

"What can I do? My father is expecting me—I can't loiter any longer. However, you can read Pelouse and Frémy's *Notions générales de chimie.* It's a good book, quite clearly written. You'll find everything you need in it."

"But don't you remember, you assured me that a book can't replace ... I've forgotten how you put it, but you know what I mean.... Don't you remember?"

"What can I do?" Bazarov repeated.

"Why leave?" Mrs. Odintsov asked, lowering her voice.

He glanced at her. She'd tilted her head toward the back of her easy chair and had folded her arms, which were bare to the elbow, across her chest. She seemed paler by the light of a single lamp covered with a perforated paper shade. A full white gown completely enfolded her; even the tips of her feet, which she'd also crossed, were barely visible.

"Why stay?" Bazarov responded.

Mrs. Odintsov turned her head slightly. "How can you ask why? Haven't you enjoyed yourself with me? Or do you think you won't be missed here?"

"I'm sure of it."

Mrs. Odintsov fell silent for a moment. "You're wrong in thinking that. But I don't believe you. You couldn't say that in all seriousness." Bazarov remained motionless. "Evgenii Vasilich, why don't you say something?"

"What should I say to you? People generally aren't worth missing, and I less than most."

"Why so?"

"I'm a pragmatic, uninteresting person. I don't know how to talk."

"You're fishing for compliments, Evgenii Vasilich."

"That's not a custom of mine. Don't you yourself recognize that I've got nothing in common with the elegant side of life, the side you prize so highly?"

Mrs. Odintsov nibbled the corner of her handkerchief.

"You may think what you like, but I'll be bored when you go away."

"Arkadii will stay," Bazarov observed.

Mrs. Odintsov shrugged her shoulders slightly. "I'll be bored," she repeated.

"Really? In any case, you won't be bored for long."

"What makes you think that?"

"Because you yourself told me that you're only bored when your regimen is disrupted. You've organized your life with such impeccable regularity that there can't be any room in it for either boredom or sadness ... for any unpleasant emotions."

"And do you find that I'm so impeccable ... that is, that I've organized my life so regularly?"

"Absolutely! Here's an example—in a few minutes, the clock will strike ten, and I know in advance that you'll send me away."

"No, I won't send you away, Evgenii Vasilich. You may stay. Open that window.... It seems stuffy to me somehow."

Bazarov rose and pushed on the window. It flew open with a bang.... He hadn't expected it to open so easily—besides which, his hands were shaking. The mild, dark night seemed to fill the room with its nearly black sky, its faintly rustling trees, and the fresh fragrance of its pure, flowing air.

"Draw the blinds and sit down," Mrs. Odintsov told him. "I want to chat with you before you go away. Tell me something about yourself—you never talk about yourself."

"I try to discuss useful subjects with you, Anna Sergeevna."

"You're very modest.... But I'd like to know something about you, about your family—about your father, for whom you're forsaking us."

"Why is she saying these things?" Bazarov wondered.

"None of that is the least bit interesting," he said aloud, "especially for you. We aren't prominent people."

"And I'm an aristocrat, in your opinion?"

Bazarov raised his eyes to look at Mrs. Odintsov.

"Yes," he said with exaggerated sharpness.

She smiled. "I see that you don't know me very well, although you maintain that all people are alike. I'll tell you about my life sometime ... but, first, tell me about yours."

"I don't know you very well," Bazarov reiterated. "Maybe

you're right—maybe everyone really is a riddle. You, for instance. You avoid society, you're oppressed by it—and you've invited two students to visit you. What makes you live in the countryside, with your intellect, with your beauty?"

"What? What was that you said?" Mrs. Odintsov interjected eagerly. "With my ... beauty?"

Bazarov scowled. "It doesn't matter," he muttered. "I meant to say that I don't fully understand why you've settled down in the countryside."

"You don't understand it.... But do you nevertheless explain it to yourself somehow?"

"Yes.... I assume that you constantly remain in the same place because you've spoiled yourself, because you're quite fond of comfort and convenience and quite indifferent to everything else."

Mrs. Odintsov smiled again. "You absolutely refuse to believe that I'm capable of being carried away by anything?"

Bazarov glanced at her mistrustfully. "By curiosity, possibly, but not by anything else."

"Really? Well, now I understand why we've become such good friends—you're just the same as I am, you see."

"We've become such good friends ...," Bazarov uttered in a choked voice.

"Yes! ... Why, I'd forgotten that you want to leave."

Bazarov stood up. The lamp was burning dimly in the middle of the dark, luxurious, isolated room; from time to time, the bitingly fresh night air wafted through the swaying blinds with its mysterious whispers. Mrs. Odintsov didn't move a muscle, but she was gradually being seized by secret agitation.... It communicated itself to Bazarov. He suddenly realized that he was alone with a beautiful young woman....

"Where are you going?" she asked slowly.

He didn't reply, and sank into a chair.

"So you consider me to be a placid, coddled, spoiled creature," she continued in the same voice, never taking her eyes off the window, "whereas I know that I'm very unhappy."

"You're unhappy? Why? Surely you can't attach any importance to idle gossip?"

Mrs. Odintsov frowned. It annoyed her that he'd interpreted her words that way.

"Such gossip can't possibly affect me, Evgenii Vasilevich, and I'm too proud to allow it to disturb me. I'm unhappy because ... I have no desires, no appetite for life. You look at me incredulously—you think that this is being said by an 'aristocrat' who's dressed all in lace, sitting in a velvet armchair. I don't conceal the fact that I love what you call comfort, and at the same time, I have little desire to live. Explain that contradiction any way you can. But this is all romanticism in your eyes."

Bazarov shook his head. "You're healthy, independent, and rich. What else could you possess? What do you want?"

"What do I want?" echoed Mrs. Odintsov, and she sighed. "I'm very tired, I'm old—I feel as if I've lived for a very long time. Yes, I'm old," she added, gently drawing the ends of her lace mantilla over her bare arms. Her eyes met Bazarov's, and she blushed faintly. "I already have so many memories—my life in Petersburg, wealth, then poverty, then my father's death, then marriage, then the inevitable trip abroad.... So many memories, yet nothing to remember. And in the future that's ahead of me—there's a long, long road, but no goal.... I have no desire to go on."

"Are you so disillusioned?" asked Bazarov.

"No," Mrs. Odintsov replied with emphasis, "but I'm not satisfied. I think that if I could firmly attach myself to something...."

"You want to fall in love," Bazarov interrupted her, "but you can't fall in love—therein lies your misfortune."

Mrs. Odintsov began to examine the edges of her mantilla.

"Is it true that I can't fall in love?" she inquired.

"Hardly! Only I was wrong in labeling that a misfortune. On the contrary, someone is more deserving of disdain than pity when such a thing occurs."

"When what occurs?"

"Falling in love."

"And how do you know that?"

"Hearsay," Bazarov responded angrily.

"You're flirting," he thought. "You're bored, and you're teasing me from the lack of anything better to do, while I ..." His heart actually felt as though it were being torn to pieces.

"Besides, maybe you're too demanding," he suggested, bending his entire body forward and playing with the fringe of the chair.

"Maybe. In my opinion, it's all or nothing. A life for a life— take mine, give up yours, and do so without regret, without turning back. Nothing else will suffice."

"So?" Bazarov rejoined. "Those are fair terms, and I'm surprised that thus far you ... haven't found what you wanted."

"But do you think it'd be easy to surrender oneself completely to something, whatever that might be?"

"It isn't easy, if you begin to think, to wait, and to attach value to yourself, to prize yourself, I mean. But to surrender yourself to something without thinking is very easy."

"How can one help prizing oneself? If I have no value, who'd need my devotion?"

"That isn't my business—it's someone else's business to discover what my value is. The main thing is to be able to surrender yourself."

Mrs. Odintsov leaned forward in her chair. "You speak," she began, "as though you'd had experience with all this."

"It happened to come up, Anna Sergeevna. As you know, all this isn't my sort of thing."

"But could you surrender yourself?"

"I don't know. I don't want to boast."

Mrs. Odintsov didn't respond, and Bazarov fell silent. The sounds of the piano floated up to them from the drawing room.

"Why is Katia playing so late?" Mrs. Odintsov wondered.

Bazarov stood up. "Yes, it really is late now. It's time for you to go to bed."

"Wait a bit. Where are you rushing off to? ... I want to say a word to you."

"What is it?"

"Wait a bit," Mrs. Odintsov whispered.

Her eyes rested on Bazarov. It seemed as though she were examining him closely.

He walked across the room, then suddenly went up to her, hurriedly said, "Goodbye," squeezed her hand so hard she almost screamed, and left. She raised her crushed fingers to her lips, blew on them, and then suddenly, impulsively rising from her low chair, she moved toward the door with rapid steps, as though she wanted to bring Bazarov back.... A maid entered the room, carrying a decanter on a silver tray. Mrs. Odintsov stopped, told her to leave, sat down again, and sank into thought once more. Her hair came unbound and fell to her shoulders in a dark coil. The lamp burned in Anna Sergeevna's room for a long time, and she remained motionless for a long time, just occasionally chafing her hands, which ached slightly from the night's coolness.

Bazarov went back to his bedroom two hours later, disheveled and morose, his boots wet with dew. He found Arkadii seated at the desk holding a book in his hands, his coat buttoned up to the throat.

"You haven't gone to bed yet?" Bazarov asked, as if annoyed.

"You stayed with Anna Sergeevna for a long while this evening," Arkadii remarked, without answering his question.

"Yes, I stayed with her the whole time you were playing the piano with Katia Sergeevna."

"I wasn't playing ...," Arkadii began, and then stopped. He felt tears coming to his eyes, and he didn't want to cry in front of his sarcastic friend.

# XVIII

The following morning, when Mrs. Odintsov came down to have some tea, Bazarov, who was sitting still, bending over his teacup, suddenly glanced up at her.... She turned toward him as though he'd struck her, and he thought that her face had become slightly paler since the previous night. She went back to her own room shortly thereafter and didn't reappear until noontime. It had been raining from early morning on; there was no possibility of going for a walk. The entire group assembled in the drawing room. Arkadii picked up the most recent issue of some journal and began to read it out loud. Typically, the princess first looked amazed, as though he were doing something improper, and then glared at him angrily, but he paid no attention to her.

"Evgenii Vasilevich," Anna Sergeevna said, "let's go to my study.... I want to ask you.... You mentioned a reference book yesterday...."

She stood up and went to the door. The princess turned around with an expression that seemed to say, "Look, look at how shocked I am!" and glared at Arkadii again. But he raised his voice, exchanging glances with Katia, by whom he was sitting, and went on reading.

Mrs. Odintsov walked to her study with rapid steps. Bazarov followed her quickly without raising his eyes, merely catching the sound of her silk dress delicately swishing and rustling as it glided ahead of him. Mrs. Odintsov sank into the same easy chair she'd sat in the previous evening, and Bazarov took his former place.

"What was the name of that book?" she began after a brief silence.

"Pelouse and Frémy, *Notions générales,*" Bazarov replied. "However, I might also recommend Ganot's *Traité élémentaire de physique expérimentale.* The illustrations in that book are clearer, and it's generally...."

Mrs. Odintsov stretched out her hand. "Evgenii Vasilich, I beg your pardon, but I didn't invite you here to discuss textbooks. I wanted to continue our conversation of last night. You went away so suddenly.... Will it bore you?"

"I'm at your service, Anna Sergeevna. But what were we talking about last night?"

Mrs. Odintsov cast a sidelong glance at Bazarov.

"We were talking about happiness, I believe. I told you about myself. By the way, I mentioned the word 'happiness.' Tell me why it is that even when we're enjoying music, for instance, or a lovely evening, or a conversation with sympathetic people, it all seems like an intimation of some immeasurable happiness existing somewhere else, rather than actual happiness, that is, the kind we ourselves possess. Why is that? Or perhaps you've never experienced a sensation like this?"

"You know the old saying, 'Happiness is to be found wherever we are not,'" Bazarov replied. "Besides, you told me yesterday that you're not satisfied. Such thoughts have certainly never entered my mind."

"Maybe they seem ridiculous to you?"

"No, but they haven't entered my mind."

"Really? You know, I'd very much like to know what you do think about."

"What? I don't understand."

"Listen to me. I've wanted to speak openly with you for a long time. There's no need to tell you—you're aware of it yourself—that you aren't an ordinary person. You're still young—all of life lies before you. What are you preparing yourself for? What sort of future is awaiting you? I mean to say—what goal do you want to attain? What are you heading toward? What's in your soul? In short, who are you? What are you?"

"You surprise me, Anna Sergeevna. You're well aware that I'm studying the natural sciences, and who I...."

"Well, who are you?"

"I've already explained to you that I'm going to become a district doctor."

Anna Sergeevna made an impatient gesture.

"Why do you say that? You yourself don't believe it. Arkadii might answer me that way, but not you."

"Why, in what way is Arkadii...."

"Stop! Is it possible that you could content yourself with such a humble career, and aren't you yourself always maintaining that you don't believe in medicine? You—with your pride—a district doctor! You answer me that way to keep me at arm's length, because you have no confidence in me. But you know, Evgenii Vasilich, I could understand you. I myself have been poor and proud, like you. Perhaps I've been through the same trials as you have."

"That's all very well, Anna Sergeevna, but you have to excuse me.... As a rule, I'm not used to talking about myself freely, and there's such a gulf between you and me...."

"What sort of gulf? You mean to tell me again that I'm an aristocrat? That's enough of that, Evgenii Vasilich. I thought I'd proved to you...."

"Even apart from that," Bazarov interrupted, "what could induce anyone to talk and think about the future, which for the most part is beyond our control? If an opportunity to do something turns up, so much the better, and if it doesn't turn up—at least you'll be glad that you didn't idly chatter about it beforehand."

"You call a friendly conversation idle chatter? Or perhaps you don't consider me, a woman, worthy of your confidence? For you despise us all."

"I don't despise you, Anna Sergeevna, and you know that."

"No, I don't know anything ... but let's assume this is so. I understand your disinclination to talk about your future career. But as to what's taking place inside you now...."

"Taking place!" Bazarov repeated. "As though I were some sort of government body or social group! In any case, it's utterly uninteresting—and besides, can someone always speak out loud about everything that's 'taking place' inside him?"

"But I don't see why you can't express everything contained in your soul."

"Can *you*?" Bazarov asked.

"Yes," Anna Sergeevna answered after a brief hesitation.

Bazarov bowed his head. "You're more fortunate than I am."

Anna Sergeevna looked at him inquiringly. "If you say so," she continued. "But still, something tells me that we haven't gotten acquainted for nothing, that we'll be close friends. I'm sure that this—what should I call it?—constraint, this reticence in you will eventually vanish."

"So you've noticed reticence ... or how did you put it ... constraint?"

"Yes."

Bazarov stood up and went to the window. "Would you like to know the reason for this reticence? Would you like to know what's taking place inside me?"

"Yes," Mrs. Odintsov repeated with a sort of dread she didn't understand at that moment.

"And you won't be angry?"

"No."

"No?" Bazarov was standing with his back toward her. "Let me tell you, then, that I love you absurdly, madly.... There, you've dragged it out of me."

Mrs. Odintsov extended both hands in front of her, while Bazarov leaned his forehead against the windowpane. He was breathing hard; his whole body was visibly trembling. But it wasn't the trembling of youthful timidity or the sweet alarm that follows an initial declaration of love that possessed him; it was passion struggling inside him, fierce, painful passion—not unlike hatred, and possibly akin to it.... Mrs. Odintsov became both frightened and sorry for him.

"Evgenii Vasilich," she began, and there was a ring of involuntary tenderness in her voice.

He quickly turned around, threw her a ravenous look—and, grasping both her hands, suddenly drew her to his breast.

She didn't immediately free herself from his embrace, but a moment later, she was already standing far away in a corner, gazing at Bazarov from there. He rushed toward her....

"You've misunderstood me," she whispered hurriedly, in alarm. It seemed that if he'd taken another step, she would have screamed.... Bazarov bit his lip and left.

Half an hour later, a maid gave Anna Sergeevna a note from Bazarov. It consisted simply of one line: "Should I go away today, or can I stay until tomorrow?"

"Why should you go? I didn't understand you—you didn't understand me," Anna Sergeevna wrote him in reply; she thought to herself, "I didn't understand myself, either."

She didn't appear until dinnertime. She continually paced back and forth in her room, pausing sometimes at the window, sometimes at the mirror, slowly rubbing her handkerchief across her neck, where she seemed to feel a burning sensation. She asked herself what had induced her to "drag out" his confession, in Bazarov's words, and whether she'd suspected anything.... "I'm to blame," she declared aloud, "but I couldn't have foreseen this." She became pensive and then blushed, remembering Bazarov's almost bestial expression as he'd rushed toward her....

"Or ...?" she suddenly wondered, stopping short and shaking her curls.... She caught sight of herself in the mirror: her head was thrown back, and a mysterious smile shining in her half-closed eyes and spreading across her half-parted lips at that moment told her something about which she herself was embarrassed, it seemed....

"No," she finally decided. "God knows what it might lead to. One mustn't joke about this—after all, tranquillity is the best thing on earth."

Her tranquillity hadn't been disrupted, but she felt sad, and even shed a few tears at one juncture without knowing why—certainly not because of the insult paid to her. She didn't feel insulted; she was more inclined to feel guilty. Under the influence of various vague emotions, a sense of life passing by, and a desire for novelty, she'd forced herself to go up to a certain point, had forced herself to look ahead of her—and had seen ahead of her not even an abyss, but emptiness ... or chaos.

# XIX

As great as her self-control was, and as superior as she was to every kind of prejudice, Mrs. Odintsov felt awkward when she went into the dining room for dinner. The meal proceeded fairly pleasantly, however. Porfirii Platonych arrived and related various anecdotes; he'd just come back from town. Among other things, he informed them that the governor, Bourdaloue, had ordered the officials on his special commissions to wear spurs so that they could go faster on horseback in case he sent them off anywhere. Arkadii talked to Katia in an undertone and diplomatically waited on the princess; Bazarov maintained a grim, obstinate silence. Mrs. Odintsov looked at him twice, not obliquely but straight in the face, which was bilious and forbidding, his eyes downcast, contemptuous determination stamped on every feature, and she thought, "No ... no ... no...." After dinner, she strolled out into the garden with the entire group, and, realizing that Bazarov wanted to speak to her, she took a few steps to one side and stopped. He went up to her—but even then he didn't raise his eyes—and declared hollowly, "I owe you an apology, Anna Sergeevna. You can't fail to be furious with me."

"No, I'm not angry with you, Evgenii Vasilich," Mrs. Odintsov responded, "but I'm disappointed."

"So much the worse. In any event, I've been sufficiently punished. My situation is utterly idiotic, as you'll probably grant. You wrote a note to me that said, 'Why go away?' But I can't stay, and don't want to. Tomorrow I'll no longer be here."

"Evgenii Vasilich, why are you ...?"

"Why am I going away?"

"No, I wasn't going to say that."

"You can't return to the past, Anna Sergeevna ... and this was bound to happen sooner or later—hence I should go. I can only conceive of one circumstance in which I could remain, but that circumstance will never exist. Excuse my impertinence—but you don't love me and never will love me, I presume?"

Bazarov's eyes glittered for an instant under their dark brows.

Anna Sergeevna didn't reply to him. The thought "I'm afraid of this man" flashed through her brain.

"Goodbye, then," Bazarov concluded, as though he'd divined her thought, and he went back into the house.

Anna Sergeevna followed him slowly and, summoning Katia,

took her arm, not leaving her side until that evening. She didn't play cards and laughed more than usual, which didn't accord in the slightest with her pale, troubled face. Arkadii was bewildered, and looked at her the way all young people do—that is, as if he were constantly asking himself, "What does all this mean?" Bazarov locked himself in his room; he came back down for tea, however. Anna Sergeevna longed to say some kind word to him, but she didn't know how to initiate a conversation with him....

An unexpected event relieved her of her discomfort: the steward announced the arrival of Sitnikov.

It's difficult to convey in words how birdlike the young apostle of progress seemed as he fluttered into the room. Even though his characteristic impudence had led him to decide to travel to the countryside to visit a woman he hardly knew, who'd never invited him to come but with whom, according to some information he'd gathered, such intelligent, intimate friends of his were staying, he was nevertheless trembling to the very marrow of his bones. Instead of making the apologies and paying the compliments he'd memorized ahead of time, he muttered some inanity about Evdoksia Kukshina having sent him to inquire after Anna Sergeevna's health, and after Arkadii Nikolaevich's, too, having always referred to him in the highest terms.... At this point he faltered, losing his presence of mind so completely that he sat down on his own hat. However, since no one sent him away and Anna Sergeevna even introduced him to her aunt and her sister, he quickly recovered himself and began to chatter volubly. The appearance of the banal is often useful during the course of life: it relieves excessive tension and tempers overly self-confident or self-sacrificing impulses by recalling the close kinship it has with them. Upon Sitnikov's arrival, everything became somehow duller—and simpler; they all even ate more supper and went to bed half an hour earlier than usual.

"I might repeat to you now," Arkadii said to Bazarov, who was getting undressed as Arkadii lay down in bed, "what you once said to me: 'Why are you so sad? One would think you'd fulfilled some sacred duty.'" For some time now, the two young men had been carrying on a sort of pseudocasual bantering, which is always a sign of secret displeasure or unspoken suspicions.

"I'm leaving for my father's tomorrow," Bazarov announced.

Arkadii raised himself up and leaned on his elbow. He felt both surprised and, for some reason, pleased. "Ah!" he responded. "And is that why you're sad?"

Bazarov yawned. "You'll get old if you know too much."

"And Anna Sergeevna?" Arkadii persisted.

"What about Anna Sergeevna?"

"I mean, will she let you go?"

"I'm not her hired help."

Arkadii fell into thought as Bazarov lay down and turned his face to the wall.

Several minutes went by in silence. "Evgenii!" Arkadii suddenly cried.

"What?"

"I'll leave with you tomorrow as well."

Bazarov didn't reply.

"Only I'll go home," Arkadii continued. "We'll travel together as far as Khokhlovskii, where you can get some horses at Fedot's. I'd be delighted to meet your family, but I'm afraid of being in their way and yours. You're coming back to visit us later, aren't you?"

"I've left all my things with you," Bazarov pointed out, without turning over.

"Why doesn't he ask me why I'm going just as suddenly as he is?" Arkadii wondered. "In fact, why am I going, and why is he going?" he reflected further. He couldn't find any satisfactory answers to his own questions, and his heart became filled with some bitter feeling. He sensed that it might be hard to say goodbye to this life, to which he'd grown so accustomed, but that it'd be somehow odd for him to stay by himself. "Something's happened between them," he reasoned to himself. "What good would it do me to hang around after he's gone? She's utterly sick of me, and I'll lose the last bit of respect she has for me." He began to picture Anna Sergeevna to himself; then other features gradually eclipsed the lovely image of the young widow.

"I'm sorry to leave Katia, too!" Arkadii whispered to his pillow, on which a tear had already fallen.... Suddenly he tossed his head and said aloud, "What the devil made that fool Sitnikov turn up here?"

Bazarov first stirred in bed a bit, then uttered the following rejoinder: "You're a fool, too, my friend, I can see that. Sitnikovs are indispensable to us. I—do you understand?—I need dolts like him. In reality, it's not up to gods to bake bricks!..."

"Aha!" Arkadii thought to himself, and only then did the fathomless depths of Bazarov's pride dawn on him in a flash. "Are you and I gods? At least, you're a god—but am I a dolt, then?"

"Yes," Bazarov affirmed morosely, "you're a fool, too."

Mrs. Odintsov expressed no particular surprise the next day when Arkadii told her that he was leaving with Bazarov; she seemed tired and distracted. Katia looked at him silently and seriously; the princess actually crossed herself under her shawl in a way he couldn't help noticing. Sitnikov, by contrast, was utterly disconcerted. He'd just come in to eat wearing a fashionable new outfit not, on this occasion, in the Slavophile style; the evening before, he'd astonished the servant who'd been told to wait on him by the quantity of linen he'd brought with him—and now his comrades were suddenly deserting him! He took a few tiny steps, doubled back like a hunted rabbit at the edge of a forest, and abruptly, almost with dismay, almost with a wail, announced that he proposed to leave as well. Mrs. Odintsov didn't attempt to detain him.

"I have a very comfortable carriage," added the unfortunate young man, turning to Arkadii. "I can take you, and Evgenii Vasilich can take your carriage, so it'll be even more convenient."

"For heaven's sake, it's not on your way at all, and it's quite far to where I live."

"That's nothing, that's nothing. I've got plenty of time, and besides, I've got business in that direction."

"Selling gin?" Arkadii inquired, somewhat too contemptuously.

But Sitnikov was in such despair that he didn't even laugh the way he usually did. "I assure you, my carriage is exceedingly comfortable," he mumbled, "and there'll be room for everyone."

"Don't disappoint Monsieur Sitnikov by refusing," urged Anna Sergeevna.

Arkadii glanced at her, and nodded his head significantly.

The visitors left right after they'd eaten. As she said goodbye to Bazarov, Mrs. Odintsov held out her hand to him and remarked, "We'll see one another again, won't we?"

"That's for you to decide," Bazarov replied.

"In that case, we will."

Arkadii descended the steps first and got into Sitnikov's carriage. A servant tucked him in respectfully, but Arkadii could have cheerfully punched him or burst into tears. Bazarov took a seat in the other carriage. When they reached Khokhlovskii, Arkadii waited until Fedot, the innkeeper, had harnessed the horses and then, going up to Bazarov's carriage, said with his old smile, "Evgenii, take me with you. I want to go to your house."

"Get in," Bazarov muttered through his teeth.

Sitnikov, who'd been walking around the wheels of his equipage whistling briskly, could merely gape when he heard these words, while Arkadii coolly pulled his luggage out of Sitnikov's carriage, took his seat beside Bazarov, and, after bowing politely to his former traveling companion, called out, "Go ahead!" Their carriage rolled away and quickly disappeared from sight.... Utterly confused, Sitnikov looked at his coachman, but the latter was flicking his whip above the trace horse's tail. Sitnikov proceeded to jump into his own carriage, and growling at two passing peasants, "Put your caps on, you idiots!," he rode back to town, where he arrived very late and where, the next day at Mrs. Kukshin's, he verbally dispensed with the "two disgusting, stuck-up boors."

When seated in the carriage beside Bazarov, Arkadii shook his hand warmly and said nothing for a long while. It seemed as though Bazarov understood and appreciated both the handshake and the silence. He hadn't slept the entire previous night, hadn't smoked, and hadn't eaten much of anything for several days. His narrow profile stood out gloomily and sharply under his cap, which was pulled down to his eyebrows.

"Well, my friend," he finally said, "give me a cigarette. But look at me—I wonder, is my tongue yellow?"

"Yes, it is," Arkadii confirmed.

"Hmm ... and the cigarette doesn't taste good. The machine's out of order."

"You've definitely looked different lately," Arkadii observed.

"It's nothing! I'll be all right soon. One thing's a bore—my mother is so tenderhearted, if you don't grow a big belly and eat ten times a day, she gets all upset. My father's all right—he's been everywhere and has known both feast and famine. No, I can't smoke," he added, and he flung the cigarette into the dust of the road.

"Is it twenty-five versts to your house?" Arkadii inquired.

"Yes. But you should ask this sage here." He pointed at the peasant sitting on the carriage box, a laborer from Fedot's.

But the sage merely replied, "Who can tell—versts aren't measured hereabouts," and he proceeded to swear at the shaft horse under his breath for "kicking with her headpiece," that is, for pulling with her head down.

"Yes, yes," Bazarov began, "let it be a lesson to you, an instructive example, my young friend. The devil knows what nonsense it all is! All human beings hang by a thread, an abyss may open under their feet at any moment, and yet they have to go and invent all sorts of difficulties for themselves and spoil their lives."

"What are you hinting at?" Arkadii asked.

"I'm not hinting at anything. I'm saying straight out that we've both behaved quite stupidly. What's the point of analyzing it? Still, I've noticed in hospital clinics that the man who's furious at his illness will invariably get over it."

"I don't completely understand you," Arkadii remarked. "I'd have thought you didn't have anything to complain about."

"Since you don't completely understand me, I'll tell you this—in my opinion, it's better to break stones on the highway than to let a woman control even the tip of one's little finger. All that is ..." Bazarov was about to utter his favorite word, "romanticism," but he checked himself and said, "nonsense. You don't believe me now, but I tell you this—you and I found ourselves in female society, and it was very pleasant for us. But forsaking that society is just like taking a dip in cold water on a hot day. A man doesn't have the time to devote himself to such trivia—a man should remain untamed, as an excellent Spanish proverb says. Now you, I suppose," he added, turning to the peasant sitting on the box, "you're a smart man—have you got a wife?"

The peasant turned his flat face and dull eyes toward the two friends.

"A wife? I do. Who doesn't have a wife?"

"Do you beat her?"

"My wife? Everything happens sometimes. I don't beat her without a reason."

"That's fine. Well, does she beat you?"

The peasant tugged on the reins. "That's a funny thing you've said, master. It's all a joke to you...." He was obviously offended.

"Do you hear, Arkadii Nikolaevich? But we've taken a beating.... That's what comes of being educated people."

Arkadii gave a forced laugh. Bazarov turned away and didn't open his mouth again during the entire journey.

The twenty-five versts seemed like at least fifty to Arkadii. But eventually, the small hamlet where Bazarov's parents lived appeared on the gentle slope of a hill. Next to it, a small house with a thatched roof was visible amid a young birch grove. Two peasants wearing hats were standing beside the closest hut, exchanging insults.

"You're a huge sow," said one, "and uglier than a little suckling pig."

"Your wife's a witch," returned the other.

"From their unconstrained behavior," Bazarov remarked to Arkadii, "and their playful retorts, you can deduce that my father's peasants aren't overly oppressed. Why, there he is himself, coming out on the steps of his house. He must have heard the bells on the harness. It's he, it's he—I recognize his shape. Aha! He's gotten so gray, though, the poor man!"

# XX

Bazarov leaned out of the carriage, and Arkadii thrust his head out behind his companion's back, thereby catching sight of a tall, thinnish man with disheveled hair and a narrow aquiline nose, dressed in an old, unbuttoned military coat, standing on the steps of the small manor house. His legs spread wide apart, he was smoking a long pipe and squinting to keep the sun out of his eyes.

The horses came to a stop.

"You've arrived at last," Bazarov's father remarked, continuing to smoke, although the pipe was nearly leaping up and down between his fingers. "Well, get out, get out and let me hug you!" He embraced his son. . . .

"Eniusha, Eniusha," rang out a tremulous female voice. The door flew open, and a plump little old woman in a white cap and a short striped jacket appeared in the doorway. She gasped, staggered, and probably would have fallen if Bazarov hadn't reached out to support her. Her plump little arms instantly entwined around his neck, her head pressed against his breast, and a hush fell over everything. The only sound to be heard was that of her broken sobs.

The elder Bazarov inhaled deeply and squinted harder than ever.

"There now, that's enough, that's enough, Arisha! Stop it," he urged, exchanging glances with Arkadii, who remained standing next to the carriage, while even the peasant on its box turned his head away. "That's not the least bit necessary. Please stop it."

"Ah, Vasilii Ivanych," faltered the elderly woman, "how many ages, my treasure, my darling, Eniusha...," and without unclasping her hands, she drew back her wrinkled face, which was wet with tears while exuding tenderness, and gazed at Bazarov with somehow blissful, foolish eyes, then collapsed against him again.

"Well, now, to be sure, this is all in the nature of things," Vasilii Ivanych declared, "only we'd better go inside. Here's a visitor who's come with Evgenii. You must excuse us," he added, turning toward Arkadii and shuffling his feet slightly. "You understand—a woman's weakness, and, well, a mother's heart...."

His own lips and eyebrows were twitching, and his beard was quivering ... but he was obviously trying to control himself and appear almost nonchalant. Arkadii bowed.

"Let's go inside, Mother, really," Bazarov said, and he led the overwrought elderly woman into the house. Settling her into a comfortable armchair, he hurriedly embraced his father once more and introduced Arkadii to him.

"I'm extremely happy to make your acquaintance," Vasilii Ivanovich affirmed, "but you mustn't expect great things. Here in my house everything's done in a plain way, on a military footing. Arina Vlasevna, calm down, I beg of you. What is this weakness? Our gentleman guest will think badly of you."

"My dear sir," the elderly woman spoke up through her tears, "I don't have the honor of knowing your first name and patronymic...."

"Arkadii Nikolaich," Vasilii Ivanych reported solemnly, in a low voice.

"Please excuse a silly woman like me." Arina Vlasevna blew her nose, and bending her head first to the right and then to the left, she carefully wiped one eye after the other. "Please excuse me. You see, I thought I'd die without living long enough to see my da-a-arling."

"Well, you see, we've lived long enough after all, my lady," interjected Vasilii Ivanovich. "Taniushka," he continued, turning to a bare-legged little girl of about thirteen wearing a bright red cotton dress, who was timidly peering in at the door, "bring your mistress a glass of water—on a tray, do you hear? And you, gentlemen," he added with some sort of old-fashioned joviality, "let me invite you into the study of a retired veteran."

"Just let me embrace you once more, Eniusha," moaned Arina Vlasevna. Bazarov bent down toward her. "Why, what a handsome fellow you've become!"

"Well, handsome or not," Vasilii Ivanovich observed, "he's a man, as the saying goes, *ommfay*. And now I hope that, having satisfied your maternal heart, Arina Vlasevna, you'll turn your thoughts to satisfying the appetites of our dear guests, because, as the saying goes, even nightingales can't be fed on fairy tales."

The elderly woman got up from her chair. "The table will be set this very minute, Vasilii Ivanovich. I myself will run to the kitchen and have the samovar brought in. Everything will be taken care of, everything. Why, I haven't seen him, I haven't given him anything to eat or drink these past three years. Is that easy?"

"Well, then, good mother, start bustling, don't embarrass us. Meanwhile, gentlemen, I beg you to follow me. Here Timofeich comes to pay his respects to you, Evgenii. He's delighted too, I'll wager, the old dog. Eh, aren't you delighted, you old dog? Be so kind as to follow me."

And Vasilii Ivanovich fussily led the way, shuffling and flapping the slippers he was wearing, which were worn down at the heel.

His whole house consisted of six tiny rooms. One of them—the one to which he led our friends—was called the study. A thick-legged table littered with papers darkened from an accumulation of ancient dust, as though they'd been preserved by smoke, occupied the entire space between the two windows; on the walls hung Turkish firearms, whips, a saber, two maps, some anatomical diagrams, a portrait of Hufeland, a sampler woven from horsehair in a dark frame, and a diploma under glass. A leather sofa, the cushions of which were worn into hollows and torn in places, was situated between two huge birchwood cupboards, on whose shelves books, boxes, stuffed birds, jars, and phials were jumbled together at random; in one corner stood a broken electric generator.

"I warned you, my dear Arkadii Nikolaich," Vasilii Ivanych began, "that we live on bivouac, so to speak...."

"Now stop that. What are you apologizing for?" Bazarov interrupted. "Kirsanov knows very well that we're not Croesuses, and that you don't have a butler. Where are we going to put him?—that's the question."

"For heaven's sake, Evgenii, I have a fine room out in the little lodge. He'll be very comfortable there."

"So you've had a lodge built?"

"Why, yes, where the bathhouse is," Timofeich put in.

"That is, next to the bathhouse," Vasilii Ivanych added hurriedly. "It's summer now.... I'll run right over there and arrange everything. Meanwhile, Timofeich, you bring in their things. Naturally, I'll offer you my study, Evgenii. *Suum cuique.*"

"There you have it! A most amusing old fellow, and extremely good-natured," Bazarov remarked as soon as Vasilii Ivanych had gone out. "Just as much of an eccentric as yours, only in a different way. He chatters too much."

"And your mother seems to be an awfully nice woman," Arkadii commented.

"Yes, there isn't anything artificial about her. You'll see what a dinner she'll give us."

"They didn't expect you today, sir—they haven't gotten any beef," said Timofeich, who'd just dragged in Bazarov's suitcase.

"We'll get along perfectly well without beef—there's no use asking for the stars. Poverty is no vice, they say."

"How many serfs does your father have?" Arkadii suddenly inquired.

"The estate isn't his, it's my mother's. There are fifteen serfs, as I recall."

"Twenty-two in all," Timofeich noted with an air of displeasure.

The flapping of slippers became audible, and Vasilii Ivanovich reappeared. "Your room will be ready to receive you in a few minutes," he cried triumphantly. "Arkadii … Nikolaich? That's correct, isn't it? And here's a servant for you," he added, pointing at a short-haired boy who'd entered with him, wearing a blue caftan that had ragged elbows and a pair of boots that didn't belong to him. "His name is Fedka. Again, I must repeat, even though my son tells me not to, that you shouldn't expect much. He knows how to fill a pipe, though. You smoke, of course?"

"I generally smoke cigars," Arkadii replied.

"And you do so very sensibly. I myself prefer cigars, but it's exceedingly difficult to obtain them in these isolated parts."

"There, now, that's enough humble pie," Bazarov interrupted again. "It'd be much better for you to sit down here on the sofa and let us have a look at you."

Vasilii Ivanovich laughed and sat down. His face was quite similar to his son's, except that his forehead was lower and narrower and his mouth somewhat wider. He was constantly in motion, shifting his shoulders as though his jacket were cutting him under the armpits, blinking, clearing his throat, and gesticulating with his fingers, whereas his son was distinguished by a kind of nonchalant immobility.

"Humble pie!" echoed Vasilii Ivanovich. "Evgenii, you mustn't think that I want to appeal to our guest's sympathies, so to speak, by suggesting that we live in such a godforsaken place. Quite the contrary—I maintain that for anyone who thinks, no place is godforsaken. At least I try as hard as I can not to get rusty, as they say, not to fall behind the times."

Vasilii Ivanovich drew a new yellow silk handkerchief out of his pocket, one he'd managed to snatch up on his way to Arkadii's room, and flourishing it in the air, he proceeded: "I'm not alluding to the fact that, not without considerable sacrifice to myself, for example, I've put my peasants on the rent system and have given my land to them in return for half the profits—I regarded that as my duty. Common sense itself reigns in such circumstances, although other landowners don't even dream about doing so. I'm alluding to the sciences, to education."

"Yes, I see that you have *The Friend of Health* from 1855 here," Bazarov remarked.

"It was sent to me by an old comrade, out of friendship," Vasilii Ivanovich hastened to respond, "but we even have some idea of phrenology, for instance," he added, addressing himself principally to Arkadii, however, pointing to a small plaster model of a head divided into numbered squares standing on one of the cupboards. "We aren't even unacquainted with Schönlein and Rademacher."

"Why, do people still believe in Rademacher in this province?" asked Bazarov.

Vasilii Ivanovich cleared his throat. "In this province.... Of course, gentlemen, you know far better. How could we keep up with you? For you've come to take our places. In my day, too, there was some sort of humoralist named Hoffmann, and someone named Brown, with his vitalism—they seemed quite ridiculous to us, but they'd also made a lot of noise at one time or another, of course. Someone new has replaced Rademacher for you—you look up to that man—but in another twenty years, it'll probably be his turn to be laughed at."

"For your consolation," Bazarov interjected, "I'll tell you that nowadays we laugh at medicine in general, and don't look up to anyone."

"How can that be? Why, you still want to be a doctor, don't you?"

"Yes, but the one doesn't preclude the other."

Vasilii Ivanovich poked his third finger into his pipe, where a bit of smoldering ash remained. "Well, perhaps, perhaps—I'm not going to argue. After all, what am I? A retired army doctor, *volatu.* Now I've taken to farming. I served in your grandfather's brigade," he addressed Arkadii again. "Yes, sir, yes, sir, I've seen many sights in my day. And I've been thrown into all quarters of society, I've come into contact with all sorts of people! I myself, the man you see before you now, have felt the pulse of Prince Wittgenstein, and of Zhukovskii! They were in the southern army, in the fourteenth, you understand." (Vasilii Ivanovich compressed his lips significantly at this point.) "I knew each and every one of them. Still, all in all, my business was on the sidelines. I knew my lancet, and that was enough! Your grandfather was a very honorable man, a real soldier."

"Come on, confess that he was a typical blockhead," Bazarov countered lazily.

"Ah, Evgenii, how can you use such an expression? Have some respect.... Of course, General Kirsanov wasn't one of the...."

"Well, now, drop the subject," Bazarov interrupted. "I was pleased to see your birch grove as I was arriving here. It's spread out gloriously."

Vasilii Ivanovich brightened up. "And you have to see what a little garden I've got now! I planted every tree myself. There are fruit trees, as well as berries, and all kinds of medicinal herbs. However clever you young gentlemen may be, old Paracelsus spoke the sacred truth: *in herbis, verbis et lapidibus....* For I've retired from practice, you know, but two or three times a week it happens that I'm recalled to my old duties. They come for advice—I can't drive them away. Sometimes the poor turn to me for help. And indeed, there aren't any doctors around here anyway. One of the local inhabitants, a retired major, also tries to cure people, if you can imagine that. I ask the question, 'Has he studied medicine?' and they tell me, 'No, he hasn't. He does it more out of philanthropy.' ... Ha! Ha! Ha! Out of philanthropy! What do you think of that? Ha! Ha! Ha!"

"Fedka, fill me a pipe!" Bazarov demanded rudely.

"And there's another doctor here who'd just reached a patient once," Vasilii Ivanovich persisted with some sort of desperation, "when the patient had already gone *ad patres.* The servant didn't let the doctor in. 'You're no longer needed,' he told him. The doctor hadn't expected this, got confused, and asked, 'Well, did your master hiccup before he died?' 'Yes.' 'Did he hiccup a lot?' 'Yes.' 'Ah, well, that's good,'—and off he went again. Ha! Ha! Ha!"

The elderly man was the only one to laugh; Arkadii forced himself to smile, and Bazarov merely stretched. The conversation continued this way for about an hour. Arkadii had time to go and see his room, which turned out to be an anteroom attached to the bathhouse but was very snug and clean. Taniusha finally came in and announced that dinner was ready.

Vasilii Ivanovich stood up first. "Let's go, gentlemen. Please be magnanimous and pardon me if I've bored you. I'm certain that my capable wife will satisfy you better."

The dinner, although prepared in haste, turned out to be very good, and even abundant. Only the wine wasn't quite up to the mark, as they say—it was some nearly black sherry purchased by Timofeich in town at a well-known merchant's, which had a faintly coppery, resinous flavor—and the flies were a terrible nuisance. On ordinary days, a young serf drove them away with a large green branch, but Vasilii Ivanych had dismissed him on this occasion for fear of being criticized by the younger generation. Arina Vlasevna had had time to change clothes: she'd put on a tall cap with silk ribbons and a pale-blue flowered shawl. She burst into tears again as soon as she caught sight of her Eniusha, but her husband didn't need to admonish her; she herself hurriedly wiped away her tears in order to avoid getting spots on her shawl.

Only the young men ate anything; the master and mistress of the house had dined much earlier. Fedka waited on the table, obviously encumbered by the unusual requirement that he wear boots; he was assisted by a woman with a masculine cast of face and only one eye whose name was Anfisushka; she performed the duties of housekeeper, poultrywoman, and laundress. Vasilii Ivanovich paced back and forth all during dinner, talking about the deep-seated anxiety he felt over Napoleonic politics and the intricacies of the Italian question with a perfectly happy, even beatific countenance. Arina Vlasevna paid no attention to

Arkadii; she didn't even urge him to eat. She leaned her round face—to which full, cherry-colored lips, as well as little moles on her cheeks and above her eyebrows, imparted a highly good-natured expression—on her closed little fist and didn't take her eyes off her son. She sighed repeatedly; Arina Vlasevna was dying to know how long he intended to stay but was afraid to ask him. "What if he says for two days?" she thought, and her heart sank.

After the main course had been consumed, Vasilii Ivanovich disappeared for a moment and returned with an opened half-bottle of champagne. "You see," he cried, "even though we live in a remote area, we do have something to celebrate with on festive occasions!" He filled three champagne glasses and a little wineglass, proposed the health of "our inestimable guests," and downed his glass all at once, in military fashion; he also made Arina Vlasevna drain her glass to the last drop. When the time came for dessert, although he couldn't bear anything sweet, Arkadii nonetheless deemed it his duty to taste four different kinds of preserves that had been freshly made, the more so since Bazarov flatly refused to have any and immediately began to smoke a cigarette. Tea subsequently appeared, along with cream, butter, and cookies. Then Vasilii Ivanovich led everyone out into the garden to admire the beauty of the evening. As they passed a garden bench, he whispered to Arkadii: "I love to contemplate philosophy in this spot as I watch the sunset—it suits a recluse like me. Over there, a little farther off, I've planted some of the trees beloved by Horace."

"What trees?" Bazarov asked, overhearing this.

"Oh ... acacias."

Bazarov began to yawn. "I suspect that it's time our travelers were in the arms of Morpheus," observed Vasilii Ivanovich.

"That is, it's time for bed," Bazarov added. "That's a fair conclusion. It's definitely time."

Bidding good night to his mother, he kissed her on the forehead; she embraced him and, stealthily, behind his back, made the sign of the cross over him three times. Vasilii Ivanovich con-

ducted Arkadii to his room and wished him "as refreshing a re-
pose as I enjoyed at your delightful age." And Arkadii did in
fact sleep extremely well in his bathhouse; it smelled of mint,
and two crickets behind the fireplace exchanged soporific chirps
with one another. Vasilii Ivanovich went from Arkadii's room to
his study, and, perching on the sofa at his son's feet, was about
to begin to chat with him. But Bazarov promptly sent his father
away, saying that he was sleepy—yet he didn't fall asleep until
dawn. His eyes wide open, he angrily stared into the darkness;
childhood memories had no power over him, and besides, he still
hadn't had time to efface his recent, bitter impressions. Arina
Vlasevna first prayed to her heart's content, then had a long, long
conversation with Anfisushka, who stood stock-still facing her
mistress, fixing her single eye upon her, and conveyed all her observations and conclusions about Evgenii Vasilevich in a secre-
tive whisper. The elderly woman's head was spinning from
happiness and wine and cigar smoke; her husband tried to talk to
her, but he gave up with a wave of his hand.

Arina Vlasevna was an authentic Russian gentlewoman of a
bygone era; she ought to have lived about two centuries earlier,
in the days of old Moscow. She was deeply devout and quite sensitive; she believed in fortune-telling, charms, dreams, and
omens of every possible type; she believed in holy wanderers, in
house-goblins, in wood-goblins, in unlucky encounters, in the
evil eye, in folk remedies; she ate specially prepared salt on
Holy Thursday; she believed that the end of the world was at
hand, that if the candles didn't go out at vespers on Easter Sunday, then there'd be a good crop of buckwheat, and that a mush-
room won't grow after it's been seen by a human eye; she
believed that the devil likes to be wherever there's water, and
that all Jews have a bloodstained patch on their chests. She was
afraid of mice, snakes, frogs, sparrows, leeches, thunder, cold
water, drafts, horses, goats, red-haired people, and black cats; she
regarded crickets and dogs as unclean beasts; she never ate veal,
doves, crayfish, cheese, asparagus, artichokes, rabbits, or water-
melons, because a sliced-open watermelon recalled the head of

John the Baptist; she couldn't speak about oysters without a shudder; she was fond of eating—and rigorously fasted; she slept ten hours out of every twenty-four—and never went to bed at all if Vasilii Ivanovich even had a headache; she'd never read a single book except *Alexis, or the Cottage in the Forest;* she wrote one or two letters a year at most, but was adept at keeping house, preserving fruits, and making jam, even though she never touched a thing with her own hands and was generally disinclined to get up from her chair.

Arina Vlasevna was very kind and, in her own way, not at all stupid. She knew that the world is divided into gentry, whose duty it is to give orders, and plain people, whose duty it is to obey them—and thus she felt no repugnance toward servility or submissive bows. But she treated her servants gently and affectionately, never let a single beggar go away empty-handed, and never spoke ill of anyone, although she did occasionally indulge in gossip. In her youth, she'd been quite pretty, had played the clavichord, and had spoken a little French; but in the course of many years of traveling with her husband, whom she'd married against her will, she'd grown stout, and had forgotten what music and French she knew. She loved and feared her son beyond words; she'd handed the management of her estate over to Vasilii Ivanovich and no longer interfered in anything; she'd simply groan, wave her handkerchief, and raise her eyebrows higher and higher with horror when her elderly husband began to discuss impending government reforms and his own plans. She was apprehensive, constantly expecting some dire misfortune, and began to cry as soon as she recollected anything sad.... Such women aren't common nowadays—God knows whether we ought to rejoice!

# XXI

When he arose, Arkadii opened the window—and the first object that met his view was Vasilii Ivanovich. Attired in a Bokharan robe fastened around the waist with a scarf, he was industriously digging away in the garden. He noticed his young visitor, and leaning on his spade, he called out: "The best of health to you! How did you sleep?"

"Wonderfully," Arkadii replied.

"Here I am, as you see, like some Cincinnatus, marking out a bed for the late turnips. The time has now come—and thank God that it has!—when everyone is obligated to produce their food with their own hands. There's no point in relying on other people—one must perform the labor oneself. And it turns out that Jean-Jacques Rousseau was right. Half an hour ago, my dear young man, you would have seen me in an entirely different situation. A peasant woman arrived who was complaining of looseness—that's how they put it, or, as we put it, dysentery— and I . . . how can I best express this? I administered opium to her. And I extracted a tooth for someone else. I offered that woman an anesthetic . . . but she wouldn't consent. I do all that *gratis— anamater.* Nevertheless, I'm thoroughly used to it. You see, I'm a plebeian, *homo novus*—I don't come from high society, like my good wife. . . . But wouldn't you like to join me out here, in the shade, to inhale the fresh morning air before we have some tea?"

Arkadii went outside.

"Welcome once again," Vasilii Ivanovich declared, raising his hand in military fashion to the dirty skullcap that covered his head. "You're accustomed to luxury and various comforts, I know, but even the luminaries of this world don't object to spending a brief period of time under a cottage roof."

"Good heavens!" Arkadii protested. "As though I were one of the luminaries of this world! And I'm not accustomed to luxury."

"Pardon me, pardon me," Vasilii Ivanovich rejoined with a polite simper. "Although I've been relegated to the archives at this point, I've seen something of the world, too—I can tell a bird by its flight. I'm also a psychologist in my own way, as well as a physiognomist. If I hadn't been endowed with those gifts, I venture to say, I'd have fallen by the wayside long ago—I wouldn't have stood a chance, a poor man like me. I must tell you, without the least bit of flattery, that I'm sincerely delighted by the friendship I observe between you and my son. I've just seen him. He got up very early, as he usually does—no doubt you're well aware of that—and went rambling around the neighborhood. Permit me to inquire—have you known my son long?"

"Since last winter."

"Indeed. And permit me to ask further—but hadn't we better sit down? Permit me, as a father, to ask with complete candor—what's your opinion of my Evgenii?"

"Your son is one of the most remarkable men I've ever met," Arkadii responded emphatically.

Vasilii Ivanovich's eyes suddenly opened wide, and his cheeks became faintly flushed. The spade dropped out of his hand.

"And so you expect . . . ," he began.

"I'm convinced," Arkadii interjected, "that your son has a great future in store for him—that he'll bring honor to your name. I've been certain of that ever since I first met him."

"How . . . how did that happen?" Vasilii Ivanovich inquired with an effort. His wide mouth had spread into a triumphant smile that wouldn't dissolve.

"Would you like me to tell you how we met?"

"Yes . . . and generally. . . ."

Arkadii began to tell him that story, speaking about Bazarov with even greater warmth, with even greater enthusiasm, than he'd displayed the evening he'd spent the mazurka with Mrs. Odintsov.

Vasilii Ivanovich listened intently, blinking repeatedly, rolling his handkerchief up into a ball with both hands, clearing his throat, and running his hands through his hair, until he finally couldn't restrain himself any longer—he leaned over toward Arkadii and kissed him on the shoulder.

"You've made me perfectly happy," he announced, never ceasing to smile. "I ought to tell you that I . . . idolize my son. I won't even speak about my wife—we all know what mothers are like!—but I don't dare to express my feelings around him, because he doesn't like it. He's averse to any display of emotion.

Many individuals even criticize him for such firmness of character, regarding it as a sign of pride or indifference, but people like him shouldn't be judged by ordinary standards, should they? Right here, for example, many others in his place would have been a constant burden on their parents, but he—would you believe it?—has never taken a kopeck more than he could help, by God, from the day he was born!"

"He's an unselfish, honorable man," Arkadii observed.

"Just so—he's unselfish. Not only do I idolize him, Arkadii Nikolaich, I'm proud of him, and the height of my ambition is that the following lines will appear in his biography someday: 'The son of a simple army doctor who nonetheless was capable of divining his greatness early on and spared nothing for his education....'" The elderly man's voice broke.

Arkadii squeezed his hand.

"What do you think," Vasilii Ivanovich inquired after a brief silence, "will it be in the field of medicine that he attains the celebrity you predict for him?"

"Probably not in medicine, even though he'll be one of the leading scientists in that field."

"Then in which field, Arkadii Nikolaich?"

"It's hard to say right now—but he'll be famous."

"He'll be famous!" the elderly man echoed, and he sank into thought.

"Arina Vlasevna sent me to invite you inside for tea," Anfisushka informed them, walking up carrying a huge dish of ripe raspberries.

Vasilii Ivanovich was startled. "Will there be chilled cream for the raspberries?"

"Yes."

"Make sure it's chilled! Don't stand on ceremony, Arkadii Nikolaich—take some more. Why hasn't Evgenii come back?"

"I'm in here," Bazarov's voice rang out from Arkadii's room.

Vasilii Ivanovich turned around quickly. "Aha! You wanted to pay a visit to your friend, but you were too late, *amice*, and we've already had a long conversation with him. Now we have to go and drink some tea—your mother is calling us. By the way, I want to have a brief talk with you."

"About what?"

"There's a little peasant here who's suffering from icterus. . . ."

"You mean jaundice?"

"Yes, a chronic, quite obstinate case of icterus. I've prescribed centaury and Saint-John's-wort for him, ordered him to eat carrots, and given him baking soda, but those are all merely palliative measures. We need some more efficacious treatment. Even though you laugh at medicine, I'm certain you can give me some useful advice. But we'll talk about that later. Now come in for tea."

Vasilii Ivanovich briskly jumped up from the garden seat and hummed a few bars from *Robert le Diable:*

> To rule, the rule, the rule we set ourselves,
> To live ... to live ... to live for joy!

"Remarkable vitality!" Bazarov commented, stepping back from the window.

———

Midday arrived. The sun was shining fiercely behind a thin veil of unbroken whitish clouds. Everything was hushed; there was no sound in the village except that of cocks irritably crowing at one another, which produced a strange sensation of drowsiness and boredom in everyone who heard them; somewhere, high up in the treetops, the incessant, plaintive peep of a young hawk could be heard. Arkadii and Bazarov were lying in the shade of a small haystack, having placed two armfuls of dry and rustling but still green, fragrant grass beneath them.

"This aspen tree," Bazarov began, "reminds me of my childhood. It's growing at the edge of the hole where a brick barn once stood, and in those days, I firmly believed that this hole and this aspen tree possessed special, talismanic powers—I was never bored when I was near them. At the time, I didn't realize that I wasn't bored because I was a child. Well, now I've grown up, and the talisman has lost its power."

"How long did you live here in all?" Arkadii inquired.

"Two years in a row. Then we started to move around. We led an itinerant life for the most part, drifting from town to town."

"And was this house built a long time ago?"

"Yes. My grandfather built it—my mother's father."

"Who was your grandfather?"

"The devil knows. Some sort of major. He served with Suvorov, and was always telling stories about crossing the Alps—lies, probably."

"There's a portrait of Suvorov hanging in your drawing room. I like these little houses like yours—they're so warm and old-fashioned, and they always have some special sort of odor."

"The smell of lamp oil and clover," Bazarov noted, yawning. "And the flies in these lovely little houses ... ugh!"

"Tell me," Arkadii requested after a brief pause, "did they discipline you much when you were a child?"

"You can see what my parents are like. They aren't the strict type."

"Do you love them, Evgenii?"

"I do, Arkadii."

"They love you so much!"

Bazarov fell silent for a while. "Do you know what I'm thinking about?" he eventually asked, clasping his hands behind his head.

"No, what?"

"I'm thinking that my parents have a good life. At the age of sixty, my father is bustling around, talking about 'palliative' measures, ministering to people, playing the role of bountiful master to the peasants—having the time of his life, in sum. And my mother's well-off, too—her day is so filled to the brim with all sorts of activities, and sighs, and groans, that she doesn't even have time to consider herself, whereas I...."

"Whereas you ...?"

"Whereas I think: I'm lying here by a haystack.... The tiny space I occupy is so infinitesimal in comparison with the rest of space, which I don't occupy and which has no relation to me. And the period of time in which I'm fated to live is so insignificant beside the eternity in which I haven't existed and won't exist.... And yet in this atom, this mathematical point, blood is circulating, a brain is working, desiring something.... What chaos! What a farce!"

"Allow me to observe that what you're saying applies to everyone...."

"You're right," Bazarov broke in. "I was going to say that they—my parents, I mean—are busy, and don't worry about their own insignificance. It doesn't sicken them ... whereas I ... I experience nothing but boredom and anger."

"Anger? Why anger?"

"Why? How can you ask why? Have you forgotten?"

"I remember everything—but I still don't concede that you have any right to be angry. You're unhappy, I'll admit, but...."

"Hah! Then I can see that you, Arkadii Nikolaevich, regard love the way all modern young men do—you summon the hen, cluck, cluck, cluck, but if the hen comes near you, you pray to God you can get away. I'm not that type. But enough of this. What can't be helped shouldn't be discussed." He turned over on his side. "Aha! There goes a valiant ant dragging off a half-dead fly. Take her away, friend, take her away! Don't pay any attention to her resistance. It's your privilege as an animal to ignore the feeling of compassion—not like us self-damaging humans!"

"You shouldn't say that, Evgenii! When have you ever damaged yourself?"

Bazarov raised his head. "That's the only thing I pride myself on. I haven't damaged myself, so a woman can't damage me. Amen! It's all over! You won't hear another word about it from me."

Both friends lay in silence for some time.

"Yes," Bazarov began again, "human beings are strange animals. When you get a distant, oblique view of the solitary lives our 'fathers' lead here, you think, 'What could be better?' You eat and drink and know that you're acting in the most reasonable, the most correct manner possible. But no—you're consumed by boredom. One wants to come into contact with people, if only to criticize them, but at least to come into contact with them."

"One ought to organize one's life so that every moment in it is significant," Arkadii stated reflectively.

"Who says so? Significance is enjoyable however illusory— but one could even make one's peace with what's insignificant. Whereas pettiness, pettiness ... that's the trouble."

"Pettiness doesn't exist for people as long as they refuse to acknowledge it."

"Hmm ... what you've just said is the antithesis of a trite phrase."

"What? What do you mean by that expression?"

"I'll tell you. To say that education is beneficial, for instance, is to employ a trite phrase, but to say that education is harmful is to employ the antithesis of a trite phrase. It has more style to it, as it were, but essentially it's all the same."

"And where's the truth—on which side?"

"Where? Like an echo I'll reply, 'Where?' "

"You're in a melancholy mood today, Evgenii."

"Really? The sun must have softened my brain, I suppose— and I shouldn't eat so many raspberries, either."

"In that case, a nap wouldn't hurt," Arkadii suggested.

"Probably not—only don't look at me. Everyone's face looks silly when they're asleep."

"But do you care what people think about you?"

"I don't know what to say to you. A real person shouldn't care. A real person is someone there's no point in thinking about, someone you have to either defer to or detest."

"It's strange! I don't detest anybody," Arkadii remarked after a moment's thought.

"And I detest so many people. You're a tender soul, a softie— how could you detest anyone? ... You get intimidated. You don't have much confidence in yourself...."

"And you?" Arkadii interrupted. "Do you have confidence in yourself? Do you have a high opinion of yourself?"

Bazarov paused. "When I meet someone who isn't inferior to me," he said, dwelling on each syllable, "then I'll change my opinion of myself. I know what it means to detest someone! You said today, for instance, as we walked past our bailiff Filipp's cottage—the one that's so nice and clean—there, you said, Russia will achieve perfection when the poorest peasant has a place like that, and each of us ought to strive to make this happen.... Whereas I've come to detest this poor peasant, this Filipp or Sidor, for whom I'm supposed to be ready to jump out of my skin, who won't even thank me for doing so ... and why should he thank me? Well, suppose he'll be living in a clean house while the nettle plants are growing out of me—well, what then?"

"Hush, Evgenii.... Listening to you today, one would be driven to agree with those who reproach us for a lack of principles."

"You talk like your uncle. There are no general principles—haven't you even figured that out yet? There are only products of the senses. Everything depends on them."

"How so?"

"Why, for instance, I take negative positions because of the products of my senses. It's pleasurable for me to negate—my brain's made that way—and that's that! Why do I like chemistry? Why do you like apples? Because of the products of my senses. It's all the same thing. Human beings will never get any deeper than that. Not everyone will tell you this, and in fact I won't tell you this a second time."

"What? Is even honesty a product of the senses?"

"Absolutely!"

"Evgenii," Arkadii began in a dejected voice.

"Well, what? Isn't all this to your liking?" Bazarov interrupted him. "No, my friend. If you've decided to mow everything down, don't spare your own legs. But we've done enough philosophizing. 'Nature breathes the silence of sleep,' as Pushkin said."

"He never said anything of the sort," Arkadii protested.

"Well, if he didn't, he could and should have said it, as a poet. By the way, he must have served in the military."

"Pushkin was never in the military!"

"For heaven's sake, on every page he writes, 'To arms! To arms! For Russia's honor!' "

"What stories you invent! This is sheer calumny."

"Calumny? That's a weighty matter! What a word he's found to frighten me with! Whatever calumny you may utter against someone, you can be sure he actually deserves twenty times worse than that."

"We'd better go to sleep," Arkadii recommended in frustration.

"With the greatest of pleasure," Bazarov responded.

But neither of them went to sleep. A feeling of near enmity crept over both young men. Five minutes later, they opened their eyes and silently exchanged glances.

"Look," Arkadii said suddenly, "a dry maple leaf has become detached and is falling to the ground. Its movement looks exactly like a butterfly's flight. Isn't that strange? The most sad and lifeless phenomenon so resembles the most cheerful and vital."

"Oh, my friend, Arkadii Nikolaich!" Bazarov cried. "I beg one thing of you—don't speak eloquently."

"I speak the best way I can.... And this is the ultimate despotism. An idea came into my head—why shouldn't I express it?"

"Fair enough—but why shouldn't I express my ideas as well? I think that eloquent speech is—indecent."

"And what's decent? Swearing?"

"Ha! Ha! I see that you really do intend to follow in your uncle's footsteps. How pleased that idiot would be if he could hear you!"

"What did you call Pavel Petrovich?"

"I called him an idiot, quite appropriately."

"But this is intolerable!" Arkadii exclaimed.

"Aha! Family feeling revealed itself there," Bazarov commented coolly. "I've noticed how stubbornly it clings to people. Someone is ready to forsake everything and abandon every prejudice, but to admit, for instance, that his brother who steals handkerchiefs is a thief—that's beyond his strength. For, in fact, he thinks, it's *my* brother, *mine*—and he's no genius.... Is this possible?"

"It was a simple sense of justice in me that revealed itself, not family feeling in the least," Arkadii asserted vehemently. "But since that's a feeling you don't understand—since you don't have that *product of the senses*—you can't appreciate it."

"In other words, Arkadii Kirsanov is too exalted for my comprehension. I'll bow down to him and say no more."

"Don't go on, Evgenii, please. We'll really quarrel in the end."

"Ah, Arkadii! Do me a favor—let's quarrel for once in earnest, to the limit, to the point of exhaustion."

"But then perhaps we'd wind up by...."

"Fighting?" Bazarov put in. "So what? Here, on the hay, in these idyllic surroundings, far from civilized society and people's eyes, it wouldn't matter. But you couldn't handle me. I'd have a hold of you by the throat in no time...."

Bazarov spread out his long, cruel fingers.... Arkadii turned around and, as though in jest, prepared to resist.... But his friend's face struck him as so sinister, such grave menace seemed to manifest itself both in the smile that distorted Bazarov's lips and in his glittering eyes, that Arkadii instinctively felt apprehensive....

"Ah! So this is where you've betaken yourselves!" the voice of Vasilii Ivanovich rang out at that moment, and the old army doctor appeared before the young men wearing a homemade linen jacket and a straw hat, also homemade, on his head. "I've been looking for you everywhere.... Well, you've picked out a wonderful place, and you're extremely well employed. Lying on 'earth,' gazing up at 'heaven.' You know, there's some sort of special significance in that!"

"I never gaze up at heaven except when I want to sneeze," Bazarov growled, and turning to Arkadii, he added in an undertone, "It's a shame he interrupted us."

"Come on, now, that's enough!" Arkadii whispered, and he

furtively grasped his friend's hand. But no friendship can withstand such blows for long.

"I look at you, my youthful interlocutors," Vasilii Ivanovich was saying in the meantime, nodding his head and leaning his folded arms on a rather cleverly bent stick he himself had carved that had the figure of a Turk for a knob, "I look at you, and I can't refrain from admiring you. You have such strength, such blooming youth, such abilities, such talents! Simply ... Castor and Pollux!"

"There you go again—spouting mythology!" Bazarov observed. "You can immediately see that he was a great Latinist in his day! Why, I seem to remember that you won a silver medal for composition, didn't you?"

"The Dioscuri, the Dioscuri!" Vasilii Ivanovich reiterated.

"Now that's enough, Father. Don't show off."

"Surely it's permissible, once in a while," murmured the elderly man. "However, I haven't been looking for you to pay you compliments, gentlemen, but, in the first place, to inform you that we'll be having dinner soon, and, in the second, to prepare you, Evgenii.... You're an intelligent person, you know what people are like, you know women—and consequently, you'll forgive.... Your mother wanted to have a service of thanksgiving sung upon the occasion of your arrival. Don't imagine that I'm asking you to attend this service—indeed, it's already over. But Father Aleksei...."

"The village priest?"

"Well, yes, the priest. He ... is going to eat ... with us.... I didn't expect this, and didn't even recommend it ... but somehow it happened.... He didn't understand me.... And, well, Arina Vlasevna.... Besides, he's a very decent, sensible man."

"He won't eat my share of dinner, I presume?" Bazarov queried.

Vasilii Ivanovich laughed. "For heaven's sake, what an idea!"

"Well, that's all I ask. I'm prepared to sit down at the dinner table with anyone."

Vasilii Ivanovich straightened his hat. "I was certain before I spoke," he said, "that you were superior to any kind of prejudice. Here I am, an old man of sixty-two, and I have none." (Vasilii Ivanovich didn't dare to confess that he himself had desired the service.... He was no less religious than his wife.) "And Father Aleksei very much wanted to meet you. You'll like him, you'll see. He doesn't even object to playing cards, and he occasionally— but this is between us—smokes a pipe."

"That's all right. We'll play a round of whist after dinner, and I'll clean him out."

"Ha! Ha! Ha! We shall see what we shall see!"

"Well, aren't you a past master?" Bazarov remarked with particular emphasis.

Vasilii Ivanovich's tanned cheeks became faintly flushed.

"Shame on you, Evgenii.... What's done is done. Ah, well, I'm prepared to admit in front of this gentleman that I had precisely that passion in my youth—and I paid for it, too! It's so hot, though! Let me sit down by you. I won't be in your way, I trust?"

"No, not at all," Arkadii replied.

Sighing, Vasilii Ivanovich lowered himself on the hay. "Your present quarters, my dear sirs," he began, "remind me of my military life in bivouacs, of the aid stations we set up somewhere like this, near a haystack, and we thanked God even for that." He sighed. "I've experienced many, many things in my day. For example, if you'll allow me, I'll tell you about an unusual episode involving the plague in Bessarabia."

"For which you received the Vladimir Cross?" interjected Bazarov. "We know, we know.... By the way, why aren't you wearing it?"

"Why, I told you that I don't have any prejudices," Vasilii Ivanovich muttered (he'd had the red ribbing taken off his coat just the previous evening), and he proceeded to relate that episode. "Why, he's fallen asleep," Vasilii Ivanovich suddenly whispered to Arkadii, pointing at Bazarov and winking good-naturedly. "Evgenii! Get up!" he added loudly. "Let's go in and have dinner."

Father Aleksei, an attractive, stout man with thick, carefully combed hair and an embroidered belt tied around his lilac silk cassock, turned out to be someone of great wit and tact. He hastened to be the first to offer his hand to Arkadii and Bazarov, as though realizing in advance that they didn't want his blessing, and he generally behaved quite informally. He neither compromised his own dignity nor gave any offense to anyone else's; he laughed a bit at seminary Latin in passing and stood up for his bishop; he drank two small glasses of wine but refused a third; he accepted a cigar from Arkadii but didn't proceed to smoke it, saying he'd take it home with him. The only thing that wasn't altogether appealing about him was a habit he had of slowly and carefully raising his hand from time to time to catch flies as they landed on his face and then occasionally crushing them. He took his seat at the card table with a mild expression of satisfaction, and ended up winning two and a half rubles in paper money from Bazarov—they never considered betting with silver in Arina Vlasevna's house....

She was sitting near her son, as before (she didn't play cards), her cheek propped on her little fist, as before; she only got up to give orders for some new treat to be served. She was afraid to caress Bazarov, and he gave her no encouragement; he never invited her caresses. Besides, Vasilii Ivanovich had advised her not to "worry" him too much. "Young people aren't fond of that sort of thing," he assured her. (It's unnecessary to describe what the dinner was like that day: Timofeich had personally galloped off at the crack of dawn for special Circassian beef; the bailiff had headed in another direction for turbot, perch, and crayfish; forty-two copper kopecks had been paid to peasant women for mushrooms alone.) Arina Vlasevna's eyes, steadfastly trained on Bazarov, expressed not only devotion and tenderness: sorrow was visible in them as well, mingled with awe and curiosity; some sort of humble reproach could also be discerned.

Bazarov, however, was in no mood to analyze the precise expression in his mother's eyes; he seldom turned toward her, and then only with some brief question. Once he asked to hold her hand "for luck"; she gently laid her soft little hand on top of his rough, broad palm.

"Well," she asked, after waiting a bit, "did it help?"

"Worse luck than ever," he replied with a careless laugh.

"He plays too rashly," Father Aleksei declared with seeming compassion, and he stroked his handsome beard.

"Napoleon's rule, good father, Napoleon's rule," interjected Vasilii Ivanovich, leading an ace.

"It brought him to St. Helena, though," Father Aleksei observed as he trumped the ace.

"Would you like some currant tea, Eniusha?" Arina Vlasevna inquired.

Bazarov merely shrugged his shoulders.

"No!" he said to Arkadii the next day. "I'm leaving here tomorrow. I'm bored. I want to work, but that's impossible here. I'll go back to your place in the countryside—I've left all my equipment there, anyway. At least at your house it's possible to lock myself up, whereas here my father always says to me, 'My study's at your disposal—nobody will interfere with you,' but he himself never moves even a step away from me. And I feel so guilty somehow if I shut myself off from him. It's the same thing with my mother, too. I hear her sighing on the other side of the wall, yet if I go in to see her, I can't find anything to say."

"She'll be bitterly disappointed," Arkadii observed, "and so will he."

"I'll come back to see them again."

"When?"

"Well, on my way to Petersburg."

"I feel particularly sorry for your mother."

"Why's that? Has she won you over with her berries, or what?"

Arkadii lowered his eyes. "You don't understand your mother, Evgenii. She's not only an extremely nice woman, she's very intelligent, really. This morning she talked to me quite sensibly and interestingly for half an hour."

"She was probably holding forth about me the whole time, wasn't she?"

"We didn't just talk about you."

"Maybe. You see better from the outside. If a woman can keep up a conversation for half an hour, that's always a good sign. But I'm leaving, all the same."

"It won't be very easy for you to break the news to them. They keep discussing what we're going to do two weeks from now."

"No, it won't be easy. Some demon drove me to tease my father today. He had one of his rent-paying peasants flogged the other day, and did so quite rightly, too—yes, yes, don't look at me with such horror—he did so quite rightly, because this peasant is a terrible thief as well as a drunkard. Only my father had no idea that I was cognizant of the facts, as they say. He got very embarrassed, and now I'll have to distress him even more.... Never mind! He'll get over it!"

Bazarov had said, "Never mind," but a whole day went by before he could bring himself to inform Vasilii Ivanovich of his intentions. Finally, just as he was saying good night to his father in the study, he remarked with a feigned yawn, "Oh ... I almost forgot to tell you.... Send someone to Fedot's for our horses tomorrow."

Vasilii Ivanovich was dumbfounded. "Is Mr. Kirsanov leaving us, then?"

"Yes. And I'm going with him."

Vasilii Ivanovich virtually reeled. "You're leaving?"

"Yes ... I have to go. Please make the arrangements about the horses."

"All right ...," faltered the old man, "to Fedot's ... all right.... Only ... only.... Why are you doing this?"

"I have to go and stay with him for a little while. I'll come back here again later."

"Ah! For a little while.... All right." Vasilii Ivanovich drew out his handkerchief, and, blowing his nose, bent over nearly to the ground. "Oh, well ... everything will be arranged. I thought you were going to be with us ... a little longer. Three days.... After three years, it's not very much—it's not very much, Evgenii!"

"But I'll come back soon, I tell you. I'm obligated to go."

"Obligated.... Oh, well! One must do one's duty before anything else. So I should send for the horses? All right. Arina and I didn't expect this, of course. She's just asked a neighbor for some flowers—she wanted to decorate your room." (Vasilii Ivanovich didn't mention the fact that every morning, just after dawn, he conferred with Timofeich, standing with his bare feet in slippers, pulling out one dog-eared ruble note after another with trembling fingers and ordering him to make various purchases, with special emphasis on good things to eat and red wine, which, as far as he could tell, the young men liked very much.) "Freedom—that's the main thing. That's my rule.... I don't want to constrain you ... not...."

He suddenly stopped talking and made for the door.

"We'll see each other again soon, Father, honestly."

But Vasilii Ivanovich merely waved his hand without turning around, and went out. When he got back to his bedroom, he found his wife in bed, and began saying his prayers in a whisper to avoid waking her up. She did wake up, however. "Is that you, Vasilii Ivanovich?" she asked.

"Yes, Mother."

"Have you just left Eniusha? You know, I'm afraid that he isn't comfortable sleeping on that sofa. I told Anfisushka to give him your portable mattress and the new pillows. I would have given him our featherbed, but I seem to remember he doesn't like too soft a bed...."

"Never mind, Mother, don't worry. He's all right. Lord, have mercy on me, a sinner," he went on praying under his breath. Vasilii Ivanovich felt sorry for his elderly wife—he didn't intend to tell her that night what sorrow lay in store for her.

—

Bazarov and Arkadii set off the next day. From early morning on, dejection reigned throughout the house; Anfisushka let dishes slip out of her hands; even Fedka was distressed, and ended up taking off his boots. Vasilii Ivanovich bustled around more than ever—he was obviously trying to put up a good front, talking loudly and stamping his feet, but his face looked haggard and his gaze studiously avoided his son. Arina Vlasevna was crying quietly; she would have utterly broken down and couldn't have controlled herself at all if her husband hadn't spent two whole hours early that morning exhorting her to do so. When, after repeated promises to come back in not more than a month, Bazarov had finally torn himself from the embraces detaining him and taken his seat in the carriage; when the horses had set off, the harness bells ringing and the wheels turning, and it no longer did any good to try to see them; when the dust had settled and Timofeich, stooped over and walking unsteadily, had crept back to his little room; when the elderly couple had been left alone in their little house, which suddenly seemed to have grown smaller and more decrepit—only then did Vasilii Ivanovich, after a few more moments of heartily waving his handkerchief from the porch steps, sink into a chair and let his head slump onto his breast.

"He's forsaken us, he's forsaken us," he murmured. "He's forsaken us. He got bored with us. We're alone, all alone!" he repeated several times, holding the index finger of one hand out in front of him. After a while, Arina Vlasevna went up to him and, leaning her gray head against his gray head, said: "There's nothing we can do, Vasia! A son is a separate piece of us that's been cut off. He's like the falcon that flies home and flies away again as he chooses, while you and I are like mushrooms in the hollow of a tree—we sit side by side and never stir from our place. Only I remain eternally constant to you, as you remain to me."

Vasilii Ivanovich took his hands away from his face and embraced his wife, his friend, more warmly than he'd ever embraced her in his youth—she comforted him in his sorrow.

# XXII

Our friends traveled as far as Fedot's mostly in silence, rarely exchanging a few insignificant words. Bazarov wasn't altogether pleased with himself—and Arkadii was definitely displeased with him. He was also feeling the baseless melancholy known only to very young people. The coachman changed the horses, and, climbing up onto the box, he inquired, "Do we go right or left?"

Arkadii was startled. The road to the right led to town, and from there to his home; the road to the left led to Mrs. Odintsov's.

He looked at Bazarov.

"To the left, Evgenii?" he asked.

Bazarov turned away. "What foolishness is this?" he muttered.

"I know that it's foolishness," Arkadii replied. "But what difference does that make? It isn't the first time."

Bazarov pulled his cap down over his forehead.

"Whatever you decide," he finally said.

"Turn to the left," Arkadii shouted.

The carriage rolled off in the direction of Nikolskoe. But having resolved to pursue this foolishness, the friends became more obstinately silent than before, and even seemed to be angry.

As soon as the steward met them on the steps of Mrs. Odintsov's house, the friends could tell that they'd acted imprudently in yielding to such a sudden passing impulse. They obviously hadn't been expected; they sat in the drawing room for a fairly long while, looking fairly silly. Mrs. Odintsov finally came in to greet them. She addressed them with her customary politeness, but was surprised at their hasty return and, as far as one could judge from the deliberateness of her gestures and words, wasn't terribly pleased by it. They hastened to announce that they'd merely dropped in along their way, and had to proceed to town within four hours. She confined herself to a slight exclamation, begged Arkadii to remember her to his father, and sent for her aunt. The princess made her entrance looking very sleepy, which gave her wrinkled old face a more malicious expression than ever. Katia wasn't feeling well, and didn't leave her room. Arkadii suddenly realized that he was at least as eager to see Katia as to see Anna Sergeevna herself. The four hours passed in trivial discussions of one thing or another; Anna Sergeevna both listened and spoke without smiling. It was only at the very moment they were departing that her former friendliness seemed to revive, as it were.

"I'm suffering from a bout of depression right now," she said, "but you mustn't pay any attention to that, and must come again—I say this to you both—before very long."

Bazarov and Arkadii each responded with a silent bow, took a seat in the carriage, and, without stopping again anywhere, went straight to Marino, where they arrived safely the evening of the following day. During the course of the entire journey, neither one even mentioned Mrs. Odintsov's name. Bazarov in particular hardly opened his mouth and kept staring off to the side, away from the road, with some sort of fierce tension in his face.

Everyone at Marino was exceedingly pleased to see them. His son's prolonged absence had begun to worry Nikolai Petrovich; he uttered a cry of delight and jumped for joy, kicking his feet up, when Fenechka ran in to find him and with sparkling eyes informed him of the arrival of the "young gentlemen." Even Pavel Petrovich was conscious of a certain degree of pleasurable excitement, and smiled condescendingly as he shook hands with the returning wanderers. Conversation and questions followed; Arkadii talked the most, especially at supper, which lasted until long after midnight. Nikolai Petrovich ordered some bottles of ale that had just been sent from Moscow to be served, and partook of the festive beverage until his cheeks turned crimson; he kept producing a half-childish, half-nervous laugh. The servants were infected by the general exhilaration as well: Duniasha ran back and forth like someone possessed, slamming doors, while Petr, even at three o'clock in the morning, kept attempting to strum a cossack melody on the guitar. The strings emitted a sweet, plaintive sound in the still air, but, with the exception of a brief preliminary flourish, nothing came of the cultured valet's efforts—nature had given no more musical talent to him than to anyone else.

Meanwhile, things weren't going too smoothly at Marino, and poor Nikolai Petrovich was having a hard time. Difficulties on the farm were springing up every day—pointless, depressing difficulties. The troubles with the hired laborers had become intolerable—some asked for their wages to be paid in full or for a raise, while others ran off with the wages they'd received in advance; the horses got sick; a harness fell to pieces as though it'd been set on fire; work was done carelessly; one threshing machine that had been ordered from Moscow turned out to be useless because of its vast weight, and another broke down the first time it was used; half the cattle sheds burned to the ground when one of the house servants, a blind old woman, went out with a burning torch in windy weather to fumigate her cow.... To be sure, the old woman maintained that the entire disaster was due to the master's plan to begin production of newfangled cheeses and milk products. The overseer suddenly got lazy and even began to grow fat, the way all Russians grow fat when they obtain a "snug berth." When he caught sight of Nikolai Petrovich in the distance, he'd fling a stick at a passing pig or threaten some half-naked urchin, but he generally slept the rest of the time. The peasants who'd been put on the rent system didn't bring their money on time and stole the forest lumber; the watchmen caught some peasants' horses in the farm meadows almost every night and sometimes forcibly rounded them up. Then Nikolai Petrovich would assess a monetary fine for the damages, but after the horses had been kept for a day or two, eating the master's fodder, these incidents usually concluded with the return of the horses to their owners.

To cap it all off, the peasants began to quarrel among themselves: brothers asked for their property to be divided because their wives couldn't get along together in the same house; suddenly, as though at a given signal, a squabble would boil up, and everyone in the village would come running to the office steps at the same time, often drunk, their faces battered, crowding in to see the master, demanding justice and retribution; a great hue and cry would arise, the women's shrill wails mingling with the men's curses. Then he had to question the opposing parties and shout himself hoarse, knowing all the while that he could never arrive at a fair verdict anyway.... There weren't enough workers to gather the harvest; one neighboring landowner with a most benevolent countenance had contracted to supply him with reapers for a commission of two rubles an acre and had cheated him in the most shameless fashion; his own peasant women demanded unheard-of sums, and in the meantime, the grain spoiled; now they weren't proceeding with the mowing, and the Council of Guardians was threatening him, demanding prompt, non-negotiable payment of a percentage....

"It's beyond my strength!" Nikolai Petrovich cried in despair more than once. "I can't flog them myself. And my principles don't permit me to call in the police captain—yet it's impossible to accomplish anything without the fear of punishment!"

*"Du calme, du calme,"* Pavel Petrovich would remark in response to all this, but even he would mutter to himself, knit his eyebrows, and tug at his moustache.

Bazarov held himself aloof from these "trivial" matters—and indeed, as a guest, it wasn't appropriate for him to meddle in other people's business. The day after his arrival at Marino, he went to work on his frogs, his amoebae, and his chemical experiments, keeping constantly occupied with them. By contrast, Arkadii considered it his duty, if not to help his father, at least to appear to be prepared to help him. He provided a patient audience, and once even offered him some advice, not with any notion of its being followed but to demonstrate his interest. The prospect of managing a farm didn't arouse any aversion in him—he'd even dreamed about agronomical work with pleasure—but his brain was swarming with other ideas at this point in time. To his own astonishment, Arkadii incessantly thought about Nikolskoe. Formerly he just would have shrugged his shoulders if anyone had told him that he could ever be bored while living under the same roof as Bazarov—and the roof was his father's! Yet he actually was bored, and yearned to escape. He tried going for long walks to wear himself out, but that didn't help.

In a conversation with his father one day, he learned that Nikolai Petrovich had several rather interesting letters written by Mrs. Odintsov's mother to his wife in his possession, and Arkadii gave his father no rest until he got hold of the letters, for which Nikolai Petrovich had to rummage through twenty different drawers and boxes. Having obtained possession of these half-crumbling pieces of paper, Arkadii felt calmer, as if it were, as though he'd caught a glimpse of the goal toward which he ought to proceed. "I say this to you both," he constantly whispered—she'd added that herself! "I'll go, I'll go, the devil take it!" Only then he'd recall the last visit, the cold reception, his former discomfort, and timidity would get the better of him.

But the "adventurousness" of youth, the secret desire to try his luck, to test his abilities on his own, without anyone's protection, finally won out. Before ten days had elapsed after his return to Marino, on the pretext of studying how Sunday schools work, he took a carriage to town, and from there to Nikolskoe. Ceaselessly urging the driver on, he flew along like a young officer riding to battle; he felt both terrified and lighthearted, and was breathless with impatience. "The main thing is not to think," he kept repeating to himself. His driver happened to be an intrepid individual; he halted before every inn, inquiring, "Do we want a drink or not?" But to make up for that, having had something to drink, he didn't spare his horses.

At last, the lofty roof of the familiar house came into sight.... The thought "What am I doing?" flashed through Arkadii's mind. "Well, there's no turning back now!" The three horses galloped in unison; the driver whooped and whistled at them. Now the bridge was groaning under the hoofs and wheels, and now the avenue of sculpted pines seemed to be coming forward to meet them.... A woman's pink dress glimmered amid the dark green, a young face peeped out from under the delicate fringe of a parasol.... He recognized Katia, and she recognized him. Arkadii told the driver to stop the galloping horses, leaped out of the carriage, and walked up to her. "It's you!" she cried, a deep blush gradually spreading across her face. "Let's go find my sister—she's out here in the garden. She'll be pleased to see you."

Katia led Arkadii into the garden. His encountering her struck him as a particularly favorable omen; he was as delighted to see her as though she were a relative of his. Everything had turned out so well: no steward, no formal entrance. At a turn in the path, he caught sight of Anna Sergeevna. She was standing with her back to him. Hearing footsteps, she slowly turned around.

Arkadii started to grow uncomfortable again, but her first words immediately put him at ease. "Welcome back, runaway!" she said in her measured, caressing voice, and walked over to him, smiling and frowning at the same time to keep the sun and wind out of her eyes. "Where did you find him, Katia?"

"I've brought you something, Anna Sergeevna," he began, "that you in no way expect...."

"You've brought yourself—that's the best thing of all."

# XXIII

Having seen Arkadii off with amused compassion, and having made it clear that he wasn't the least bit deceived as to the real object of Arkadii's journey, Bazarov went into total seclusion; he was overwhelmed by a feverish desire to work. He no longer argued with Pavel Petrovich, especially since the latter regularly assumed an extremely aristocratic demeanor in Bazarov's presence and expressed his opinions more in inarticulate sounds than in words. Only once did Pavel Petrovich begin a debate with the "nihilist" on the issue—much discussed at that time— of the rights of the nobility in the Baltic provinces, but he suddenly stopped of his own accord, remarking with icy politeness,

"However, we can't understand one another. Or at least, I don't have the honor of understanding you."

"Of course not!" Bazarov cried. "Someone's capable of understanding anything—how the atmosphere vibrates and what occurs on the sun—but he's incapable of understanding how other people can blow their noses differently than he does."

"Oh—is that witty?" Pavel Petrovich remarked quizzically, and he walked away.

Nonetheless, he occasionally requested permission to attend Bazarov's experiments, and once even lowered his fragrant face, cleansed with the very finest soap, to the microscope to see how a transparent amoeba swallowed a green speck and busily gulped it down by means of two very rapidly moving sorts of rods located in its throat. Nikolai Petrovich visited Bazarov much oftener than his brother; he would have come every day "to study," as he put it, if his difficulties with the farm hadn't distracted him. He didn't hinder the young scientific researcher; he'd sit down somewhere in a corner of the room and watch attentively, occasionally permitting himself a discreet question. During mealtimes, he often tried to turn the conversation to physics, geology, or chemistry, since all other topics, even agriculture—to say nothing of politics—might lead, if not to conflict, at least to mutual dissatisfaction.

Nikolai Petrovich suspected that his brother's hatred of Bazarov hadn't diminished in the slightest. One minor incident, among many others, confirmed his suspicions. Cholera began to appear in some places around the region, and even "carried off" two people at Marino itself. One night Pavel Petrovich happened to have a rather severe attack. He was in pain until morning, but didn't avail himself of Bazarov's skills. And when he encountered Bazarov the following day, still quite pale but scrupulously groomed and shaven, in reply to Bazarov's inquiry as to why he hadn't sent for him, Pavel Petrovich observed, "But I seem to recall that you yourself said you didn't believe in medicine."

Thus the days went by. Bazarov stubbornly and grimly continued to work.... Meanwhile, there was one creature in Nikolai Petrovich's house to whom, if Bazarov didn't open his soul, he was at least eager to talk.... This creature was Fenechka.

He'd encounter her for the most part early in the morning, in the garden or the courtyard; he never went to her room to see her, and she'd only come to his door once, to ask whether she ought to let Mitia have his bath or not. It wasn't just that she trusted him, that she wasn't afraid of him; she was more relaxed, more informal around him than around Nikolai Petrovich himself. It's hard to say why this had happened—perhaps it was because she unconsciously sensed in Bazarov the absence of all the gentility, all the superiority, that both attracts and overawes. In her eyes, he was at once an excellent doctor and an ordinary man. She cared for her baby without any constraint in his presence; one day, when she suddenly felt dizzy and had a headache, she accepted a spoonful of medicine from his hand. In front of Nikolai Petrovich, she kept her distance from Bazarov, as it were; she didn't behave this way out of cunning, but out of some sort of feeling of propriety. She feared Pavel Petrovich more than ever; he'd been watching her for some time, and would appear all of a sudden, as though he'd sprung up out of the earth behind her back, wearing his English suit, his face alert but immobile, his hands in his pockets. "It's like having a bucket of cold water thrown on you," Fenechka complained to Duniasha. The latter sighed in response and thought about another "unfeeling" man: without the slightest suspicion of the fact, Bazarov had become the "cruel tyrant" of her heart.

Fenechka liked Bazarov; he liked her, too. His face was actually transformed when he talked to her—it assumed a radiant, almost kindly expression—and his habitual nonchalance was replaced by some sort of jocular attentiveness. Fenechka was getting prettier every day. There's a time in the lives of young women when they suddenly begin to grow and bloom like summer roses; this time had arrived for Fenechka. Everything contributed to this, even the July heat that was then prevailing.

Wearing a delicate white dress, she herself seemed whiter and more delicate; she wasn't tanned by the sun, but the heat, from which she couldn't shield herself, spread a slight flush across her cheeks and ears, diffusing a tranquil indolence throughout her entire body that was reflected by a dreamy languor in her lovely eyes. She was virtually incapable of working; her hands seemed to fall naturally into her lap. She barely moved around at all, and was constantly sighing and complaining with comical helplessness.

"You should go swimming more often," Nikolai Petrovich told her. He'd created a large pool covered by an awning in the one of the farm's ponds that hadn't quite disappeared yet.

"Oh, Nikolai Petrovich! By the time you get to the pond, you could die, and coming back you could die again. You see, there isn't any shade in the garden."

"That's true, there isn't any shade," Nikolai Petrovich replied, rubbing his forehead.

One day, as he was returning from a walk at about seven o'clock in the morning, Bazarov came across Fenechka in the lilac arbor, which had long since blossomed but was still thick and green. She was sitting on a bench and had thrown a white kerchief over her head as usual; near her lay a whole pile of red and white roses that were still wet with dew. He said good morning to her.

"Ah! Evgenii Vasilich!" she responded, lifting the edge of her kerchief slightly to look at him; in doing so, her arm was bared to the elbow.

"What are you doing here?" Bazarov inquired, sitting down beside her. "Are you making a bouquet?"

"Yes—for the table at noon. Nikolai Petrovich likes that."

"But it's still a long while until noon. What a mass of flowers!"

"I gathered them now because it'll be hot then, and you can't go out. Now is the only time you can breathe. I've gotten so weak from the heat—I'm already afraid that I might get sick."

"What an idea! Let me feel your pulse." Bazarov took her

hand, found the rhythmically beating pulse, and didn't even begin to count its throbs. "You'll live for a hundred years!" he declared, releasing her hand.

"Ah, God forbid!" she exclaimed.

"Why? Don't you want to live a long time?"

"Well, yes—but a hundred years! There was an old woman living near us who was eighty-five years old—and what a martyr she was! Gray, deaf, stooped, and coughing all the time. She was nothing but a burden to herself. What sort of life is that?"

"So it's better to be young?"

"Well, isn't it?"

"But how is it better? Tell me!"

"How can you ask how? Why, here I am now, I'm young, I can do everything—come and go and carry things, without needing to ask anyone for anything.... What could be better?"

"Whereas it's all the same to me whether I'm young or old."

"What do you mean—it's all the same? What you say isn't possible."

"Well, judge for yourself, Fedosia Nikolaevna—what good is my youth to me? I live alone, a poor bachelor...."

"That's entirely your own fault."

"It isn't my fault at all! If only someone would take pity on me."

Fenechka cast a sidelong glance at Bazarov, but said nothing. "What's this book you have?" she inquired after a short pause.

"This one? This is a scientific book, a very difficult one."

"Are you still studying? And don't you get bored? You already know everything, I'd say."

"Not everything, evidently. Try to read a little."

"But I won't understand any of it. Is it Russian?" Fenechka asked, picking up the heavily bound book with both hands. "It's so thick!"

"Yes, it's Russian."

"All the same, I won't understand anything."

"Well, I didn't give it to you for you to understand. I wanted to look at you while you were reading. When you read, the tip of your little nose moves so prettily."

Fenechka, who'd quietly begun to try to read through an article on "creosote" that she'd happened to select, laughed and put the book down.... It slipped from the bench onto the ground.

"I also like it when you laugh," Bazarov observed.

"That's enough of that!"

"I like it when you talk. It's just like a little brook babbling."

Fenechka turned her head away. "What a silly thing to say!" she remarked, separating the flowers with her fingers. "And how can you like to listen to me? You've had conversations with such intelligent ladies."

"Ah, Fedosia Nikolaevna! Believe me, all the intelligent ladies in the world aren't worth your little elbow."

"Well now, that's something else you've made up!" Fenechka murmured, clasping her hands.

Bazarov picked the book up off the ground.

"That's a medical book—why are you throwing it away?"

"It's medical?" Fenechka echoed, and she turned toward him again. "Do you know what? Ever since you gave me those drops—do you remember?—Mitia has slept so well! I truly can't imagine how to thank you. You're so kind, really."

"But these days you have to pay doctors," Bazarov commented with a smile. "Doctors, as you yourself know, are greedy people."

Fenechka raised her eyes, which looked even darker than usual in contrast to the whitish reflection the kerchief cast on the upper part of her face, and gazed at Bazarov. She didn't know whether he was joking or not.

"If you like, we'll be delighted.... I'll have to ask Nikolai Petrovich...."

"Why, do you think I want money?" Bazarov interrupted her. "No, I don't want money from you."

"What, then?" Fenechka asked.

"What?" Bazarov repeated. "Guess!"

"I'm no good at guessing!"

"Then I'll tell you. I want ... one of those roses."

Fenechka laughed again and even clapped her hands, so amusing did Bazarov's request seem to her. She laughed, and at the same time felt flattered. Bazarov looked at her intently.

"By all means," she finally said, and bending over the bench, she began to pick through the roses. "Which do you want—a red one or a white one?"

"Red—and not too large."

She straightened up again. "Here, take this one," she suggested, but instantly drew back her outstretched hand, glanced toward the entrance of the arbor, biting her lips, and started to listen.

"What is it?" Bazarov inquired. "Nikolai Petrovich?"

"No.... He's gone out to the fields.... Besides, I'm not afraid of him ... but Pavel Petrovich ... I thought...."

"What?"

"I thought that *he* was coming here. No ... no one's there. Take this." Fenechka gave Bazarov the rose.

"What reason do you have to be afraid of Pavel Petrovich?"

"He always scares me. Most people talk readily—he doesn't talk, he just looks around knowingly. And even you don't like him. You remember, you always used to quarrel with him. I don't know what you were quarreling about, but I could see you twisting him around this way and that."

Fenechka demonstrated with her hands the way Bazarov twisted Pavel Petrovich around, in her opinion.

Bazarov smiled. "But if he started to give me a beating," he probed, "would you come to my defense?"

"How could I come to your defense? But no—no one could get the better of you."

"Do you think so? I know a hand that could conquer me with one finger if it wanted to."

"Which hand is that?"

"Why, don't you really know? Smell the delicious fragrance of this rose you gave me."

Fenechka stretched her little neck forward and put her face close to the flower.... The kerchief slipped off her head onto her shoulders; the soft masses of her dark, shining, slightly ruffled hair became visible.

"Wait—I want to smell it with you," Bazarov declared. He bent over and kissed her firmly on her parted lips.

She flinched and put both hands on his chest to push him back, but only pushed weakly, so that he was able to renew and prolong his kiss.

A dry cough sounded behind the lilac bushes. Fenechka instantly moved to the other end of the bench. Pavel Petrovich appeared, made a slight bow, and, remarking with some sort of hostile dejection "You're here," he retreated. Fenechka immediately gathered up all her roses and left the arbor. "That was sinful of you, Evgenii Vasilevich," she whispered as she was leaving. There was a note of genuine reproach in her whisper.

Bazarov recalled another recent scene, and felt both ashamed and contemptuously annoyed. But he promptly shook his head, sarcastically congratulated himself "on his formal assumption of the role of Lothario," and went off to his own room.

Pavel Petrovich left the garden and made his way to the forest with deliberate strides. He stayed there for a fairly long while, and when he returned at noon, Nikolai Petrovich anxiously asked whether he was quite well—his face had gotten so dark.

"You know I sometimes suffer from a liver ailment," Pavel Petrovich responded tranquilly.

# XXIV

Two hours later, Pavel Petrovich knocked on Bazarov's door.

"I must apologize for interrupting your scientific pursuits," he began, seating himself on a chair by the window and resting both hands on a handsome cane with an ivory handle (he ordinarily walked without a cane), "but I'm forced to beg you to spare me five minutes of your time ... no more."

"My time is completely at your disposal," Bazarov replied. Some unusual expression had flashed across his face as soon as Pavel Petrovich had crossed the threshold.

"Five minutes will suffice for me. I've come to ask you a single question."

"A question? What's it about?"

"I'll tell you, if you'll be so kind as to hear me out. Early on during your stay in my brother's house, before I'd deprived myself of the pleasure of conversing with you, I had the opportunity to hear your opinions about many subjects. But, if memory serves, we never discussed the subject of single combat or dueling in general, nor did you ever discuss it in my presence. May I inquire what your opinion on that subject is?"

Bazarov, who'd risen to greet Pavel Petrovich, sat down on the edge of a table and crossed his arms.

"My opinion," he said, "is that, from a theoretical point of view, dueling's absurd. From a practical point of view, however— it's a different propostion."

"That is, you mean to say—if I understand you correctly— whatever your theoretical view of dueling might be, in practice, you wouldn't allow yourself to be insulted without demanding satisfaction?"

"You've thoroughly grasped my meaning."

"Excellent. I'm very glad to hear you say so. Your words relieve me of uncertainty...."

"Of indecision, you mean to say."

"It's all the same. I express myself so as to be understood— I ... I'm not a creature of the seminary. Your words save me from a certain regrettable necessity. I've decided to fight a duel with you."

Bazarov's eyes opened wide. "With me?"

"Indubitably."

"But why, for heaven's sake?"

"I could explain the reason to you," Pavel Petrovich began, "but I'd prefer to remain silent about it. To my way of thinking,

your presence here is an imposition. I can't endure you. I despise
you. And if that isn't enough for you...."

Pavel Petrovich's eyes glittered.... Bazarov's were also flash-
ing.

"All right," he assented. "There's no need for further explanations. You've conceived a whim to test your sense of chivalry out
on me. I might deny you this pleasure, but—so be it!"

"I'm deeply obliged to you," Pavel Petrovich replied. "May I
then rely upon your acceptance of my challenge without my
being compelled to resort to violent measures?"

"I take it you're alluding to that cane, to speak nonmetaphori-
cally?" Bazarov remarked coolly. "You're perfectly correct—it's
quite unnecessary for you to insult me. Indeed, it wouldn't be altogether safe. You can remain a gentleman.... And I accept your
challenge in equally gentlemanly fashion."

"That's excellent," Pavel Petrovich responded, depositing his
cane in a corner. "We'll say a few words about the conditions of
our duel in a moment, but I'd like to ascertain first whether you
deem it necessary to resort to the formality of some trifling dispute that might serve as a pretext for my challenge?"

"No. It's better without any formalities."

"I think so myself. I presume that it's also inappropriate to
delve into the actual basis of our dispute. We can't abide one another. What more could be required?"

"What more, indeed?" Bazarov repeated sarcastically.

"In regard to the conditions of the encounter itself, seeing
that we won't have any seconds—for where could we get them?"

"Just so—where could we get them?"

"I therefore have the honor to present the following proposal
to you: the duel should take place early tomorrow morning, at
six, let's say, beyond the grove, with pistols, at a distance of ten
paces...."

"Ten paces? That will do—we hate one another at that distance."

"We might make it eight," Pavel Petrovich noted.

"We might."

"Each of us will fire twice, and in order to be prepared for any eventuality, let's each put a brief letter in one of his pockets that blames himself for his own demise."

"Now, I don't approve of that at all," Bazarov declared. "That's like something out of a French novel, something quite implausible."

"Perhaps. You do agree, however, that it might be unpleasant to incur the suspicion of having committed murder?"

"I agree on that. But there's a way to avoid such a lamentable accusation. We won't have any seconds, but we can have a witness."

"Who, if you'll allow me to inquire?"

"Why, Petr."

"Which Petr?"

"Your brother's valet. He's a man who's scaled the heights of contemporary culture, and will perform his part with all the *comilfo* required in such circumstances."

"It seems to me that you're joking, my dear sir."

"Not in the slightest. If you think my suggestion over, you'll become convinced that it's full of common sense and simplicity. You can't make a silk purse out of a sow's ear, but I'll endeavor to prepare Petr in a suitable manner and bring him to the field of battle."

"You persist in joking," Pavel Petrovich commented, rising from his chair. "But after the courteous cooperation you've given me, I have no right to hold this against you.... And so, everything's been arranged.... By the way, do you have any pistols?"

"Where would I get any pistols, Pavel Petrovich? I'm not in the army."

"In that case, let me offer you mine. You may rest assured that it's been five years since I've fired one."

"That's a very consoling piece of information."

Pavel Petrovich picked up his cane.... "And now, my dear sir, it merely remains for me to thank you and leave you to your studies. I have the honor to bid you good day."

"Until we have the pleasure of meeting again, my dear sir," Bazarov responded, conducting his visitor to the door.

Pavel Petrovich went out. Bazarov remained standing in front of the door for a minute, then suddenly exclaimed: "What the devil! How refined—and how idiotic! What a farce we've enacted! Like trained dogs dancing on their hind legs. But refusing was out of the question. Why, for all I know, he'd have struck me, and then...." (Bazarov turned pale at the very thought; his pride was instantly aroused.) "At that point, it might have come to my strangling him like a kitten." He went back to his microscope, but his heart was pounding, and the composure needed to make scientific observations had vanished. "He saw us today," Bazarov thought, "but would he really behave like this on his brother's behalf? And how important is a kiss? There must be something else to it. Bah! Maybe he's in love with her himself. Of course, he's in love—it's as clear as day. What a development!... It's a bad business!" he finally concluded. "It's a bad business, whichever way you look at it. In the first place, it'll be necessary to risk having a bullet put through my brains and then, in any case, to go away. In the second, there's Arkadii ... and that dear, innocent lamb, Nikolai Petrovich. It's a bad, bad business."

The day passed in some sort of special quietude and languor. Fenechka seemed to have disappeared from the face of the earth; she sat in her little room like a mouse in its hole. Nikolai Petrovich looked preoccupied—he'd just learned that blight had begun to invade his wheat, upon which he'd particularly rested his hopes. Pavel Petrovich overwhelmed everyone, even Prokofich, with his icy courtesy. Bazarov began a letter to his father, but tore it up and threw it under the table.

"If I die," he thought, "they'll find out—but I'm not going to die. No, I'll struggle along on this planet for a good while yet." He ordered Petr to come and see him about important business the next morning, as soon as it was light; Petr imagined that Bazarov wanted to take him along to Petersburg. Bazarov went to bed late, and was tormented by chaotic dreams all night long.... Mrs. Odintsov kept appearing in them: first she was his mother, followed by a kitten with black whiskers, which turned out to be Fenechka; then Pavel Petrovich took the shape of a huge forest, with which he nonetheless had to fight. Petr awakened Bazarov at four o'clock; he promptly got dressed and went outside with Petr.

It was a lovely, fresh morning; tiny striped clouds hovered overhead like little curls of fleece in the pale, clear blue sky; fine drops of dew lay on the leaves and grass, sparkling on spiders' webs like silver; the damp, dark earth still seemed to retain traces of the rosy dawn; larks' songs came pouring from every corner of the sky. Bazarov walked as far as the grove, sat down in the shade at its edge, and only then disclosed to Petr the nature of the service required of him. The cultured valet became mortally frightened, but Bazarov calmed Petr down by assuring him that he wouldn't have to do anything except stand at a distance and observe, that he wouldn't incur any sort of responsibility. "And in the meantime," Bazarov added, "just think what an important role you have to play!" Petr gestured helplessly, lowered his gaze, and leaned against a birch tree, turning green with terror.

The road from Marino skirted the grove; light dust lay across the road, which hadn't been disturbed by wheel or foot since the previous day. Bazarov involuntarily stared along this road, then pulled and sucked on a blade of grass while he kept repeating to himself, "What stupidity!" The early-morning chill made him shiver twice.... Petr looked at him dejectedly, but Bazarov merely smiled—he wasn't afraid.

The tramp of horses' hoofs on the road became audible.... A peasant came into sight from behind the trees. He was driving two horses that had been hobbled together ahead of him, and, as he passed Bazarov, he looked at him somewhat strangely, without touching his cap, which evidently struck Petr as a bad omen. "There's someone else who's up early," Bazarov mused, "but at least he's gotten up for work, whereas we...."

"It seems the gentleman's coming," Petr suddenly whispered.

Bazarov raised his head and saw Pavel Petrovich. Dressed in a light checked jacket and snow-white trousers, he was rapidly walking down the road carrying a box wrapped in green cloth under his arm.

"I beg your pardon—I believe I've kept you waiting," he began, bowing first to Bazarov and then to Petr, whom he treated with respect at that moment as something like a second. "I didn't want to awaken my valet."

"It doesn't matter," Bazarov responded. "We've just arrived ourselves."

"Ah! So much the better!" Pavel Petrovich took a look around. "There's no one in sight—no one will hinder us. Can we proceed?"

"Yes, let's proceed."

"You don't require any fresh explanation, I presume?"

"No, I don't."

"Would you like to load these?" Pavel Petrovich inquired, taking the pistols out of the box.

"No, you load them, and I'll measure out the paces. My legs are longer," Bazarov added with a smile. "One, two, three...."

"Evgenii Vasilevich," Petr mumbled with an effort (he was trembling as though he had a fever), "no matter what you say, I'm going farther away."

"Four ... five.... Go ahead, my friend, go ahead. You can even get behind a tree and cover your ears—just don't shut your eyes. And if anyone falls, run and pick him up. Six ... seven ... eight...." Bazarov stopped. "Is that enough?" he asked, turning toward Pavel Petrovich, "or should I add two more paces?"

"It's up to you," replied the latter, inserting a second bullet.

"Well, let's make it two more." Bazarov drew a line on the ground with the toe of his boot. "There's the barrier, then. By the way, how many paces may each of us step back from the barrier? That's an important question, too. The issue wasn't discussed yesterday."

"I'd think ten," Pavel Petrovich answered, handing Bazarov both pistols. "Will you be so good as to choose?"

"I will. But you must admit, Pavel Petrovich, that our duel is unusual to the point of absurdity. Just look at the countenance of our second."

"You're inclined to laugh at everything," Pavel Petrovich retorted. "I don't deny that our duel is strange, but I consider it my duty to warn you that I intend to duel in earnest. *A bon entendeur, salut!*"

"Oh! I don't doubt that we've made up our minds to annihilate one another, but why not laugh, too, and unite *utile dulci*? So you speak French to me, whereas I speak Latin to you."

"I'm going to duel in earnest," Pavel Petrovich repeated, and he walked over to his position. Bazarov, for his part, counted off ten paces from the barrier and stood still.

"Are you ready?" asked Pavel Petrovich.

"Perfectly."

"Then we can approach one another."

Bazarov moved forward slowly, and Pavel Petrovich, his left hand thrust into his pocket, advanced toward him, gradually raising the muzzle of his pistol.... "He's aiming straight at my nose," Bazarov observed to himself, "and he's aiming carefully, the villain! This isn't a pleasant sensation, though. I'm going to look at his watch chain."

Something suddenly whizzed right past his ear, and at the same instant, the sound of a shot rang out. The thought "I heard it, so it must be all right" had time to flash through Bazarov's brain. He took one more step and, without aiming, pulled the trigger.

Pavel Petrovich shuddered slightly and clutched at his thigh. A stream of blood began to trickle down his white trousers.

Bazarov flung his pistol aside and went over to his antagonist. "Are you wounded?" he queried.

"You had the right to summon me to the barrier," Pavel Petrovich declared, "but that's of no consequence. According to our agreement, each of us has one more shot."

"Well, forgive me, but that can occur another time," Bazarov replied, seizing hold of Pavel Petrovich, who was beginning to turn pale. "Now I'm not a duelist, I'm a doctor, and I have to take a look at your wound before anything else occurs. Petr! Come here, Petr! Where are you hiding?"

"That's all nonsense.... I don't need anyone's assistance," Pavel Petrovich affirmed jerkily, "and ... we must ... again...." He tried to tug at his moustache, but his hand went limp, his eyes grew dim, and he lost consciousness.

"Here's a new twist! A fainting fit! What next?" Bazarov involuntarily exclaimed as he laid Pavel Petrovich on the grass. "Let's have a look and see what's wrong." He pulled out a handkerchief, wiped away the blood, and began feeling around the wound.... "The bone hasn't been broken," he muttered through his teeth. "The bullet didn't go deep—one muscle, *vastus externus,* was grazed. He'll be dancing in three weeks!... And he faints! Oh, I'm so sick of these high-strung types! My, what delicate skin!"

"Is he dead?" Petr's tremulous voice inquired from behind Bazarov's back.

Bazarov looked around. "Go get some water as quickly as you can, my friend, and he'll outlive us all."

But the modern servant didn't seem to comprehend his words, and didn't move. Pavel Petrovich slowly opened his eyes. "He's dying!" Petr whispered, and began crossing himself.

"You're right.... What a foolish countenance!" the wounded gentleman remarked with a forced smile.

"Well, go get some water, you devil!" Bazarov shouted.

"There's no need.... It was momentary *vertige....* Help me sit up ... there, that's right.... I just need something to bind this scratch, and I can go home on foot, or else you can send a cart for me. If it's all right with you, the duel won't be renewed. You've behaved honorably ... today, I emphasize, today."

"There's no need to recall the past," Bazarov rejoined, "and as for the future, it isn't worth it for you to trouble your head about that, either, because I intend to head out without delay. Let me bandage your leg now—your wound isn't serious, but it's always best to stop any bleeding. I have to bring this mortal to his senses first, though."

Bazarov shook Petr by the collar and sent him to fetch a cart.

"Be sure that you don't frighten my brother," Pavel Petrovich told him. "Don't you dream of informing him about this."

Petr raced off, and while he hastily sought a cart, the two antagonists sat on the ground without speaking. Pavel Petrovich tried not to look at Bazarov; he still didn't want to become reconciled with him. He was ashamed of his own haughtiness and of his failure; he was ashamed of the whole situation he'd created, even though he felt that it couldn't have ended in a more fortuitous manner. "At any rate, there won't be any scandal," he consoled himself, "and I'm grateful for that." The silence was prolonged, awkward, and distressing; both of them were uncomfortable. Each was aware that the other understood what he was feeling. This awareness is always pleasant for friends, and always most unpleasant for those who aren't friends, especially when it's impossible either to confront one another or to go separate ways.

"Have I bound your leg too tightly?" Bazarov finally inquired.

"No, not at all, it's fine," Pavel Petrovich answered, and, after a brief pause, he added, "We won't be able to deceive my brother. We'll have to tell him that we quarreled about politics."

"That's fine," Bazarov assented. "You can say I insulted all Anglomaniacs."

"That will do beautifully. What do you suppose this man thinks about us now?" Pavel Petrovich continued, pointing to the same peasant who'd driven the hobbled horses past Bazarov a few minutes prior to the duel, who now, returning along the road, took off his cap at the sight of the "gentry."

"Who on earth knows?" Bazarov responded. "Most likely, he doesn't think anything. The Russian peasant is the mysterious unknown that Mrs. Radcliffe once analyzed at such length. Who can understand him? He doesn't understand himself!"

"Ah! So that's your attitude!" Pavel Petrovich began, and then he suddenly cried, "Look what your fool Petr has done! Here comes my brother galloping out to find us!"

Bazarov turned around and caught sight of the pale face of Nikolai Petrovich, who was sitting in the cart. He jumped out of it well before it stopped and rushed up to his brother.

"What does this mean?" he asked in an agitated voice. "Evgenii Vasilich, for heaven's sake—what is all this?"

"It's nothing," answered Pavel Petrovich. "They've alarmed you in vain. I had a minor dispute with Mr. Bazarov, and I've had to pay for it a little bit."

"But why did all this happen, for God's sake?"

"What can I tell you? Mr. Bazarov alluded to Sir Robert Peel disrespectfully. I must hasten to add that I'm the only person to blame in all this, while Mr. Bazarov has behaved most honorably. I challenged him."

"But you're all covered with blood, for heaven's sake!"

"Well, did you suppose I had water in my veins? But this bloodletting is actually beneficial to me. Isn't that so, Doctor? Help me get into the cart, and don't succumb to melancholy. I'll be perfectly well tomorrow. There, that's fine. Go ahead, driver."

Nikolai Petrovich walked behind the cart; Bazarov was going to stay where he was....

"I have to ask you to look after my brother," Nikolai Petrovich said to him, "until we get another doctor from town."

Bazarov silently nodded his head. Within an hour's time, Pavel Petrovich was lying in bed with a skillfully bandaged leg. The entire household was upset; Fenechka felt sick. Nikolai Petrovich kept stealthily wringing his hands, while Pavel Petrovich laughed and joked, especially with Bazarov. Pavel Petrovich put on a delicate cambric nightshirt and an elegant morning robe, as well as a fez, didn't allow the blinds to be drawn, and humorously complained about the need to be deprived of food.

Toward nightfall, however, he grew feverish; his head started to ache. The doctor arrived from town. (Nikolai Petrovich wouldn't listen to his brother, and indeed, Bazarov himself didn't want him to. Bazarov had spent the whole day in his room, looking jaundiced and malevolent, and had only stopped in to see the patient for the briefest possible periods; he'd happened to run into Fenechka twice, but she'd shrunk away from him in horror.) The new doctor advised a diet of cool foods; he confirmed Bazarov's assessment that there was no danger, however. Nikolai

Petrovich told him that his brother had wounded himself by accident, to which the doctor responded, "Hmm!" But after twenty-five silver rubles were slipped into his hand on the spot, he remarked, "You don't say so! Well, that often happens, to be sure."

No one in the house went to bed, or even undressed. Nikolai Petrovich kept tiptoeing in to look at his brother and tiptoeing out again; Pavel Petrovich dozed, groaned slightly, told him in French, *"Couchez-vous,"* and asked for something to drink. Nikolai Petrovich sent Fenechka to bring him a glass of lemonade; Pavel Petrovich gazed at her intently and downed the liquid to the last drop. Toward morning, the fever increased a bit; a slight delirium developed. Pavel Petrovich uttered incoherent words at first; then he suddenly opened his eyes, and, seeing his brother standing close to his bed, anxiously bending over him, he said, "Nikolai, don't you think that Fenechka looks somewhat like Nellie?"

"Which Nellie is that, Pavel dear?"

"How can you ask? Princess R——. Especially in the upper part of the face. *C'est de la même famille.*"

Nikolai Petrovich didn't reply, but he marveled inwardly at the persistence of youthful passions in human beings. "It's at times like these when they come to the surface," he thought.

"Ah, how I love that hollow creature!" Pavel Petrovich moaned, drearily clasping his hands behind his head. "I can't stand the thought that any insolent upstart would dare to touch ...," he whispered a few moments later.

Nikolai Petrovich merely sighed; he didn't in the least suspect to whom those words referred.

Bazarov presented himself to Nikolai Petrovich at eight o'clock the next morning. He'd already managed to pack and to set all his frogs, insects, and birds free.

"Have you come to say goodbye to me?" Nikolai Petrovich inquired, standing up as Bazarov came in.

"Just so."

"I understand what you're doing, and fully approve. My poor brother is to blame, of course, and he's been punished for it. He himself told me that he made it impossible for you to act otherwise. I believe that you couldn't have avoided this duel, which ... which is explained alone to some extent by the almost constant antagonism of your respective views." (Nikolai Petrovich was getting his words slightly mixed up.) "My brother is a man of the old school, he's hot-tempered and stubborn.... Thank God it's ended the way it has. I've taken every precaution to avoid all public attention...."

"I'm leaving you my address, in case there's any trouble," Bazarov remarked nonchalantly.

"I hope there won't be any sort of trouble, Evgenii Vasilich.... I'm very sorry that your stay in my house should have come to such a ... such an end. It's all the more distressing for me that Arkadii...."

"I'll probably be seeing him," Bazarov observed—"explanations" and "protestations" of every sort always made him impatient. "In case I don't, I beg you to say goodbye to him for me, and to accept the expression of my regret."

"And I beg ... ," Nikolai Petrovich responded with a bow. But Bazarov went out without waiting for the end of his sentence.

When he learned of Bazarov's intended departure, Pavel Petrovich expressed a desire to see him, and shook his hand. But Bazarov remained as cold as ice even then—he realized that Pavel Petrovich wanted to play the role of the magnanimous nobleman. He didn't manage to say goodbye to Fenechka; he merely exchanged glances through one window. Her face looked sad to him. "She'll probably have some hard times," he said to himself.... "But she'll pull though somehow!" Petr was so overwhelmed by emotion that he wept on Bazarov's shoulder until Bazarov stifled him by asking whether he had an endless supply of moisture in his eyes; Duniasha was forced to run off into the grove to hide her distress. The man guilty of causing all the misery got into a carriage, lit a cigar, and at a bend in the road after the fourth verst, where the Kirsanovs' farm buildings and new house were visible in a long row, he merely spat, muttering, "Damned snobs!" and wrapped himself more tightly in his coat.

———

Pavel Petrovich began to improve shortly thereafter, but he had to stay in bed for about a week. He bore his captivity, as he called it, quite patiently, merely taking great pains with his toilette and having everything scented with eau de cologne. Nikolai Petrovich read him journals; Fenchka waited on him as usual, bringing him soup, lemonade, hard-boiled eggs, and tea, but she was filled with concealed dread whenever she went into his room. Pavel Petrovich's unexpected actions had alarmed everyone in the house—and her more than anyone else. Prokifich was the only person who wasn't concerned; he discoursed upon the way in which gentlemen in his day used to fight duels, albeit "only with real gentlemen. They used to have low curs like that horsewhipped at the stables for their insolence."

Fenechka's conscience barely reproached her, but she was periodically tormented by the thought of the true cause of the dispute. And Pavel Petrovich looked at her so strangely . . . in such a way that she could feel his eyes on her even when her back was turned. She grew thinner from the ceaseless inner agitation and, as so often happens, became even lovelier as a result.

One day—this incident occurred in the morning—Pavel Petrovich felt better and moved from his bed to the sofa, while Nikolai Petrovich, having assured himself that his brother really was better, went off to the threshing barn. Fenechka brought Pavel Petrovich a cup of tea, and setting it down on a little table, was about to withdraw. He detained her.

"Where are you going in such a hurry, Fedosia Nikolaevna?" he began. "Are you busy?"

"No, sir . . . yes, sir . . . I have to pour the tea."

"Duniasha will do that without you. Sit here for a while with a poor invalid. Anyway, I want to have a chat with you."

Fenechka silently sat down on the edge of an easy chair.

"Listen," Pavel Petrovich said, tugging at his moustache, "I've wanted to ask you something for a long time. Are you afraid of me for some reason?"

"Me?"

"Yes, you. You never look at me—as though your conscience weren't clear."

Fenechka was starting to blush, but she glanced at Pavel Petrovich. He seemed somewhat strange to her, and her heart began to throb quietly.

"Is your conscience clear?" he inquired.

"Why shouldn't it be clear?" she faltered.

"Goodness knows why! Besides, whom could you have wronged? Me? That's not likely. Anyone else in the house here? That's also improbable. Could it be my brother? But you love him, don't you?"

"I do love him."

"With all your soul, with all your heart?"

"I love Nikolai Petrovich with all my heart."

"Truly? Look at me, Fenechka." (It was the first time he'd used this name.) "You know, it's a terrible sin to lie!"

"I'm not lying, Pavel Petrovich. If I were to stop loving Nikolai Petrovich—I wouldn't want to live after that."

"And you'll never forsake him for anyone else?"

"For whom would I forsake him?"

"For whom, indeed! Well, how about that gentleman who's just left here?"

Fenechka stood up. "My God, Pavel Petrovich, why are you torturing me? What have I done to you? How can you say such things?"

"Fenechka," Pavel Petrovich addressed her in a sorrowful voice, "you know that I saw...."

"What did you see?"

"Out there ... in the arbor."

Fenechka blushed to the roots of her hair. "How was I to blame for that?" she inquired with an effort.

Pavel Petrovich lifted himself up. "You weren't to blame? No? Not at all?"

"I love Nikolai Petrovich and no one else in the world, and I'll always love him!" Fenechka exclaimed with sudden force, and her throat seemed to be nearly bursting with sobs. "As for what you saw, I'll declare on the final day of judgment that I'm not to blame and wasn't to blame for it, and I'd rather die right now than have people suspect me of doing anything to hurt my bene-factor, Nikolai Petrovich...."

Her voice broke at this point, and at the same point, she felt Pavel Petrovich grasping and squeezing her hand.... She looked at him and became almost petrified. He'd turned even paler than before; his eyes were shining and, most surprising of all, a large, solitary tear was rolling down his cheek.

"Fenechka," he said in some sort of wonderful whisper, "love him—love my brother! He's such a kind, decent man! Don't for-sake him for anyone in the world! Don't listen to anyone else! Think about it—what can be more terrible than to love and not to be loved? Never leave my poor Nikolai!"

Fenechka's eyes dried and her terror subsided, so great was her astonishment. But even greater was her astonishment when Pavel Petrovich, Pavel Petrovich himself, put her hand to his lips and seemed to pierce it without kissing it, merely heaving con-vulsive sighs from time to time....

"My Lord," she thought, "is he having some kind of attack?"

At that instant, his entire ruined life was crumbling inside him.

The staircase creaked under rapidly approaching foot-steps.... He pushed her hand away from him and let his head fall back on the pillow. The door opened and Nikolai Petrovich en-tered, looking cheerful, refreshed, and ruddy. Mitia, as refreshed and ruddy as his father, wearing nothing but a light shirt, was frisking on Nikolai Petrovich's shoulder, catching his little bare toes on the big buttons of his father's coarse country coat.

Fenechka virtually flung herself at Nikolai Petrovich, and clasping him and her son together in her arms, she let her head fall against his shoulder. Nikolai Petrovich was surprised: Fenechka, the reserved, shy Fenechka, had never embraced him in the presence of a third party.

"What's the matter?" he asked, and glancing at his brother, he handed Mitia to her. "Do you feel worse?" he asked next, approaching Pavel Petrovich.

Pavel Petrovich buried his face in a cambric handkerchief. "No ... not at all.... On the contrary, I feel much better."

"You were in too much of a rush to move to the sofa. Where are you going?" Nikolai Petrovich added, turning around to address Fenechka. She'd already closed the door behind her, however. "I was bringing my young hero in to show you—he's been missing his uncle. Why has she taken him away? What's wrong with you, though? Has anything happened between the two of you, eh?"

"Brother!" Pavel Petrovich began solemnly.

Nikolai Petrovich flinched. He felt dismayed, although he himself couldn't have said why.

"Brother," Pavel Petrovich repeated, "give me your word that you'll carry out my sole request."

"What request? Tell me."

"It's very important—the happiness of your entire life depends on it, in my opinion. I've been thinking a great deal this whole time about what I want to say to you now.... Brother, do your duty, the duty of an honorable, generous man. Put an end to the scandal and the bad example you're setting—you, the best of men!"

"What do you mean, Pavel?"

"Marry Fenechka. She loves you. She's the mother of your son."

Nikolai Petrovich retreated a step and threw up his hands. "Is it you who's saying this, Pavel? You, whom I've always regarded at the most steadfast opponent of such marriages! You're saying this? Don't you know that it's been purely out of respect for you that I haven't done what you so rightly call my duty?"

"You were wrong to respect me, in that case," Pavel Petrovich responded with a weary smile. "I'm beginning to think that Bazarov was right in accusing me of aristocratism. No, my dear brother, let's not worry about the world's opinion anymore. We're old, humble people now—it's time we set aside all sorts of vanity. Let's just do our duty, as you say, and you'll see—we'll obtain happiness in the bargain."

Nikolai Petrovich rushed over to hug his brother.

"You've finally opened my eyes!" he cried. "I was right in always affirming that you are the most intelligent, kindhearted person in the world, and now I see that you're just as wise as you are generous."

"Gently, gently," Pavel Petrovich interrupted him. "Don't hurt the leg of your wise brother who, at the age of nearly fifty, fought a duel like an ensign. So then, it's settled. Fenechka will become my ... *belle soeur*."

"My dearest Pavel! But what will Arkadii say?"

"Arkadii? He'll be ecstatic, for heaven's sake! Marriage is against his principles, but then again, his sense of equality will be gratified. And, after all, what significance do class distinctions have *au dix-neuvième siècle*?"

"Ah, Pavel, Pavel! Let me kiss you once more! Don't be afraid—I'll be careful."

The brothers embraced one another.

"What do you think—shouldn't you inform her of your intentions right away?" Pavel Petrovich inquired.

"Why hurry?" Nikolai Petrovich responded. "Has there been any sort of discussion between the two of you?"

"A discussion between us? *Quelle idée!*"

"Well, that's all right, then. First of all, you have to get well, and meanwhile, there's plenty of time. We should think it through carefully, and consider...."

"But your mind's made up, I trust?"

"Of course my mind's made up, and I thank you from the bottom of my heart. I'll leave you now—you should rest. Any excitement is bad for you.... But we'll talk it over again later. Sleep well, dear one, and God bless you!"

"Why is he thanking me so much?" Pavel Petrovich wondered when he'd been left alone. "As though it didn't depend on him!

I'll go away as soon as he gets married, somewhere far away—
Dresden or Florence—and I'll live there until I die."

Pavel Petrovich moistened his forehead with eau de cologne
and closed his eyes. Illuminated by the bright light of day, his
handsome, emaciated head lay on the white pillow like the head
of a dead man ... and, indeed, he was a dead man.

# XXV

At Nikolskoe, Katia and Arkadii were sitting in the garden on a
sod bench beneath the shade of a tall ash tree. Fifi had settled
herself on the ground near them, arranging her slender body in
that graceful position known among dog fanciers as "the hare
curve." Both Arkadii and Katia were silent; he was holding a
book half-open in his hands, while she was picking out the few
crumbs of bread left in a basket and throwing them to a small
family of sparrows who, with their typical cowardly impudence,
were hopping and chirping right at her feet. A faint breeze stirring the ash tree's leaves slowly scattered pale-gold flecks of sunshine up and down across the path and over Fifi's tawny back. A
patch of unbroken shade covered Arkadii and Katia; from time to
time, a bright streak of light gleamed on her hair. Both were
silent, but the very way in which they were silent, the way in
which they were sitting together, bespoke trustful intimacy; both
of them seemed utterly unaware of any companion, while secretly rejoicing in one another's presence. Even their faces had
changed since we last saw them: Arkadii's looked more tranquil,
Katia's, more animated and bold.

"Don't you think," Arkadii began, "that the ash has been quite
aptly named *iasen** in Russian? No other tree is as delicate and
'transparent' in the air as it is."

Katia raised her eyes upward and said, "Yes," while Arkadii

*The adjective *iasnyi* means "clear" or "transparent."

thought, "Well, she doesn't reproach me for speaking eloquently."

"I don't like Heine," Katia declared, glancing toward the book Arkadii was holding in his hands, "when he either laughs or cries. I like him when he's pensive and mournful."

"Whereas I like him when he laughs," Arkadii remarked.

"Those are the remnants of your satirical tendencies...." ("The remnants!" Arkadii thought. "If only Bazarov could hear that!") "Wait a little while—we'll transform you."

"Who'll transform me? You?"

"Who? My sister. Profirii Platonovich, with whom you no longer quarrel. My aunt, whom you escorted to church the day before yesterday."

"Well, I couldn't refuse! And as for Anna Sergeevna, she agreed with Evgenii about many things—do you remember?"

"My sister was under his influence then, just as you were."

"Just as I was? Do you really think that I'm free of his influence now?"

Katia didn't say anything.

"I know," Arkadii continued, "that you never liked him."

"I can't form an opinion about him."

"Do you know, Katerina Sergeevna, that whenever I hear this reply, I distrust it.... There's no one about whom each of us couldn't form an opinion! That's simply an evasion."

"Well, then, I'll admit that I don't.... It's not exactly that I don't like him—but I sense that he's different from me, and that I'm different from him ... and that you're different from him as well."

"How so?"

"What can I say to you?... He's a wild animal, whereas you and I are tame."

"Even I'm tame?"

Katia nodded.

Arkadii scratched his ear. "Let me tell you, Katerina Sergeevna, that this is deeply insulting."

"Why, would you like to be wild?"

"Not wild, but strong, energetic."

"It's pointless to want to be that. . . . Your friend doesn't want to be that, you see, but it's inside him all the same."

"Hmm! So you believe he wielded a great deal of influence over Anna Sergeevna?"

"Yes. But no one can maintain the upper hand over her for long," Katia added under her breath.

"Why do you think that?"

"She's very proud. . . . I didn't mean that. . . . She highly prizes her independence."

"Who doesn't prize it?" Arkadii asked, but the thought flashed through his mind: "What good is it?" "What good is it?" Katia wondered as well. When young people frequently spend time together in friendly fashion, they constantly stumble onto the same ideas.

Arkadii smiled, and drawing slightly closer to Katia, he said in a whisper, "Confess that you're a little bit afraid of *her*."

"Of whom?"

*"Her,"* Arkadii repeated meaningfully.

"And what about you?" Katia asked in turn.

"I am, too. Notice that I said, 'I am, *too.*' "

Katia shook her finger at him. "I'm surprised at that," she observed. "My sister's never been as well-disposed toward you as she's recently been—much more so than when you first came."

"Really?"

"Why, haven't you noticed? Aren't you glad?"

Arkadii grew thoughtful.

"How have I managed to earn Anna Sergeevna's good opinion? Was it because I brought her your mother's letters?"

"Both because of that and other reasons, which I won't tell you."

"Why not?"

"I won't say."

"Oh! I know that you're extremely stubborn."

"Yes, I am."

"And observant."

Katia gave Arkadii a sidelong look. "Maybe so. Does that irritate you? What are you thinking about?"

"I'm wondering how you've gotten to be as observant as you actually are. You're so shy, so reserved. You keep everyone at a distance...."

"I've lived alone a great deal—that forces one to become contemplative involuntarily. But do I really keep everyone at a distance?"

Arkadii threw a grateful glance at Katia. "That's all very well," he continued, "but people in your situation—I mean, in your financial circumstances—don't often possess that gift. It's as hard for them to reach the truth as it is for tsars."

"But I'm not rich, you see."

Arkadii was taken aback, and didn't immediately understand what Katia meant. The thought "Why, of course—the property all belongs to her sister!" suddenly struck him. This thought didn't displease him. "You said that so well!" he commented.

"What?"

"You said that well—simply, without either being ashamed or bragging. By the way, I believe that there must always be something special, some unique sort of pride, in the emotional state of individuals who know they're poor, and say so."

"I've never experienced anything of that sort, thanks to my sister. I merely referred to my financial circumstances now because the subject happened to come up."

"True, but you must admit that you have a portion of the pride I just mentioned."

"How so, for instance?"

"For instance, you—please forgive the question—you wouldn't marry a rich man, would you?"

"If I loved him very much.... No, I think that I wouldn't marry him even then."

"There! You see!" Arkadii cried. And after a short pause, he added, "And why wouldn't you marry him?"

"Because of what's said in ballads about unequal matches."

"Maybe you want to have control, or...."

"Oh, no! Why would I? On the contrary, I'm ready to obey someone. But inequality is oppressive. To respect oneself and obey someone else—that I can understand, that's happiness. But a subordinate existence.... No, I've had enough of that as it is."

"You've had enough of that as it is," Arkadii echoed Katia's words. "Yes, yes," he continued, "you're not Anna Sergeevna's sister for nothing. You're just as independent as she is, but you're more reserved. I'm sure that you aren't the one to express this feeling first, however intense and sacred it might be...."

"Well, what would you expect?" Katia inquired.

"You're equally intelligent, and you've got as much strength of character, if not more than she...."

"Please don't compare me to my sister," Katia hurriedly interrupted him. "It works too much to my disadvantage. You seem to have forgotten that my sister is beautiful and intelligent and.... You in particular, Arkadii Nikolaevich, shouldn't say such things—with such a serious face, moreover."

"What do you mean by 'you in particular'—and what makes you suppose I'm joking?"

"Of course you're joking."

"Do you think so? But what if I'm convinced of what I say? What if I believe I still haven't put it strongly enough?"

"I don't understand what you mean."

"Really? Well, now I see—I clearly took you to be more observant than you are."

"How so?"

Arkadii didn't reply. He turned away, while Katia sought out a few more crumbs in the basket and started to throw them to the sparrows. But she moved her arm too vigorously, and they flew away without stopping to pick up the crumbs.

"Katerina Sergeevna!" Arkadii began suddenly. "It's probably of no consequence to you, but let me tell you that I wouldn't trade you, not only for your sister, but for anyone else on earth."

He stood up and left quickly, as though frightened by the words that had fallen from his lips.

Katia let her hands drop into her lap alongside the basket and stared for a long while at the path Arkadii had taken, her head bowed. A faint crimson flush gradually spread across her cheeks, but her lips didn't smile, and her dark eyes filled with a look of perplexity, as well as some other, still undefined emotion.

"Are you alone?" she heard the voice of Anna Sergeevna speaking next to her. "I thought you came into the garden with Arkadii."

Katia slowly raised her eyes to look at her sister (she was standing in the path, elegantly, even elaborately dressed, tickling Fifi's ears with the tip of her open parasol), and slowly replied, "Yes, I'm alone."

"So I see," Anna Sergeevna responded with a smile. "I suppose he's gone back to his room?"

"Yes."

"Were you reading together?"

"Yes."

Anna Sergeevna put her hand under Katia's chin and tilted her sister's face upward.

"You haven't been quarreling, I hope?"

"No," Katia said, and she calmly moved her sister's hand away.

"How solemnly you reply! I expected to find him here, and meant to suggest that he come for a walk with me—he's always asking to do that. They've sent you some shoes from town—go try them on. I just noticed yesterday that your old ones are quite shabby. You never think enough about such things, and you have such charming little feet! Your hands are nice, too . . . only they're quite large. So you have to make the most of your little feet. But you're not a coquette."

Anna Sergeevna proceeded further along the path with a quiet rustle of her beautiful dress. Katia rose from the bench and left as well, taking Heine with her—but not to try on her shoes.

"Charming little feet!" she thought as she slowly and lightly mounted the stone steps of the terrace, which were hot from the sun's rays. "Charming little feet, you say. . . . Well, he's going to end up falling at them."

But she suddenly felt ashamed, and swiftly ran upstairs.

Arkadii had started down a corridor toward his room when the steward overtook him and announced that Mr. Bazarov was waiting for him.

"Evgenii!" Arkadii murmured almost in dismay. "Did he arrive a long time ago?"

"Mr. Bazarov just arrived this minute, sir, and gave orders not to announce his arrival to Anna Sergeevna, but to take him straight up to your room."

"Can something bad have happened at home?" Arkadii wondered, and hurriedly running up the stairs, he threw open the door to his room. Bazarov's expression immediately reassured him, although a more experienced eye might well have discerned signs of inner agitation in the gaunt, albeit still energetic, form of his unexpected visitor. With a dusty coat thrown round his shoulders and a cap on his head, he was sitting at the window; he didn't even stand up when Arkadii flung his arms around his visitor's neck, voicing loud exclamations.

"This is so unexpected! What good fortune has brought you here?" he kept repeating, bustling around the room like someone who imagines—and wishes to demonstrate—that he's delighted. "I presume that everything's all right at home—they're all well, aren't they?"

"Everything's all right, but they're not all well," Bazarov replied. "Stop chattering. Send for some kvass for me, sit down, and listen while I tell you all about it in a few but, I hope, fairly impressive sentences."

Arkadii fell silent as Bazarov described his duel with Pavel Petrovich. Arkadii was quite surprised and even saddened, but didn't deem it necessary to reveal this. He merely asked whether his uncle's wound truly wasn't serious, and upon receiving the response that it was extremely interesting, though not from a medical point of view, he gave a forced smile. At heart, however, he felt both horrified and somehow ashamed. Bazarov seemed to understand him.

"Yes, my friend," he remarked, "that's what comes of residing with feudal types—you end up becoming a feudal type yourself and find yourself taking part in knightly tournaments. Well, so I set off for my parents' house," Bazarov wound up, "and I've stopped here along the way ... to tell you all this, I'd say, if I didn't consider a useless lie tantamount to stupidity. No, I stopped here—the devil knows why. You see, sometimes it's a good thing for a man to seize himself by the scruff of the neck and pull himself up, the way you pull a radish up out of its soil. That's what I've been doing lately.... But I wanted to have one more look at what I'm parting from—at the soil where I was planted."

"I hope those words don't refer to me," Arkadii interjected agitatedly. "I hope you aren't thinking of parting from *me*."

Bazarov turned an intense, almost piercing gaze on him.

"Would that distress you so much? It strikes me that *you* have already parted from me. You look so fresh and clean.... Your dealings with Anna Sergeevna must be going very well."

"Which dealings with Anna Sergeevna?"

"Why, didn't you come here from town on her account, little bird? By the way, how are those Sunday schools progressing? Do you mean to tell me you aren't in love with her? Or have you already reached the stage of being discreet?"

"Evgenii, you know that I've always been open with you. I can assure you—I swear to you—you're mistaken."

"Hmm! That's a new word," Bazarov remarked in an undertone. "But you don't need to get excited—it's a matter of absolute indifference to me. A romantic would say, 'I feel that our paths are beginning to diverge,' but I'll simply say that we've gotten tired of one another."

"Evgenii...."

"My dear friend, that's no real disaster—one gets tired of much more than that on earth. And now I suppose we'd better say goodbye, hadn't we? I've felt absolutely vile ever since I got here, just as though I'd been reading Gogol's letters to the wife of the governor of Kaluga. In any event, I didn't tell them to unharness the horses."

"For heaven's sake, this is beyond belief!"

"Why?"

"I won't say anything more about myself, but this would be the ultimate discourtesy to Anna Sergeevna, who'll definitely want to see you."

"Oh, you're mistaken there."

"On the contrary, I'm sure I'm right," Arkadii retorted. "And what are you pretending for? If it gets down to that, haven't you come here on her account yourself?"

"That may be true—and yet you're mistaken nonetheless."

But Arkadii was right. Anna Sergeevna did want to see Bazarov and sent the steward to ask him to come and chat with her. Bazarov changed his clothes before doing so—it turned out that he'd packed his new suit in order to be able to get it out easily.

Mrs. Odintsov met him not in the room where he'd so unexpectedly told her he loved her, but in the drawing room. She cordially extended her fingertips to him, and yet her face betrayed involuntary tension.

"Anna Sergeevna," Bazarov hastened to say, "before anything else transpires, I should set your mind at ease. In front of you stands a poor mortal who came to his senses long ago and hopes that other people have also forgotten his foolish behavior. I'm going away for a long while, and even though I'm not a particularly sensitive creature, as you'll agree, it'd be hard for me to carry away the thought that you remember me with distaste."

Anna Sergeevna heaved a deep sigh, like someone who's just climbed a high mountain, and her face brightened with a smile. She held out her hand to Bazarov a second time, and returned the pressure of his.

"Let's let bygones be bygones," she said, "all the more so because my conscience tells me that I was to blame then, too, for flirtatiousness—or for something else. In a word, let's be friends the way we were before. The rest was a dream, wasn't it? And who ever remembers dreams?"

"Who remembers them? And besides, love ... is a purely contrived feeling, you know."

"Really? I'm very pleased to hear that."

Thus spoke Anna Sergeevna and thus spoke Bazarov; they both believed that they were speaking the truth. Was there truth, absolute truth, in their words? They themselves didn't know, nor does the author. But their conversation continued precisely as though they thoroughly believed one another.

Anna Sergeevna asked Bazarov, among other things, what he'd been doing at the Kirsanovs'. He was on the verge of telling her about his duel with Pavel Petrovich, but he checked himself with the thought that she might conclude he was trying to make himself appear interesting, and replied that he'd been working the entire time.

"Whereas I had a bout of depression at first," Anna Sergeevna observed. "God only knows why. I even made plans to go abroad, if you can imagine that!... Then the depression went away, your friend Arkadii Nikolaich arrived, and I lapsed back into my old routine. I assumed my present role again."

"Which role is that, may I ask?"

"The role of aunt, guardian, mother—call it whatever you like. By the way, do you know, I didn't understand your close friendship with Arkadii Nikolaich very well before—I considered him somewhat undistinguished. But now I've gotten to know him better and have become convinced he's quite intelligent.... And he's young, he's young ... that's the main thing ... not like you and me, Evgenii Vasilich."

"Is he still as shy as ever in your company?" Bazarov inquired.

"Why, was he ...?" Anna Sergeevna began, and after a brief pause, she added, "He's become more trusting now—he talks to me, whereas he used to avoid me. Of course, I didn't seek out his companionship, either. He's friendlier with Katia."

Bazarov got annoyed. "A woman can't help being devious!" he thought. "You say he used to avoid you," Bazarov remarked aloud with an icy smile, "but has it remained a secret to you that he was in love with you?"

"What? He was too?" fell from Anna Sergeevna's lips.

"He was too," Bazarov repeated with a submissive bow. "Is it possible that you didn't know this, that I've told you something new?"

Anna Sergeevna lowered her eyes. "You're mistaken, Evgenii Vasilich."

"I don't think so. But maybe I shouldn't have mentioned it." "Just don't try to be devious in the future," he added to himself.

"Why not? Yet I imagine that you're attributing too much importance to a passing impression in this matter as well. I begin to suspect that you're inclined to exaggeration."

"We'd better not talk about it, Anna Sergeevna."

"Oh, why not?" she responded, but she herself turned the conversation in another direction. She was still uncomfortable with Bazarov, even though she'd told him and had assured herself that everything had been forgotten. While she was exchanging the simplest sentences with him, even while she was joking with him, she felt a faint undercurrent of dread. Thus do people sailing on a steamship converse and laugh carelessly, precisely as though they were on dry land, but should the slightest untoward incident occur, should the least sign of anything out of the ordinary arise, then an expression of special alarm betraying the constant awareness of constant danger immediately appears on every face.

Anna Sergeevna's conversation with Bazarov didn't last long. She became absorbed in thought, replied abstractedly, and finally suggested that they go into the main hall, where they found the princess and Katia. "But where's Arkadii Nikolaich?" inquired the lady of the house, and upon learning that he hadn't been seen for more than an hour, she sent for him. He couldn't be found right away; he'd betaken himself to the very densest part of the garden where, with his chin propped on his folded hands, he was sitting lost in meditation. It was deep, serious, but not mournful meditation. He knew that Anna Sergeevna was alone with Bazarov and yet he didn't feel jealous, the way he once had; on the contrary, his face slowly brightened. He seemed to be simultaneously surprised and joyful, and to have made up his mind about something.

# XXVI

The deceased Odintsov hadn't liked innovations, but he'd tolerated "the fine arts within certain limits," and had consequently erected an edifice that resembled a Greek portico, made of Russian brick, in the garden between the greenhouse and the pond. Along the blank rear wall of this portico, or gallery, were niches for six statues, which Odintsov had intended to order from abroad. These statues were supposed to represent Solitude, Silence, Contemplation, Melancholy, Modesty, and Sensitivity. One of them, the goddess of Silence, her finger on her lips, had been received and set up, but some of the boys on the estate had broken off her nose that very same day. And even though a local plasterer had attempted to make her a new nose "twice as good as the old one," Odintsov had nonetheless ordered her to be removed, and she'd ended up in a corner of the threshing barn, where she'd stood for many years, a source of superstitious terror to the peasant women. The front section of the portico had become overgrown by thick vegetation long ago; only the capitals of the columns could be seen above the dense verdure. It was cool beneath the portico itself, even at midday. Anna Sergeevna hadn't liked to visit this spot ever since she'd seen a snake there, but Katia often came and sat on a wide stone seat under one of the niches. Here, in the midst of the shade and the coolness, she read or studied or gave herself over to the sensation of perfect peace that's probably familiar to each of us, the charm of which consists in the barely conscious, silent recognition of life's vast current constantly flowing both around and inside us.

The day after Bazarov's arrival, Katia was sitting on her beloved stone seat, and Arkadii was sitting beside her once more. He'd asked her to come to the portico with him.

There was about an hour to go before their midday meal; the dewy morning had already given way to a sultry day. Arkadii's face had retained the expression of the preceding day; Katia's had a preoccupied look. Immediately after having had their morning tea, her sister had summoned Katia to her study, and after some preliminary caresses, which always scared Katia a little, she'd advised Katia to be more guarded in her behavior toward Arkadii, and in particular to avoid solitary conversations with him, since they were likely to attract the attention of their aunt, as well as the rest of the household. Moreover, Anna Sergeevna hadn't been in a good mood the previous evening, and Katia herself had been uncomfortable, as though she'd felt guilty for having done something wrong. In acceding to Arkadii's request, she told herself that it was for the last time.

"Katerina Sergeevna," he began with some sort of bashful familiarity, "while I've had the pleasure of living in the same house with you, I've discussed many things with you, but there's still one question that's very important ... for me, which I haven't touched on until now. You remarked yesterday that I've been changed during my stay here," he went on, at once noticing and avoiding the inquiring gaze Katia turned toward him. "I've definitely changed a great deal, and you know that better than anyone else—you're in essence the one to whom I owe this change."

"I? ... To me? ..." Katia responded.

"I'm no longer the conceited boy that I was when I came here," Arkadii continued. "I haven't reached the age of twenty-three for nothing. I want to be useful, just as I did before; I want to devote all my energies to the pursuit of truth. But I no longer look for my ideals where I did before—they've presented themselves to me ... much closer to hand. Up until now, I didn't understand myself, I set myself tasks that were beyond my strength.... My eyes have been opened recently, thanks to one feeling.... I'm not expressing myself entirely clearly, but I hope that you'll understand me...."

Katia didn't reply, but she stopped looking at Arkadii.

"I believe," he began again, this time in a more agitated voice, while a finch lightheartedly sang its song among the leaves of a birch tree above his head, "I believe that it's the duty of every honorable person to be completely open with those ... with those people who ... in a word, with those who are close to him, and so I ... I intend...."

But at this point Arkadii's eloquence deserted him; he lost his train of thought, got confused, and was forced to fall silent for a moment. Katia still didn't raise her eyes. It seemed as though she didn't understand what he was leading up to by all of this, and was waiting for something.

"I foresee that I'm going to surprise you," Arkadii began once more, pulling himself together with an effort, "especially since this feeling relates in a certain way ... in a certain way, please note ... to you. You reproached me yesterday, if you remember, for a lack of seriousness." Arkadii continued like a man who's stepped into a bog and senses that he's sinking deeper and deeper at every step, yet hurries onward in hope of crossing it as soon as possible. "This reproach is often aimed ... often falls ... on young men even when they cease to deserve it. And if I had more self-confidence...." ("Oh, help me, help me!" Arkadii was thinking in desperation, but Katia still didn't turn her head.) "If I could only hope...."

"If I could only be sure of what you're saying," Anna Sergeevna's clear voice resounded at that moment.

Arkadii instantly fell silent, and Katia turned pale. A little path ran past the bushes that screened the portico; Anna Sergeevna was walking along it, escorted by Bazarov. Katia and Arkadii couldn't see them but could hear their every word, the rustle of their clothes, their very breathing. The two walked a few steps farther and, as though on purpose, stopped directly opposite the portico.

"You see," Anna Sergeevna continued, "you and I made a mistake. We're both past our early youth—I in particular. We've experienced life, we're tired. We're both—why pretend otherwise?—intelligent. At first we piqued one another's interest, our curiosity was aroused ... and then...."

"And then I got stale," Bazarov interjected.

"You know that this wasn't the cause of our misunderstanding. But, be that as it may, we didn't need one another—that's the main thing. There was too much in us ... how shall I put it? ...

that was alike. We didn't realize it right away. By contrast, Arkadii...."

"Do you need him?" Bazarov inquired.

"Hush, Evgenii Vasilich. You say that he isn't indifferent to me, and it always seemed to me that he liked me. I know that I could easily be his aunt, but I don't want to conceal from you that I've begun to think about him more often. There's some sort of charm in such youthful, fresh emotions...."

"The word 'fascination' is more often employed in such instances," Bazarov interrupted, splenetic anger audible in his hollow if steady voice. "Arkadii was concealing something from me yesterday, and didn't refer either to you or to your sister.... That's a telling symptom."

"He's just like a brother to Katia," Anna Sergeevna commented, "and I like that in him, although perhaps I shouldn't have allowed such intimacy to develop between them."

"Is that thought prompted by ... your feelings as a sister?" Bazarov drawled.

"Naturally ... but why are we standing still? Let's go on. What a strange conversation we're having, aren't we? I never would have believed I'd be talking to you like this. You know that I'm afraid of you ... and at the same time, I trust you, because you're fundamentally so kind."

"In the first place, I'm not the least bit kind. And in the second place, I no longer mean anything to you, and yet you tell me that I'm kind.... It's like laying a wreath of flowers on the head of a corpse."

"Evgenii Vasilich, we don't control...," Anna Sergeevna began, but a gust of wind blew by, setting the leaves rustling and carrying away her words. "Of course, you're free," Bazarov declared after a brief pause. Nothing more could be distinguished; the footsteps retreated.... Everything became still.

Arkadii turned to Katia. She was sitting in the same position, but her head was bowed even lower. "Katerina Sergeevna," he said in a trembling voice, clasping his hands together tightly, "I love you infinitely and irrevocably, and I love no one but you. I wanted to tell you this, to find out what you think about me, and to ask you if you'll marry me, since I'm not rich, and I'm prepared to sacrifice everything.... Won't you answer me? Don't you believe me? Do you think I'm speaking lightly? But remember these last few days! Surely you must have realized for a long while now that everything—do you understand?—everything else vanished long ago without a trace? Look at me, say one word to me ... I love ... I love you.... Please believe me!"

Katia cast a radiant yet serious glance at Arkadii, and after a lengthy pause, just barely smiling, she said, "Yes."

Arkadii leaped up from the stone seat. "Yes! You said 'yes,' Katerina Sergeevna! What does that word mean? Only that I do love you, that you believe me ... or ... or.... I can't go on...."

"Yes," Katia repeated, and this time he understood what she meant. He grasped her large, beautiful hands and, breathless with rapture, pressed them to his heart. He could hardly stand upright, and could only whisper, "Katia, Katia ...," while she innocently began to weep, quietly laughing at her own tears. He who hasn't seen such tears in the eyes of his beloved still doesn't know to what extent someone who's faint with embarrassment and gratitude may be happy on this earth.

———

The next day, early in the morning, Anna Sergeevna summoned Bazarov to her study and, with a forced laugh, handed him a folded piece of notepaper. It was a letter from Arkadii; in it, he asked for permission to marry her sister.

Bazarov quickly scanned the letter and made an effort to control himself in order to conceal the malicious feeling that momentarily flared up in his breast.

"So that's how it is," he responded. "And only yesterday, it seems, you assumed that he loved Katerina Sergeevna like a brother. What do you intend to do now?"

"What do you advise me to do?" Anna Sergeevna inquired, still laughing.

"Well," Bazarov replied, laughing as well, although he felt

anything but cheerful, and was no more inclined to laugh than she was, "I suppose that you ought to give the young people your permission. It's a good marriage in every respect—Kirsanov's financial circumstances are passable, he's the only son, and his father's such a good-natured man that he won't try to thwart him."

Mrs. Odintsov paced around the room. Her face alternately flushed and paled. "Do you think so?" she mused. "Well, I see no obstacles.... I'm happy for Katia ... and for Arkadii Nikolaevich, too. Of course, I'll wait for his father's response—I'll send him in person to see his father. But, you see, it turns out that I was right yesterday when I told you we were both old people.... How was it that I didn't see anything? That's what surprises me!" Anna Sergeevna laughed again, and quickly turned her head away.

"Today's youth has gotten awfully devious," Bazarov remarked, and he laughed, too. "Goodbye," he spoke up again after a short silence. "I hope you'll bring this matter to a most satisfactory conclusion. I'll rejoice from a distance."

Mrs. Odintsov quickly turned toward him again. "You aren't going away? Why shouldn't you stay *now*? Stay.... It's enjoyable talking to you.... One seems to be walking on the edge of a precipice. One's intimidated at first, but one becomes braver as one goes forward. Do stay."

"Thank you for the invitation, Anna Sergeevna, and for your flattering estimation of my conversational talents. But I think I've already been moving in a sphere that isn't my own for too long. Flying fish can stay aloft for a while, but sooner or later they have to splash back into the water. Allow me to swim in my own element, too."

Mrs. Odintsov looked at Bazarov. His pale face was distorted by an embittered smile. "This man did love me!" she thought, feeling sorry for him, and she held out her hand to him in sympathy.

But he also understood her. "No!" he said, stepping back a pace. "I'm a poor man, but I've never taken charity thus far. Goodbye. Be well."

"I'm certain we aren't seeing one another for the last time," Anna Sergeevna declared with an impulsive gesture.

"Anything can happen on this earth!" Bazarov responded with a bow, and left.

"So you're considering building yourself a nest?" he said to Arkadii as he packed his suitcase the same day, crouching on the floor. "Well, it's a good thing. But you didn't need to be so cunning. I expected something completely different from you. Or maybe it took you yourself by surprise?"

"I certainly didn't expect this when I said goodbye to you," Arkadii replied, "but you're being cunning yourself, saying 'a good thing'—as though I didn't know your opinion of marriage."

"Ah, my dear friend," Bazarov cried, "the way you express yourself! Do you see what I'm doing? There's turned out to be an empty space in the suitcase, and I'm putting hay in it. That's how we treat the suitcases of our lives—we'd rather stuff them with something than accept a void. Please don't be offended— you'll undoubtedly remember what my opinion of Katerina Sergeevna has always been. Many young ladies are considered intelligent simply because they can sigh intelligently, but yours can hold her own, and, in fact, she'll do it so well that she'll get you under her thumb—indeed, that's just how it should be." He slammed the suitcase lid shut and got up from the floor.

"And now I'll say goodbye again, for it's pointless to deceive ourselves—we're saying goodbye forever, and you realize that yourself.... You've acted wisely. You aren't cut out for our bitter, rough, lonely existence. There's no insolence in you, no animosity, although there's youthful courage and youthful ardor. You aren't suited to our task. Your sort, the gentry, can never get beyond noble resignation or noble indignation, and they're worthless. For instance, you won't fight—and yet you consider yourselves gallant men. But we want to fight. Oh, well! Our dust would get in your eyes, our mud would spatter you. You aren't up to our level yet. You involuntarily admire yourselves, and you like to criticize yourselves, but we're sick of that—give us other people to deal with! We need other people to crush! You're a fine man, but you're a weak, liberal snob for all that—*e volatu*, as my estimable father likes to say."

"You're saying goodbye to me forever, Evgenii," Arkadii responded sadly, "and you have no other words for me?"

Bazarov scratched the back of his head. "Yes, Arkadii, I do have other words for you, but I'm not going to say them, because that's romanticism—that's sickeningly sweet. Still, get married as soon as you can, and build your nest, and have as many children as possible. They'll be smart ones, because they'll have been born at the right time, not like you and me. Aha! I see that the horses are ready. It's time to go. I've said goodbye to everyone else.... Well, what now? Should we embrace?"

Arkadii flung his arms around the neck of his former mentor and friend, and the tears virtually gushed from his eyes.

"That's what it means to be young!" Bazarov observed calmly. "But I have faith in Katerina Sergeevna. You'll see how quickly she'll console you! Goodbye, my friend!" he said to Arkadii when he'd gotten into the carriage. And pointing to a pair of crows sitting side by side on the stable roof, he added, "Those are for you! Study them."

"What does that mean?" Arkadii asked.

"What? Are you so weak in natural history, or have you forgotten that the crow is a most respectable family bird? They're an example for you!... Goodbye, señor!"

The carriage creaked and rolled away.

Bazarov had spoken the truth. Talking with Katia that evening, Arkadii completely forgot about his mentor. He'd already begun to defer to her; Katia was aware of this, and wasn't surprised by it. He was going to set off for Marino to see Nikolai Petrovich the next day. Anna Sergeevna wasn't inclined to put any constraints on the young people, and didn't leave them alone together too long merely for the sake of propriety. Magnanimously, she kept the princess out of their way; the latter had been reduced to a tearful frenzy by the news of the forthcoming marriage. At first, Anna Sergeevna was afraid that the sight of their happiness might prove somewhat distressing, but it turned out to be quite the opposite: this sight not only didn't distress her, it intrigued her; in the end, it even moved her. Anna Sergeevna was both pleased and saddened by this. "Evidently Bazarov was right," she thought. "It was curiosity, nothing but curiosity, and love of tranquillity, and egotism. . . ."

"Children," she said aloud, "what do you think—is love a purely contrived feeling?"

But neither Katia nor Arkadii understood what she meant. They were shy around her; the fragment of conversation they'd unintentionally overheard haunted their memories. But Anna Sergeevna soon set their minds at ease, which wasn't difficult for her—she'd set her own mind at ease.

# XXVII

Bazarov's elderly parents were overjoyed by their son's arrival, all the more because it was utterly unexpected. Arina Vlasevna got so excited and started to run around the house so energetically that Vasilii Ivanovich compared her to a "female partridge"— the tail of her short jacket actually did lend her a somewhat bird-like appearance. He himself merely mumbled, gnawed on the amber mouthpiece of his pipe, and, clutching his neck with his fingers, turned his head around as though checking to see whether it was properly attached, then suddenly opened his mouth wide and lapsed into completely noiseless laughter.

"I've come to stay with you for six whole weeks, old man," Bazarov told him. "I want to work, so please don't disturb me now."

"You'll totally forget my face—that's how much I'll disturb you!" Vasilii Ivanovich promised him.

He kept his promise. After installing his son in his study, as he had before, he nearly hid from Bazarov, and restrained his wife from any excessive displays of tenderness. "During Eniusha's first visit, my dear," he said to her, "we bothered him a little bit. We should be more prudent this time." Arina Vlasevna agreed with her husband, but that didn't matter very much, since she only saw her son at meals and had become thoroughly frightened of speaking to him. "Eniushenka," she'd occasionally say, but before he had time to look around, she'd nervously finger the tassels of her workbag and murmur, "Never mind, never mind, I only...." Then she'd go to find Vasilii Ivanovich and, resting her cheek on her hand, would say to him: "Could you find out what Eniusha would like for dinner today, darling—cabbage soup or borscht?" "But why didn't you ask him yourself?" "Oh, he'll get tired of me!"

Bazarov soon ceased to isolate himself, however; his feverish desire to work dissipated, and was replaced by dismal boredom and vague restlessness. A strange fatigue manifested itself in all his movements; even his firm, confidently bold stride changed. He gave up walking in solitude and began to seek out company; he drank tea in the drawing room, strolled around the kitchen garden with Vasilii Ivanovich, and smoked with him in silence; once, he even inquired about Father Aleksei.

Vasilii Ivanovich rejoiced over this change at first, but his joy wasn't long-lived. "Eniusha's breaking my heart," he complained to his wife in private. "It's not that he's dissatisfied or angry—that wouldn't mean anything. But he's depressed, he's sad—that's what's so terrible. He's always silent—if only he'd criticize us. He's getting thin, and the color of his face is so bad." "Lord, Lord!" whispered the old woman. "I'd hang an amulet around his neck, but you know he wouldn't let me." Vasilii Ivanovich attempted to question Bazarov several times in the most circumspect manner about his work, about his health, about Arkadii.... But Bazarov replied reluctantly and offhandedly; one day, noticing that his father was gradually trying to lead up to something in conversation, Bazarov said with annoyance: "Why do you always seem to be walking around me on tiptoe? That's even worse than the old way."

"There, there, I didn't mean any harm!" poor Vasilii Ivanovich responded hurriedly. Thus his politic hints remained fruitless. He hoped to engage his son's interest one day by beginning to talk about progress in regard to the approaching emancipation of the serfs, but Bazarov observed indifferently: "Yesterday I was walking past the fence and I heard the peasant boys here bawling out a popular song, 'The right time is coming, love is touching my heart,' instead of singing some old ballad. That's progress for you."

Sometimes Bazarov went to the village and embarked upon a conversation with some peasant in his usual bantering tone. "Well now," he'd say to the peasant, "set forth your views on life to me, my friend. You see, they say that the entire strength and future of Russia lies in your hands, that you'll begin a new epoch in history—that you'll give us our true language and our laws."

The peasant would either fail to reply at all, or would utter a few words like this: "Well, we can ... also, because, it means ... we've taken such a position, approximately...."

"Explain to me what you think the world is," Bazarov would interrupt, "and tell me—is it the same world that's said to rest on three fishes?"

"It's the earth that rests on three fishes, your worship," the peasant would explain soothingly in a patriarchal, kindly, singsong tone, "whereas opposite ours, that is, our world, it's well known, there's God's will, which is why you're our superiors. And the stricter the master is, the better for the peasant."

After listening to such a reply one day, Bazarov shrugged his shoulders contemptuously and turned away, whereupon the peasant slowly sauntered homeward.

"What was he talking about?" inquired another middle-aged peasant with a surly countenance who'd been listening to the conversation with Bazarov from a distance, at the door of his hut. "Unpaid debts, eh?"

"Unpaid debts? No indeed, my friend!" answered the first peasant. There was no longer any trace of a patriarchal singsong tone in his voice; on the contrary, some sort of disdainful gruffness could be heard in it. "Oh, he babbled away about something or other. He wanted to exercise his tongue a bit. Of course, he's a gentleman—what does he understand?"

"What could he understand?" rejoined the other peasant, and then, shoving back their caps and pushing down their belts, they proceeded to discuss their concerns and their needs. Alas! Bazarov, who shrugged his shoulders contemptuously, who knew how to talk to peasants (as he'd boasted during one argument with Pavel Petrovich), this self-confident Bazarov in no way suspected that in their eyes he was something on the order of a buffoon....

He finally found an activity to occupy him, though. One day, Vasilii Ivanovich was bandaging a peasant's wounded leg in his presence, but the elderly man's hands were shaking, and he couldn't tie the bandages properly; his son helped him, and from that point on, Bazarov began to participate in his father's practice, although at the same time he repeatedly sneered both at the remedies he himself advised and at his father, who hastened to make use of them. But Bazarov's sneering didn't perturb Vasilii Ivanovich in the least; it actually comforted him. Holding his greasy robe closed across his stomach with two fingers and smoking his pipe, he listened to Bazarov with great pleasure; the more malicious his son's sallies, the more good-naturedly did the delighted father chuckle, displaying all of his blackened teeth. He'd even repeat these sometimes flat or pointless remarks for several days, constantly reiterating without rhyme or reason, for instance, "That's not a matter of major importance!" simply because his son, upon learning that Vasilii Ivanovich was going to matins, had used this expression. "Thank God! He's stopped moping!" Vasilii Ivanovich whispered to his wife. "He really gave it to me today—it was wonderful!" Moreover, the idea of having such an assistant overjoyed him, filling him with pride. "Yes, yes," he'd say to some peasant woman wearing a man's coat and a cap shaped like a horn, as he handed her a bottle of Goulard's extract or a jar of white ointment, "you ought to be thanking God every minute, my good woman, that my son's staying with me. Now you'll be treated according to the most scientific, the most modern methods. Do you know what that means? Even the French emperor, Napoleon, has no better doctor." And the peasant woman, who'd come to complain that she felt sort of odd all over (she herself wasn't able to explain the precise meaning of these words, however), merely bowed and rummaged around her bodice, where four eggs lay tied up in the corner of a piece of cloth.

Once Bazarov even extracted a tooth for a passing cloth peddler, and despite the fact that this tooth was an average specimen, Vasilii Ivanovich preserved it as a rarity, and incessantly repeated as he showed it to Father Aleksei, "Just look—what a fang! The strength Evgenii has! The peddler virtually leaped into the air. If it'd been an oak tree, it seems, he'd have uprooted it!"

"Most impressive!" Father Aleksei eventually commented, not knowing what response to make or how to get rid of the ecstatic old man.

One day, a peasant from a neighboring village brought his brother who had typhus to see Vasilii Ivanovich. The unfortunate man, lying flat on a pile of straw, was dying: his body was covered with dark spots, and he'd long since lost consciousness. Vasilii Ivanovich expressed regret that no one had thought of obtaining medical assistance any sooner, then declared that there was no hope. And in fact, the peasant didn't make it back to his brother's home—he died in their cart.

Three days later, Bazarov came into his father's room and asked him if he had a cauterizing stone.

"Yes. What do you want it for?"

"I need it ... to burn a cut."

"For whom?"

"For myself."

"What—for yourself? Why's that? What sort of a cut? Where is it?"

"Here, on my finger. I went to the village today, you know, where they'd taken that peasant who had typhus. They were just about to cut open the body for some reason or other, and I haven't had any practice at that sort of thing for a long time."

"And so?"

"And so I asked the district doctor for permission, and I dissected it."

Vasilii Ivanovich suddenly turned completely pale, and without uttering a word, he rushed to his study, from which he immediately returned with a piece of cauterizing stone in his hand. Bazarov wanted to take it and leave.

"For God's own sake," Vasilii Ivanovich pleaded, "let me do it myself."

Bazarov smiled. "What a dedicated practitioner!"

"Please don't make jokes. Show me your finger. The cut isn't a large one. Does this hurt?"

"Press harder—don't be afraid."

Vasilii Ivanovich stopped. "What do you think, Evgenii—wouldn't it be better to burn it with a hot iron?"

"That should have been done sooner. Even the cauterizing stone is useless at this point, actually. If I've been infected, it's too late now."

"How ... too late ...?" Vasilii Ivanovich could hardly pronounce the words.

"Yes, indeed! It's been more than four hours."

Vasilii Ivanovich seared the cut a little more. "But didn't the district doctor have a cauterizing stone?"

"No."

"How could that be? My God! He's a doctor—and he doesn't have as indispensable a thing as that!"

"You should have seen his lancets," Bazarov commented as he walked out.

Up until late that evening and the entire following day, Vasilii Ivanovich seized every possible opportunity to go into his son's room. Although he didn't refer to the cut, and even tried to talk about the most unrelated subjects, he peered into his son's eyes so persistently and regarded him so anxiously that Bazarov lost his patience and threatened to leave. Vasilii Ivanovich promised not to bother him, all the more readily since Arina Vlasevna, from whom he kept everything secret, naturally, was beginning to pester him about why he couldn't sleep and what had come over him. He restrained himself for two whole days, although he didn't like the way his son looked at all; he kept watching him stealthily ... but by the third day, at dinner, he couldn't bear it any longer. Bazarov was sitting with his eyes downcast, without touching his food.

"Why aren't you eating, Evgenii?" he inquired, donning a thoroughly nonchalant expression. "The food has been prepared quite nicely, I think."

"I don't want anything, so I'm not eating."

"Don't you have any appetite? How's your head?" Vasilii Ivanovich added timidly. "Does it ache?"

"Yes, it does. Why shouldn't it ache?"

Arina Vlasevna sat up and became alert.

"Please don't be angry, Evgenii," Vasilii Ivanovich continued, "but won't you let me feel your pulse?"

Bazarov stood up. "I can tell you without feeling my pulse that I have a fever."

"Have you been shivering?"

"Yes, I've been shivering, too. I'll go lie down, and you can have someone bring me some lime tea. I must have caught a cold."

"Indeed, I heard you coughing last night," Arina Vlasevna observed.

"I've caught a cold," Bazarov reiterated, and he went out.

Arina Vlasevna busied herself preparing the lime tea, while Vasilii Ivanovich went into the next room and silently clutched at his hair.

Bazarov didn't get up again that day and spent the whole night in a heavy, semiconscious torpor. At about one in the morning, opening his eyes with an effort, he saw his father's pale face bending over him in the lamplight and told him to go away. The elderly man begged his pardon and left, but quickly came back on tiptoe and, half hidden by the cupboard door, steadily gazed at his son. Arina Vlasevna didn't go to bed either, and leaving the study door slightly ajar, she kept coming up to it to hear "how Eniusha was breathing" and to look at Vasilii Ivanovich. She couldn't see anything except his motionless, stooped back, but even that afforded her some consolation.

The next morning, Bazarov tried to get up; his head began to spin and his nose began to bleed; he lay down again. Vasilii Ivanovich attended to him in silence; Arina Vlasevna went in to see him and asked him how he was feeling. He answered, "Better"—and turned toward the wall. Vasilii Ivanovich waved his wife away with both hands; she bit her lip in order not to cry, and went out.

The whole house suddenly seemed dark; everyone's face looked drawn; a strange hush set in; one noisy rooster was moved from the yard to the village, unable to comprehend why he was being treated that way. Bazarov continued to lie still with his face turned toward the wall. Vasilii Ivanovich tried to pose various questions to him, but they exhausted Bazarov, and the elderly man sank into his armchair, merely cracking his knuckles every now and then. He went into the garden for a few moments and stood there like a statue, as though overwhelmed by inexpressible bewilderment (an astonished expression almost never left his face), then returned to his son, trying to avoid his wife's inquiries. She finally grasped him by the arm and passionately, almost menacingly, asked: "What's wrong with him?" Then he collected himself and forced himself to try to smile in reply, but to his own horror, instead of smiling, he found himself somehow overcome by a fit of laughter.

He sent for a doctor at daybreak. He deemed it necessary to inform his son of this fact, for fear he'd get angry. Bazarov suddenly rolled over on the sofa, trained a fixed, vacant gaze on his father, and asked for something to drink. Vasilii Ivanovich gave him some water and, as he did so, felt his son's forehead. It seemed to be on fire.

"Old man," Bazarov began in a slow, drowsy voice, "I'm in terrible shape. I've been infected, and you'll have to bury me in a few days."

Vasilii Ivanovich staggered as though someone had struck a blow at his legs.

"Evgenii," he faltered, "what are you saying?... God have mercy on you! You've caught a cold...."

"That's enough of that!" Bazarov interrupted him deliberately. "A doctor isn't allowed to talk like that. I have all the symptoms of infection—you know that yourself."

"Where are the symptoms ... of an infection, Evgenii?... For heaven's sake!"

"And what's this?" Bazarov asked, pulling up his shirt sleeve and showing his father the ominous red patches that were appearing on his arm.

Vasilii Ivanovich shuddered and grew cold with terror.

"Supposing," he finally said, "even supposing ... even if there's something like ... an infection...."

"Pyemia," interjected his son.

"Well, yes ... something ... like the epidemic...."

"Pyemia," Bazarov repeated abruptly and distinctly. "Have you forgotten your textbooks?"

"Well, yes—whatever you want.... In any event, we'll cure you."

"Come on—that's out of the question. But that isn't the point. I didn't expect to die so soon. It's a very unpleasant development, to tell you the truth. You and Mother ought to make the most of your deep religious faith—now's the time to put it to the test." He drank a little water. "I want to ask you about one thing ... while my mind is still under my control. Tomorrow or the next day my brain will submit its resignation, you know. I'm not even quite certain whether I'm expressing myself clearly right now. As I've been lying here, I've kept thinking that red dogs were running around me and that you were making them point at me as if I were a woodcock. It's like I was drunk. Can you understand me all right?"

"For heaven's sake, Evgenii, you're speaking perfectly coherently."

"All the better. You told me you'd sent for the doctor.... You did that to comfort yourself.... To comfort me as well, send a messenger...."

"To Arkadii Nikolaich?" interjected the elderly man.

"Who's Arkadii Nikolaich?" Bazarov asked, as though in doubt.... "Oh, yes! That little bird! No, leave him alone—he's turned into a crow now. Don't be alarmed—that's not delirium yet. Send a messenger to Mrs. Odintsov, to Anna Sergeevna. She's a lady with an estate.... Do you know her?" (Vasilii Ivanovich nodded.) "Say that Evgenii Bazarov sends his regards and sends word that he's dying. Will you do that?"

"Yes, I will.... But is it possible that you could be dying, Evgenii?... Just think! How could there be any justice after that?"

"I don't know anything about that—just send the messenger."

"I'll send one this minute, and I'll write a letter myself."

"No—what for? Say that I send my regards—nothing else is required. And now I'll go back to my dogs. It's strange! I want to focus my thoughts on death, and nothing happens. I see some sort of blur ... and nothing more."

He laboriously turned back to the wall again, while Vasilii Ivanovich left the study and, struggling as far as his wife's bedroom, helplessly dropped to his knees in front of the icons.

"Pray, Arina, pray!" he moaned. "Our son is dying."

The doctor arrived, the same district doctor who hadn't had a cauterizing stone, and after examining the patient, he advised them to continue the palliative treatments, saying a few words at that point about the possibility of recovery.

"Have you ever seen people in my condition *not* set off for Elysium?" Bazarov inquired, and suddenly grabbing the leg of a heavy table that stood near his sofa, he shook the table and pushed it out of place. "There's strength here, there's strength," he murmured. "Everything's still here, but I have to die!... An old man at least has time to divorce himself from life, but I....

Well, go try to negate death. Death will negate you, and that's all! Who's crying there?" he added after a short pause. "Mother? Poor thing! Whom will she feed her exquisite borscht to now? And you, Vasilii Ivanovich, are you whimpering, too? Well, if Christianity can't help you, be a philosopher, a Stoic, or whatever! Didn't you boast that you were a philosopher?"

"Me, a philosopher!" Vasilii Ivanovich wailed as the tears simply streamed down his cheeks.

Bazarov grew worse with every passing hour; the disease progressed rapidly, as is typical in cases of surgical poisoning. He still hadn't lost consciousness, though, and could understand what was said to him; he was still struggling. "I don't want to start raving," he'd whisper, clenching his fists. "What nonsense this is!" And then he'd say, "How much is eight minus ten?" Vasilii Ivanovich wandered around like someone possessed, proposing first one remedy, then another, and ended up doing nothing but covering his son's feet. "Try a cold pack ... an emetic ... mustard plasters on the stomach ... bleeding," he'd suggest tensely. The doctor, whom he'd begged to remain, agreed with him, ordered the patient to drink lemonade, and requested a pipe, as well as something "warming and strengthening"—that is, vodka—for himself. Arina Vlasevna sat on a low stool near the door and only left from time to time to pray. A few days earlier, a mirror had slipped out of her hands and broken, and she'd always considered this an evil omen; Anfisushka herself couldn't say anything to console her. Timofeich had gone to Mrs. Odintsov's.

Bazarov had a bad night.... He was in agony from the high fever. Toward morning, he became a little more comfortable. He asked Arina Vlasevna to comb his hair, kissed her hand, and drank two sips of tea. Vasilii Ivanovich perked up a bit. "Thank God!" he declared. "The crisis has come.... The crisis has passed."

"There, just think what a word can do!" Bazarov observed. "He's found one—he's said 'crisis'—and he feels better. It's astonishing how an individual can still believe in words. If someone tells him he's a fool, for instance, even though he doesn't suffer physically as a result, he'll be miserable. Call him an intelligent person and he'll be pleased, even if you go off without paying him."

This little speech by Bazarov, reminiscent of his former "sallies," greatly moved Vasilii Ivanovich.

"Bravo! Well said! Very good!" he exclaimed, pretending to clap his hands.

Bazarov smiled sadly.

"So what do you think," he asked, "has the crisis passed, or has it just begun?"

"You're better, that's what I see—that's what delights me," Vasilii Ivanovich replied.

"Well, that's good. Delight is never a bad thing. And that lady—did you remember to send someone to see her?"

"Of course I did."

The change for the better didn't last long. The disease resumed its onslaught. Vasilii Ivanovich remained sitting beside Bazarov. It seemed as though the elderly man were being tormented by some special anguish. He was on the verge of speaking several times—and couldn't.

"Evgenii," he began at last, "my son, my precious, adored son!"

This unfamiliar endearment had its effect on Bazarov. Turning his head somewhat and obviously trying to fight against the leaden weight of oblivion pressing down upon him, he asked, "What is it, Father?"

"Evgenii," Vasilii Ivanovich continued, and fell on his knees in front of Bazarov, although the latter had closed his eyes and couldn't see him. "Evgenii, you're getting better now. God grant that you'll get well. But make use of this time, comfort your mother and me—perform the duty of a Christian! What causes me to say this to you is horrible, but it's even more horrible ... forever and ever, Evgenii.... Think a bit about what...."

The elderly man's voice broke, and a strange look passed

across his son's face, although he lay still and kept his eyes closed.

"I won't refuse, if that can bring you any comfort," Bazarov finally declared, "but it seems to me that there's no need to rush. You yourself say that I'm getting better."

"Oh, yes, Evgenii, you're better, you're better—but who knows? It's all in God's hands, and in doing the duty...."

"No, I'll wait a little while," Bazarov interrupted him. "I agree with you that the crisis has come. And if we're wrong, what about it? They also give the sacrament to people who are unconscious, you know."

"Evgenii, for heaven's sake...."

"I'll wait a little while. Now I want to go to sleep. Don't disturb me." And he turned his head back to its previous position.

The elderly man rose from his knees, sat down in the armchair, and, clutching his beard, began biting his nails....

The sound of a carriage bouncing on springs, a sound that's particularly impressive in the depths of the countryside, suddenly reached his ears. The slender wheels rolled nearer and nearer; the neighing of horses became audible.... Vasilii Ivanovich jumped up and ran to the little window. A two-seated carriage with four horses harnessed to it entered the yard in front of his house. Without stopping to consider what this meant, with a burst of some sort of mindless joy, he ran out onto the steps.... A groom in livery was opening the carriage doors; a lady wearing a black veil and a black mantilla was getting out of it....

"I'm Mrs. Odintsov," she announced. "Is Evgenii Vasilich still alive? Are you his father? I've brought a doctor with me."

"You're nobility itself!" Vasilii Ivanovich cried, and clasping her hand, he convulsively pressed it to his lips, while the doctor Anna Sergeevna had brought, a little man with glasses who had Germanic features, slowly stepped out of the carriage. "He's still alive, my Evgenii's alive, and now he'll be saved! Wife! Wife!... An angel from heaven has come to see us...."

"What does this mean? Oh, Lord!" quavered the elderly woman, running out of the drawing room without comprehending anything. She fell at Anna Sergeevna's feet there in the hallway and began to kiss her dress like a madwoman.

"What are you doing? What are you doing?" Anna Sergeevna protested, but Arina Vlasevna didn't listen to her, while Vasilii Ivanovich could only repeat, "An angel! An angel!"

"*Wo ist der Kranke?* And where is the patient?" the doctor finally inquired, not without a certain impatience.

Vasilii Ivanovich recovered himself. "Here, here, follow me, *wertester Herr Collega,*" he added, drawing upon old memories.

"Ah!" grunted the German, grinning sourly.

Vasilii Ivanovich led him into the study. "A doctor engaged by Anna Sergeevna Odintsova is here," he said, bending down to his son's very ear, "and she's here herself."

Bazarov suddenly opened his eyes. "What did you say?"

"I said that Anna Sergeevna's here, and has brought this gentleman, a doctor, to see you."

Bazarov looked around. "She's here.... I want to see her."

"You can see her, Evgenii, but first we have to have a little chat with the doctor. I'll tell him the entire history of your illness, since Sidor Sidorych" (that was the district doctor's name) "has left, and we'll have a short consultation."

Bazarov glanced at the German.

"Well, consult quickly, but not in Latin—you see, I know what *iam moritur* means."

"*Der Herr scheint des Deutschen mächtig zu sein,*" began the new follower of Aesculapius, turning toward Vasilii Ivanovich.

"*Ich ... gabe....* We'd better speak Russian," suggested the elderly man.

"Ah, hah! So that's how it is.... If you prefer...." And the consultation began.

Half an hour later, Vasilii Ivanovich led Anna Sergeevna into the study. The doctor had managed to whisper to her that there was no hope of the patient's recovery.

She glanced at Bazarov ... and stopped in the doorway, so greatly was she struck by his flushed and yet deathlike face, whose lackluster eyes were fastened upon her. She was overcome by some sort of icy, suffocating fear; the thought that she wouldn't have felt like this if she'd really loved him instantaneously flashed through her mind.

"Thank you," he said laboriously. "I didn't expect this. You're doing a good deed. So we're seeing one another again, as you promised."

"Anna Sergeevna was so kind...," Vasilii Ivanovich began.

"Father, leave us alone. Anna Sergeevna, will you mind? Now, it seems...." With a motion of his head, he indicated his prostrate, helpless body.

Vasilii Ivanovich went out.

"Well, thank you," Bazarov repeated. "This is regal of you. Tsars also visit the dying, they say."

"Evgenii Vasilich, I hope...."

"Ah, Anna Sergeevna, let's concede the truth. It's all over for me—I've fallen under the wheel. So it turns out that there was no reason to think about the future at all. Death's an old joke, but each individual encounters it anew. So far I'm not afraid ... but unconsciousness will arrive soon, and then *pffft!*" (He waved his hand feebly.) "Well, what can I say to you? ... I loved you! There was no point in that before, and there's less than ever now. Love requires a form, and my own form is already decomposing. I'd rather talk about how lovely you are! And right now you're standing here, so beautiful...."

Anna Sergeevna involuntarily shuddered.

"Never mind, don't be distressed.... Sit down over there.... Don't come close to me—you know that my illness is contagious."

Anna Sergeevna crossed the room swiftly and sat down in the armchair near the sofa on which Bazarov was lying.

"Noble-hearted!" he whispered. "Oh, how close—and so young, and fresh, and pure ... in this loathsome room!... Well, goodbye! Live a long while—that's the best thing of all—and make the most of your life while you have time. You see what a hideous spectacle I am—a worm that's half crushed but still writhing. And, after all, I did think that I'd overcome so many things, that I wouldn't die—why should I? There are problems to solve, and I'm a giant! And now the whole problem for the giant is how to die decently, although that doesn't matter to anyone, either.... Don't worry—I'm not going to break down."

Bazarov fell silent and groped for his glass with one hand. Anna Sergeevna helped him take a sip without removing her glove, drawing her breath timidly.

"You'll forget me," he began again. "The dead are no companions for the living. My father will tell you what a man Russia is losing.... That's ridiculous, but don't contradict the old man. Whatever toy will comfort a child ... you know. And be kind to my mother. People like them can't be found in your elegant world if you search high and low.... I'm necessary to Russia.... No, it's clear that I'm not necessary. And who is necessary? The shoemaker is necessary, the tailor is necessary, the butcher ... gives us meat ... the butcher ... wait a minute, I'm getting confused.... There's a forest here...."

Bazarov put his hand on his forehead.

Anna Sergeevna bent over him. "Evgenii Vasilich, I'm here...."

He immediately took his hand away and raised himself up.

"Goodbye," he said with sudden strength, and his eyes gleamed with their last light. "Goodbye.... Listen.... You know, I didn't kiss you then.... Blow on the dying lamp, and let it go out...."

Anna Sergeevna touched her lips to his forehead.

"That's enough!" he murmured, and fell back onto the pillow. "Now ... darkness...."

Anna Sergeevna went out quietly. "Well?" Vasilii Ivanovich asked her in a whisper.

"He's fallen asleep," she replied, barely audibly.

Bazarov wasn't fated to awaken again. He sank into complete unconsciousness toward evening, and he died the following day. Father Aleksei had performed the last rites over him. When they'd anointed him in extreme unction, when the holy oil had touched his breast, one of his eyes had opened, and it seemed as though the sight of the priest in his vestments, the smoking censers, and the candles before the icon had caused something like a shudder of horror fleetingly to cross his death-stricken face.

When he'd finally drawn his last breath, and lamentation had arisen throughout the house, Vasilii Ivanovich was seized by a sudden frenzy. "I said that I'd rebel," he shrieked hoarsely, his face inflamed and distorted, shaking his fist in the air as though threatening someone, "and I rebel—I rebel!" But Arina Vlasevna, who'd dissolved in tears, threw her arms around his neck, and they fell to their knees on the ground together. "Side by side," Anfisushka reported afterward in the servants' quarters, "they bowed their poor heads like lambs in the noonday heat...."

But the noonday heat passes, evening comes, and then nighttime, when it's possible to return to some quiet refuge where it's sweet for the tortured and the weary to sleep....

# XXVIII

Six months went past. Deepest winter had set in, accompanied by its cruelly still, cloudless frosts, thick, crisp snow, rosy rime on the trees, pale emerald sky, wreaths of smoke above the chimneys, puffs of steam rushing out doors when they're opened for an instant, people's frostbitten faces, and briskly trotting, chilly horses. A January day was drawing to its close; the evening cold was keener than ever in the motionless air, and a brilliant red sunset was rapidly fading away. Lights were burning in the windows of the house at Marino; Prokofich, wearing a black dress coat and white gloves, had set the table for seven with special solemnity. A week earlier, two weddings had taken place quietly, almost without witnesses, in the small parish church—Arkadii's to Katia, and Nikolai Petrovich's to Fenechka—and this evening, Nikolai Petrovich was giving a farewell dinner for his brother, who was leaving for Moscow on business. Anna Sergeevna had also left for there as soon as the ceremony was over, after giving the young couple some very handsome presents.

They all gathered around the table at precisely three o'clock. Mitia had been brought in, too; a nurse in a glossy brocade cap appeared along with him. Pavel Petrovich took a seat between Katia and Fenechka; the husbands took their places beside their wives. Our friends had changed recently: they all seemed to have grown bigger and handsomer; only Pavel Petrovich had gotten thinner, which gave an even more elegant, "grand seigneurial" aspect to his expressive features.... Fenechka also looked different. Wearing a fresh silk dress, a wide velvet cap on her hair, and a gold chain around her neck, she sat perfectly still, exuding both self-respect and respect for everything surrounding her, and smiling as though she wanted to say, "I beg your pardon, I'm not to blame." And she wasn't alone—the others all smiled and seemed apologetic as well; they all felt a little awkward, a little sad, and essentially very happy. They served one another with comical courtesy, as though they'd all agreed to enact some sort of innocent farce. Katia was the calmest of all; she gazed around her confidently, and it was evident that Nikolai Petrovich already loved her deeply. At the end of dinner, he stood up, and taking his glass in his hand, he turned to Pavel Petrovich.

"You're leaving us ... you're leaving us, my dear brother," he began. "Not for long, of course, but still, I can't help expressing to you what I ... what we ... how much I ... how much we.... Now, the worst of it is that we don't know how to make speeches. Arkadii, you say something."

"No, Papa, I haven't prepared anything."

"As though I were so well prepared! Well, brother, let me simply hug you, wish you good luck, and tell you to return to us as soon as you can!"

Pavel Petrovich exchanged kisses with everyone, not excluding Mitia, of course. Moreover, he kissed Fenechka's hand, which she hadn't learned to offer properly yet, and draining the glass that had been refilled, he said with a deep sigh, "Be happy, my friends! *Farewell!*" The fact that he spoke this final word in English passed unnoticed, but everyone was touched.

"To the memory of Bazarov," Katia whispered in her husband's ear as she touched her glass against his. Arkadii pressed her hand warmly in return, but he didn't dare propose this toast out loud.

——

Would it appear that this is the end? But perhaps one of our readers would like to know what each of the characters we've introduced is doing now, right now. We're prepared to satisfy that reader.

Anna Sergeevna has recently gotten married, not out of love but out of prudence, to one of the future leaders of Russia, a very intelligent man—a lawyer with a vigorous, practical mind, a strong will, and remarkable verbal skills—a still young, good-natured man who's as cold as ice. They're living together in great harmony, and will live long enough, perhaps, to attain happiness ... perhaps, to attain love. The Princess Kh——is dead, having been forgotten the very day of her death.

The Kirsanovs, both father and son, have settled down at Marino; their situation is beginning to improve. Arkadii has become a zealous landowner, and the "farm" is now yielding a fairly good income. Nikolai Petrovich has ended up as one of the mediators appointed to carry out the emancipation reforms, and labors with all his might: he constantly travels throughout his district, delivering long speeches (he maintains the view that the peasants ought to be "brought around," that is, they ought to be reduced to a state of quiescence by the constant repetition of the same words). And yet, to tell the truth, he doesn't completely satisfy either the refined gentry, who at times stylishly and at times sadly speak about the "mancipation" (pronouncing the syllable "an" through their noses), or the unrefined gentry, who unceremoniously curse "the damned 'mancipation.'" He's too soft-hearted for either side. Katerina Sergeevna has had a son, little Nikolai; Mitia now runs around brashly and chatters fluently. Next to her husband and Mitia, Fenechka—Fedosia

Nikolaevna—adores no one more than her daughter-in-law, and when Katia is sitting at the piano, Fenechka would gladly spend the whole day by her side. A brief word about Petr: he's become completely ossified with stupidity and self-importance, pronouncing all his *e*'s like *u*'s, but he's married, too, having received a respectable dowry from his bride, the daughter of a town greengrocer who'd refused two perfectly good suitors only because neither of them had a watch, whereas Petr not only had a watch—he had a pair of patent leather shoes.

On the Brühl Terrace in Dresden between two and four in the afternoon—the most fashionable time for strolling—you may encounter a man of about fifty who's quite gray and looks as though he suffers from gout, but is still handsome, elegantly dressed, and has the special air exhibited only by those who spend a lot of time amid the highest strata of society. This is Pavel Petrovich. Having left Moscow, he went abroad for the sake of his health and settled permanently in Dresden, where he associates mostly with English residents and Russian travelers. He behaves simply, almost modestly, but not without dignity toward the English; they find him somewhat boring, but respect him for being, as they say, "a perfect gentleman." He's more casual with the Russians, venting his spleen and making fun of himself and them. But he does all this with great amiability, nonchalance, and propriety. He holds Slavophile views—it's well known that this is considered *très distingué* in the highest social circles. He never reads anything Russian, but he keeps a silver ashtray shaped like a peasant's bast shoe on his desk. He's much sought after by our tourists; Matvei Ilich Koliazin, finding himself "in temporary opposition," graced him with a visit on the way to a Bohemian spa. The native inhabitants, with whom, incidently, he associates quite rarely, virtually grovel at his feet. No one can obtain a ticket for the court chapel, the theater, and so forth, as easily and quickly as *der Herr Baron von Kirsanoff.* He does everything as genially as he can; he still makes a little bit of noise in the world—it isn't for nothing that he was once a social lion—but life is hard for him ... harder than he himself suspects.

One merely has to glance at him in the Russian church when, leaning against a wall to one side, he sinks into thought and remains motionless for long stretches of time, bitterly compressing his lips, then suddenly collects himself and almost imperceptibly begins to cross himself....

Mrs. Kukshin also went abroad. She's in Heidelberg now, studying not the natural sciences but rather architecture, in which, according to her, she's discovered new laws. She still fraternizes with students, especially the young Russian physicists and chemists Heidelberg is filled with, who, at first astounding the naive German professors by their sound views of things, later astound the same professors by their utter inefficiency and absolute laziness. Sitnikov roams St. Petersburg in the company of two or three such chemists, who can't tell oxygen from nitrogen but are full of skepticism and conceit—and the great Elisevich. Sitnikov is likewise preparing to become great and, according to his own assurances, is continuing the "work" of Bazarov. They say that someone recently beat him up, but he got his revenge: in an obscure little article hidden in an obscure little journal, he hinted that the man who beat him up was a coward. He calls this irony. His father bullies him as much as ever, while his wife considers him a fool ... and a man of letters.

There's a small village graveyard in one of the remote corners of Russia. Like almost all of our graveyards, it has a wretched appearance: the ditches surrounding it were overgrown long ago; the gray, wooden crosses have fallen over and lie rotting under their once-painted little roofs; the stone slabs are all tilted, as though someone had pushed them from behind; the two or three bare trees provide hardly any shade; sheep wander amid the graves unchecked.... But among those graves is one that no one touches and no animal tramples—only the birds perch on it and sing at daybreak. An iron railing runs around it; two young fir trees have been planted at each end. Evgenii Bazarov is buried in this grave.

Two quite feeble elderly people often come from the little village not far off to visit it—husband and wife. Holding one another up, they walk with heavy steps; they approach the railing, kneel down, and remain on their knees, crying long and bitterly, looking long and intently at the mute stone under which their son is lying; they exchange a brief word, wipe the dust off the stone, straighten the branch of a fir tree, and pray again, unable to tear themselves away from this spot, where they seem to be closer to their son, closer to their memories of him.... Can it be that their prayers, their tears, are fruitless? Can it be that love, sacred, devoted love, isn't omnipotent? Oh, no! However passionate, sinful, and rebellious the heart hidden in that grave may have been, the flowers growing on it gaze serenely at us with their innocent eyes. They speak to us not only of eternal peace, of that glorious peace of "indifferent" nature; they also speak to us of eternal reconciliation and life everlasting....

# NOTES

The notes to the present edition are indebted to the work of E. R. Sands. Information taken from his edition of the Russian text of *Fathers and Sons* is denoted [S].

p. xxv *Belinskii:* Influential liberal critic (1811–1848). He had praised Turgenev's major early work, *A Sportsman's Sketches* (begun in 1847), which attacked serfdom and was thought to have contributed to Aleksandr II's decision to emancipate the serfs.

CHAPTER I

p. 3, line 20 *"a farm":* The Russian transliterates the English word. Nikolai Petrovich Kirsanov is a progressive landowner who has anticipated the emancipation of the serfs in 1861 by assigning land to his peasants and replacing serf labor by hired labor [S].

line 21 *1812:* Napoleon's invasion of Russia and subsequent retreat from Moscow.

p. 4, line 27 *Petr Kirsanov:* In the Russian, misspelled "Pyotr Kirsanoff," as Kirsanov's illiterate phonetic rendering of his own name [S]. He has social pretensions: see notes below.

line 31 *Tavricheskii garden:* The garden of the Taurida Palace, built by

Catherine the Great for Potemkin after his victories in the Crimea [S].

line 31 *the English Club:* The oldest and most exclusive club in Petersburg, established in 1770 and, in 1835, having among its members such notable writers as Pushkin and Krylov [S].

p. 5, line 9 *Lesnii Institute:* The Institute of Forestry, recently established on the outskirts of Petersburg [S].

line 22 *the year 1848:* The year of revolutions in western Europe when the Russian frontiers were closed.

CHAPTER III

p. 9, line 35 *their rent:* Now paid in lieu of their earlier dues of unpaid labor in the fields.

p. 13, line 36 Eugene Onegin: The celebrated verse novel, composed between 1825 and 1831, by A. S. Pushkin (1799–1837). Nikolai Petrovich is quoting from the second stanza opening in Chapter VII.

p. 14, line 21 *Poverty Farm:* The Russian nickname actually evokes Nikolai Petrovich's widowerhood [S]: literally "Loner's Farm."

CHAPTER IV

p. 16, line 35 "s'est dégourdi": French: "has acquired some polish." Pavel Petrovich's use of French indicates his own European sophistication, as does the handshake with which he initially greets Arkadii.

p. 18, line 25 Galignani: *Galignani's Messenger,* a liberal daily newspaper published, in English, in Paris [S].

CHAPTER V

p. 23, line 14 *nihilist:* The term was not introduced into Russian by Turgenev here, as is sometimes asserted. In Russia it was first used pejoratively in 1829 to mean "a man without principles," and in 1858 to connote a skeptic. Turgenev portrays Bazarov as an elementary empiricist [S]. The term's swift historical evolution is charted from its earliest, most hostile connotations to its latest and most positive in the glosses provided by Pavel Petrovich, Nikolai Petrovich, and Arkadii respectively.

p. 24, line 3 *"good health and a general's rank":* An inaccurate quotation of A. S. Griboedov's *Woe from Wit* (1825), II. v. [S].

line 7 *"Hegelians":* G.W.F. Hegel (1770–1831), the German philosopher, was popular in Russian intellectual circles in the 1830s and 1840s [S].

The Russian here sounds disparagingly silly: "First the gegelists; now the nigilists."

p. 25, line 19 *"an Aesop":* Presumably the bailiff's overambitious coinage, like "deboshed," intended to mean "a type, an oddball."

## CHAPTER VI

p. 27, line 30 *"Liebig":* Justus, Baron von Liebig (1803–1873), German chemist, founder of agricultural chemistry, and author of *Organic Chemistry in Its Applications to Agriculture and Physiology* (1840).

## CHAPTER VII

p. 29, line 2 *Corps of Pages:* An exclusive military academy under imperial patronage.

p. 31, line 28 *Baden:* A German spa popular with the Russian aristocracy in this period.

p. 33, line 27 *Wellington at Louis Philippe's residence:* Arthur Wellesley, First Duke of Wellington (1769–1852), celebrated British soldier and statesman. After the French July Revolution of 1830, the bourgeois July Monarchy of Louis Philippe lasted until his overthrow in the February Revolution of 1848. Wellington served as foreign secretary under Sir Robert Peel from 1834 to 1835. Perhaps Pavel Petrovich's dining with both at some point in this period is envisaged. See also note for p. 167.

## CHAPTER VIII

p. 37, line 22 *"Gooseberry":* In Fenechka's slight, phonetic misspelling in the Russian [S].

line 34 *General Ermolov:* General Alexei Ermolov (1772–1861) was famous for his part in the Russo-Napoleonic war of 1812, and in 1816 was appointed commander of Russia's army in the Caucasus region [S].

p. 38, line 5 *Masalskii's* Musketeers: Masalskii was a popular historical novelist of the 1830s; his *Musketeers* came out in 1832 [S].

## CHAPTER X

p. 47, line 18 *"Büchner's* Stoff und Kraft": Ludwig Büchner (1824–1899), German physicist and materialist philosopher, author of *Kraft und Stoff* (1855).

p. 49, line 11 "Mathieu": Gallic form of the name Matvei.

p. 50, line 25 *Alexandrine era:* The reign of Aleksandr I (1801–25). In this period the upper classes spoke French: hence the reference to "the rare occasions when the nobility of that era spoke their own language," i.e., Russian.

p. 51, line 18 *"Aristocratism, liberalism, progress, principles":* In Russian the first three are unchanged loan words from English: *principles* is French in origin and audibly so in Pavel Petrovich's archaically precise pronunciation (see p. 23).

p. 54, line 5 *"we used to say":* Bazarov's argument partially paraphrases Dobroliubov's article "What Is Oblomovism?" [S]. Oblomovism I is sluggishness and indecision, as epitomized by the hero of Ivan Goncharov's novel *Oblomov* (1858).

p. 55, line 23 *"un barbouilleur":* French: a scribbler, a hack.

p. 56, line 1 *"a cheap candle":* Traditionally, the origin of the Great Fire of Moscow in 1812.

line 12 *" 'A Girl at a Fountain' ":* Exhibited in 1859, the year in which *Fathers and Sons* is set, this work by the artist Novokovich was part of a movement toward greater artistic realism, deprecated by Pavel Petrovich [S].

line 34 *"the commune":* The peasant commune, which paid dues and had a joint responsibility for working the land and is seen by some historians as the germ of agrarian socialism [S].

p. 57, line 7 *"the privileges the head of the family enjoys":* A snide reference to the *droit de seigneur,* the right to a bride's maidenhead enjoyed by patriarchal figures in many primitive societies.

line 36 "vieilli": French: passé, out-of-date.


CHAPTER XII

p. 63, line 4 *Guizot:* François Guizot (1787–1874), French statesman and historian, a leading intellectual in the July Monarchy of Louis Philippe (see note for p. 33, line 27).

line 6 routiniers: French: slaves of routine.

line 13 *the Alexandrine era:* See note for p. 50.

line 14 *Mrs. Svechin:* (1782–1859). Wife of the Russian general Svechin; for forty years she was the leader of a famous salon, and died in the year in which *Fathers and Sons* is set. Her writings on religious and mystical topics were published in 1860 and much discussed in the Russian press during the period of this novel's composition [S].

line 16 *Condillac:* Étienne de Condillac (1715–1780), French materialist philosopher, who developed the theory of sensationalism, which held that all knowledge derives from the senses.

p. 64, line 30 "il a fait son temps": French: his time is past.

p. 65, line 14 *Bourdaloue* ... "burda": Louis Bourdaloue (1632–1702) was a professor in the Jesuit College of Bruges; *burda* is a word of Turkish origin meaning a muddy, unpleasant liquid [S].

p. 66, line 36 *"the gin business":* As the Russian makes clear, Sitnikov's father held a concession in the crown monopoly on the sale of spirits, a trade repugnant to radicals like Bazarov.

## CHAPTER XIII

p. 69, line 21 "Moscow Gazette": The official weekly of the Moscow province [S].

p. 70, line 4 *"Elisevich":* A name suggestive of G. Z. Eliseyev (1821–1891), a contributor to the radical paper *Sovremennik* (The Contemporary) [S], which, under the editorship of Nekrasov, had published Turgenev's early writings and from which Turgenev was currently disassociating himself.

line 14 *"Cooper's Pathfinder":* James Fennimore Cooper (1789–1851). *The Pathfinder* (1840) appeared in Russian, also in 1840.

line 27 *Bunsen:* Robert Wilhelm Bunsen (1811–1899), chemist and inventor of the Bunsen burner (1855); with Gustav Robert Kirchhoff, the originator of spectrum analysis.

p. 71, line 30 *Proudhon:* Pierre Joseph Proudhon (1809–1865), French socialist and anarchist thinker, a critic of private property.

line 36 *Macaulay:* Thomas Babington Macaulay (1800–1859), English historian and author.

p. 72, line 10 "Domostroi": A sixteenth-century Russian treatise advocating repressive authoritarian values in religious, social, and family life. It was frequently attacked by nineteenth-century authors for its reactionary morality (and supposed espousal of wife-beating) [S].

line 19 *Michelet's book:* Jules Michelet (1798–1874), French writer and historian of the romantic school, whose *De l'amour* appeared in 1858.

## CHAPTER XIV

p. 82, line 29 "Optime": Latin: "Excellent."

p. 84, line 16 *"Like Speranskii":* Mikhail Speranskii (1772–1839), a reformer and outstanding statesman in the reigns of Aleksandr I and

Nicholas I; the son of a priest. Speranskii could easily have been an ideal for Bazarov. At Aleksandr I's request he drew up proposals for a constitution that included popular participation in legislation and limited local self-government. Aleksandr I never adopted these, although other of Speranskii's reforms, including promotion on the basis of merit and a progressive income tax on nobility, were later implemented and antagonized nobles and bureaucrats alike. Speranskii was exiled in 1812 for supposed dealings with the French prior to Napoleon's invasion of Russia. Under Nicholas I he was responsible for the codification of Russian law.

## CHAPTER XVII

p. 96, line 10 *Toggenburg:* The hero of *Ritter Toggenburg,* a ballad of chivalric love and renunciation by the German poet Friedrich von Schiller (1759–1805).

line 11 *minnesingers and troubadours:* German and French poets and musician-singers in the eleventh to the fourteenth centuries whose major theme was courtly love.

p. 99, line 1 *"Pelouse and Frémy's* Notions générales de chymie":  Published in Paris in 1853, where the authors were professors of chemistry at the École Polytechnique [S].

## CHAPTER XVIII

p. 105, line 27 *"Ganot's* Traité élémentaire de physique expérimentale": Published in Paris in 1851, and in Russian in 1862 [S], after the period in which this novel is set. Bazarov is very up-to-date.

## CHAPTER XIX

p. 113, line 10 *"it's not up to gods to bake bricks":* I.e., the Sitnikovs of life can do the dirty work.

## CHAPTER XX

p. 119, line 12 "ommfay": French: *homme fait,* "a complete man." When Bazarov or his family uses French, Turgenev transliterates into Russian, suggesting a Russified mispronunciation (mockingly deliberate on Bazarov's part). Elsewhere, other characters' French is rendered in the original. Bazarov's father uses Latin correctly.

line 36 *Hufeland:* Christoph-Wilhelm Hufeland (1762–1836), celebrated German doctor and scholar, whose *Makrbiotik* or *The Art of Prolong-*

*ing Life* (1796), was widely translated in Europe. Like father, like son: Vasilii Ivanovich shares his son's taste for the latest scientific treatise, now out-of-date by half a century.

p. 122, line 5 "The Friend of Health": A medical periodical published in Petersburg, 1833–1869 [S].

line 12 *"Schönlein and Rademacher"*: Johann-Lucas Schönlein (1793–1864) and Johann-Gottfried Rademacher (1772–1849), distinguished German medical scholars, professors at Berlin and Halle respectively [S].

line 19 *"humoralist"*: Humoral pathology, orginating with Hippocrates and refined by Galen, derived all diseases from the four humors: blood, phlegm, choler, and melancholy.

line 19 *"Hoffmann"*: Friedrich Hoffmann (1660–1742), professor at Halle; the first to describe appendicitis and German measles. His approach to physiology was mechanistic.

line 20 *"Brown"*: John Brown (1735–1788), Scottish doctor and founder of the Brunonian system. *Vitalism* postulated the existence of a life force or vital principle.

line 34 "volatu": French: *voilà tout,* "that's all."

p. 123, line 3 *"Prince Wittgenstein"*: (1768–1842). General-field-marshal distinguished for his role in the Russo-Napoleonic war [S].

line 4 *"Zhukovskii"*: Vasily Zhukovskii (1783–1852), Russian poet and translator. He was tutor to the future czar Aleksandr II, who was influenced by his liberal ideas.

line 4 *"the southern army"*: The Decembrists' uprising of December 14, 1825, protesting the accession of Nicholas I, was particularly associated with the Southern Army [S]: the Decembrists were members of secret revolutionary societies who persuaded several Petersburg regiments to refuse the oath of allegiance to the new czar and to march on the Senate. Vasilii Ivanovich clearly had radical sympathies.

line 10 *"a typical blockhead"*: It was made clear on p. 4 that Arkadii's grandfather was illiterate.

line 20 *"Paracelsus"*: Originally named Theophrastus Bombastus von Hohenheim (1493–1541), Swiss physician and alchemist, whose thought combined the fantastic philosophies of his time with pragmatic observation. He opposed the humoral theory of disease championed by Galen, advocated the use of specific remedies for specific diseases (to which Vasilii Ivanovich refers here), and noted

relationships like the hereditary pattern of syphilis, the associa-
tion of cretinism with endemic goiter, and of paralysis with head injuries.

line 21 "in herbis, verbis et lapidibus": Latin: diseases are cured "by
herbs, words and stones [minerals]."

line 34 "ad patres": Latin: he had gone "to his ancestors," i.e., he died.

p. 124, line 34 *Napoleonic politics . . . the Italian question:* The Italian struggle for independence and unity was at its height in 1859, compli-
cated by Napoleon III's betrayal of the Italian cause in his separate
peace treaty with Austria.

p. 126, line 23 *holy wanderers:* Mentally ill itinerants believed to have
holy and prophetic powers, often referred to as holy fools, who were
supported by the charity of people like Arina Vlasevna.

line 25 *salt:* Salt prepared on Maunday Thursday, the Thursday of
Holy Week, was stored under the eaves and used as a curative
throughout the year [S].

p. 127, line 5 Alexis, or the Cottage in the Forest: A French sentimental
romance by François-Guillaume Ducray-Dumesnil (1761–1819),
first published in 1788 and popular in early nineteenth-century
Russia, where it went though three editions between 1794 and
1804 [S].

line 14 *submissive bows:* Traditionally, a serf would touch his forehead to
the ground before his master.

CHAPTER XXI

p. 128, line 6 *"Cincinnatus":* Fifth-century Roman patriot. One-time
consul, twice dictator, twice emerging from retirement on his farm
to lead the Romans to victory before resigning the dictatorship once
more.

line 11 *"Jean-Jacques Rousseau":* (1712–1778). Swiss-French philosopher
and political theorist. Author of, among other works, *Sur l'Origine et
les fondements de l'inégalité parmi les hommes* (1754) and *Du contrat social*
(1762).

line 18 "anamatyer": French: *en amateur,* "as an amateur."

p. 130, line 1. "amice": Latin: friend.

p. 131, line 15 Robert le Diable: Opera by Giacomo Meyerbeer
(1791–1864), German dramatic composer [S]. It was his first "grand
opera" written in French, and very successful when premiered in
1831.

p. 132, line 13 *"Suvorov"*: Aleksandr Suvorov (1729–1800) was a great Russian field marshal in the reigns of Catherine II and Paul I, famous for his army's hazardous crossing of the Alps in 1799.

p. 138, line 8 *"Castor and Pollux"*: In classical mythology, twin heroes called the Dioscuri: great warriors noted for their mutual devotion.

p. 139, line 26 *"Vladimir Cross"*: A military order and decoration instituted by Catherine II in 1792, conferring hereditary nobility on the recipient [S]. It is not a thing Bazarov would approve of.

p. 144, line 21 *"We're alone, all alone!"*: In the Russian, Vasilii Ivanovich uses the proverbial "solitary as a single finger," which explains his gesture.

## CHAPTER XXII

p. 148, line 13 *Council of Guardians:* Originally founded by Catherine II to safeguard the interests of orphans, it gradually acquired other powers, including the provision of mortgage and credit facilities [S].

p. 149, line 13 *"I say this to you both"*: Arkadii is remembering Mrs. Odintsov's parting phrase, on p. 146.

p. 150, line 35 *the rights of the nobility in the Baltic provinces:* The Baltic landowners opposed plans for the emancipation of the serfs because they had already freed their own serfs—without land—in 1819. The proposed emancipation of the Russian serfs—*with* land— would put them into a dangerously anomalous position [S].

p. 157, line 20 *"Lothario"*: Proverbial for a philanderer. Lothario was a seducer in the play *The Fair Penitent* (1703), by Nicholas Rowe.

## CHAPTER XXIV

p. 160, line 18 "comilfo": French: *comme il faut,* "propriety."

p. 164, line 5 "A bon entendeur, salut!": French: the general sense is "So take note!"

line 8 *"unite* utile dulci": Latin: combine utility with pleasure.

p. 165, line 25 "vertige": French: dizziness, vertigo.

p. 166, line 29 *"Mrs. Radcliffe"*: Ann Radcliffe (1764–1823) was a hugely popular English gothic novelist, best known for *The Mysteries of Udolpho* (1794).

p. 167, line 7 *"Sir Robert Peel":* (1788–1850). British statesman who established the London police force. A moderate conservative who accepted the Reform Bill of 1832, espousing, in his words, further change "without infringing on established rights." A nice joke on the part of Pavel Petrovich—and Turgenev. Peel would have provided a litmus test for the divergent sympathies of Bazarov and Pavel Petrovich.

p. 168, line 9 "Couchez-vous": French: "Go to bed."

line 19 "C'est de la même famille": French: "They're the same type"; literally, "It's from the same family."

p. 174, line 12 "belle soeur": French: sister-in-law.

line 17 "au dix-neuvième siècle": French: in the nineteenth century.

line 25 "Quelle idée!": French: "What an idea!"

CHAPTER XXV

p. 175, line 31 "iasen": In Russian the adjective *iasnyi* means "clear" or "transparent."

p. 176, line 3 *"Heine"*: Heinrich Heine (1797–1856), German poet.

p. 181, line 25 *"kvass"*: A light beer made from rye flour and malt.

p. 182, line 34 *"Gogol's letters"*: Bazarov is alluding to a letter of 1846 from author Nikolay Gogol to O. A. Smirnova, which was first printed in 1860 and aroused the disgust of liberals for its sententious moralizing and reactionary quietism [S].

p. 193, line 2 "e volatu": French: *et voilà tout,* "and that's all."

CHAPTER XXVII

p. 196, line 14 *"you'll give us our true language"*: Deeply ironic: the peasant's reply is not only confused but, in the Russian, skewed by rustic vulgarisms.

line 19 *"the world that's said to rest on three fishes"*: According to primitive Russian cosmology.

p. 197, line 34 *a cap shaped like a horn:* Traditional ornate peaked headdress worn by married women on special occasions.

line 35 *Goulard's extract:* A lotion of lead acetate solution devised by the eighteenth-century French chemist Goulard [S].

p. 199, line 8 *cauterizing stone:* Silver nitrate, used for cauterizing wounds.

p. 202, line 21 *"Pyemia"*: Blood poisoning: the blood is invaded by pus-forming microorganisms.

p. 207, line 6 "Wo ist der Kranke?": German: "Where is the patient?"

line 9 "wertester Herr Collega": German: esteemed colleague.

line 24 "iam moritur": Latin: he is already dying.

line 25 "Der Herr scheint des Deutschen mächtig zu sein": German: "The gentleman seems to have a good knowledge of German."

line 27 "Ich . . . gabe": German: "I give." There is grim comedy here as Vasilii Ivanovich and the doctor attempt to find a common language. The doctor's next reply in the Russian text is given in a halting, heavily German accent.

## CHAPTER XXVIII

p. 213, line 27 *a peasant's bast shoe:* These boat-shaped shoes were made of woven lime bark and bound to the foot with strips of cloth. Pavel Petrovich's silver ashtray cast in this shape is at once absurd and sad, contradictorily epitomizing his worldly elegance and his nostalgia for Russia's rustic past.

# READING GROUP GUIDE

1. How does Arkadii and Bazarov's relationship change over the course of the novel? Why does Arkadii look up to Bazarov in the beginning? How does he see him by the end?

2. What are the attitudes of Pavel Kirsanov, Anna Odintsova, and Evgenii Bazarov toward notions of time: the past, the present, and the future? What are the effects of those differing attitudes on their characters?

3. Compare and contrast Bazarov's and Arkadii's very different notions of and attitudes toward love. How do the scenes of prosaic happiness—say, of Nikolai Kirsanov and his future wife—function in the novel? What does the narrator's attitude seem to be toward those scenes? What does the narrator's attitude seem to be toward prosaic versus aesthetic ideals of happiness and of living?

4. What is the significance of the role of order in Anna Odintsova's life? In what ways does she begin to question that role after she meets Bazarov? What does she mean when she says to Bazarov, "You know, you're the same as I am"? What kind of self-revelation does Anna Odintsova have then, and why does she retreat from Bazarov?

5. How does Turgenev's decision to have Bazarov die at the novel's end affect our understanding of the character? Why might one imagine that Turgenev made this choice? What effect does Bazarov's stoicism throughout his death scene have on our understanding of him? How might one interpret the dogs that he envisions as he's dying?

6. There was a critical storm surrounding *Fathers and Sons* when it was first published in 1862. Certain critics on the right felt Turgenev's portrayal of Bazarov was far too sympathetic and represented Turgenev's misguided search for the approval of the younger generation. Certain critics on the left felt just the opposite—that Turgenev's portrayal of Bazarov as such an extreme character was a hindrance, and very near slander, to the liberal cause, providing ammunition for the right. And some felt that Turgenev himself was not completely certain of his attitude toward Bazarov. As Isaiah Berlin succinctly put it, "What was Bazarov? How was he to be taken? Was he a positive or negative figure? A hero or a devil?" How might one think about answering these questions? From a close reading of the text, how do you think Turgenev might have felt toward Bazarov? Toward nihilism?

A NOTE ON THE TYPE

The principal text of this Modern Library edition
was set in a digitized version of Janson, a typeface that
dates from around 1690 and was cut by Nicholas Kis,
a Hungarian working in Amsterdam. The original matrices
have survived and are held by the Stempel foundry in Germany.
Herman Zapf redesigned some of the weights and sizes for
Stempel, basing his revisions on the original design.